Praise for *Boston Cream*

"From start to epilogue, *Boston Cream* is a mystery thriller of insight, compassion, with an infectious sense of urgency that drives to a conclusion both real and satisfying. Author Howard Shrier masterfully links the dialogue to the pace, the setting and the plot with an energy that makes readers feel they're absorbing the story at a rate almost too fast to take in. . . . I suggested in an earlier column that Shrier was an author to watch. In *Boston Cream*, he's arrived.   —*The Hamilton Spectator*

"Crime writers should look over their shoulders: Howard Shrier started strong, and he's only getting better. *Boston Cream* is a well-paced, atmospheric tale, with assured writing, believable characters and engaging protagonists."   —*Spinetingler Magazine*

"Shoot 'em up action mixed with clever dialogue and thought provoking conundrums."   —*Women's Post*

"As with his previous books, Shrier keeps the pace moving at a brisk clip, ups the ante with surprising . . . plot twists, and makes the reader care about Geller and Jenn."   —*Quill & Quire*

"I am so glad to have discovered Shrier. Geller is a richly different character."   —*Crimespace*

"There is a reason Shrier consistently wins the Arthur Ellis, Canada's highest crime fiction award: he tells a really good story. Relish the local color, cultural nuances, and successive waves of action."   —*Library Journal* (starred review)

"Explosive."   —*Publishers Weekly* (starred review)

Praise for HIGH CHICAGO

WINNER OF THE ARTHUR ELLIS AWARD FOR BEST CRIME NOVEL

"Shrier . . . writes with an easy assurance and a killer sense of humour. . . . *High Chicago* is a great addition to the mystery shelf."
— *NOW* (Toronto)

"Howard Shrier's first novel, *Buffalo Jump*, won the Arthur Ellis Award for best first novel. *High Chicago*, his second, will definitely be short-listed for another. It's got the same stellar characters, the same clever plotting, and, if anything, an even better story."
— *The Globe and Mail*

"*High Chicago* confirms Shrier as an author to watch for, both in Canada and abroad. It's a mystery that peels away the urban layers of big business civility to expose the raw flesh of reality underneath."
— *The Hamilton Spectator*

"Combining fast-paced action with well-structured plots, and featuring a complex but likeable protagonist, Shrier's novels are fast winning him legions of loyal fans. If you enjoy contemporary hard-boiled tales with nuanced characters, check out *High Chicago*; you won't be disappointed. "
— *Sherbrooke Record*

"Shrier is one of the most exciting new voices in the mystery genre. This sophomore effort is sure to please."
— *Village Post*

"With *High Chicago*, Shrier cements his reputation as a fine mystery writer. I suspect and hope that he and Jonah will be around for a long time to come."
— *Canadian Jewish News*

"*High Chicago* is tighter, tauter, and speedier than its predecessor. I am looking forward to the next American city to receive a flying visit from Jonah Geller and his crew."

—Yvonne Klein, reviewingtheevidence.com

"Shrier's first Jonah Geller mystery was terrific; *High Chicago* is even better."

— Linwood Barclay, bestselling author of *No Time for Goodbye* and *Too Close to Home*

"A plot brimming with greed, deceit, violence and murder makes *High Chicago* a fast-paced, entertaining read."

—José Latour, bestselling author of *Crime of Fashion*

"A fast-moving and violent tale that proves your deadliest enemy is probably the person sleeping right beside you. I hope Geller returns for a third book."

—Lee Goldberg, writer and producer

"*High Chicago* is often funny, sometimes violent, and always thoughtful, with a powerful sense of place throughout. Toronto may have just found its Spenser in PI Jonah Geller, and I can't wait for his next case."

—Sean Chercover, award-winning author of *Trigger City* and *Big City, Bad Blood*

Praise for BUFFALO JUMP

WINNER OF THE ARTHUR ELLIS AWARD FOR BEST FIRST NOVEL

"Howard Shrier's first novel, *Buffalo Jump*, is a winner."
—*National Post*

"Contemporary Canadian crime writers are not exactly plentiful in number, and . . . Howard Shrier is a welcome addition to their ranks. . . . Continue[s] the tradition of Robert B. Parker and Robert Crais with a hearty and promising Maple Leaf Twist."
—*Quill & Quire*

"Delivers a fast plot with the requisite brutalities."
—Joan Barfoot, *London Free Press*

"A great debut novel from Montreal-born Torontonian Shrier, and it introduces PI Jonah Geller in what is certainly going to be a fine series. The plot is tight, the characters engaging, and this one even has a believable—and sympathetic—bad guy."
—*The Globe and Mail*

"A debut novel with a well-juggled storyline brimming with dry humour, a cast of oddball characters, and graphic scenes that come alive with action. A must-read for summer."
—*The Hamilton Spectator*

"This first book by Shrier is top-notch, a page-turner to rate with the best of them and with some memorable characters. It also contains just the right dose of cynicism and dark humour, both of which mark the best of the private-eye novels."
—*The Guelph Mercury*

"A cast of compelling oddballs; a complex, funny and always surprising hero, and a plot as fresh and twisty as today's headlines—Shrier juggles them all deftly and nails his first crime novel with the aplomb and impact of a seasoned pro. A completely satisfying read that made me wish Jonah Geller could work cases on my shows."

—René Balcer, Emmy-winning executive producer/ head writer of *Law & Order*, creator of *Law & Order Criminal Intent*, winner of the Peabody Award, and of four Edgar Awards from the Mystery Writers of America

"A crime story that is both thrilling and thoughtful."

—Kelley Armstrong, bestselling author of the Women of the Otherworld series

"Jonah Geller has a strong and individual voice. . . . He is contemporary, appealing, and fresh in several senses of the word."

—Yvonne Klein, *reviewingtheevidence.com*

"Journalist turned actor turned author Howard Shrier has a great new first novel." —Craig Rintoul, *bookbits.ca*

Also by Howard Shrier

Buffalo Jump*
High Chicago**
Boston Cream

* Arthur Ellis Award Winner for Best First Novel
** Arthur Ellis Award Winner for Best Crime Novel

MISS MONTREAL

HOWARD SHRIER

VINTAGE CANADA

Published in Canada by Vintage Canada, a division of Random House of Canada Limited, Toronto, in 2013. Distributed by Random House of Canada Limited.

Vintage Canada with colophon is a registered trademark.

www.randomhouse.ca

Lyrics from Blue Rodeo's "Montreal" used with permission from Jim Cuddy/Greg Keelor and Thunder Hawk Music.

Library and Archives Canada Cataloguing in Publication

Shrier, Howard
        Miss Montreal / Howard Shrier.

(Jonah Geller mystery series ; 4)
Issued also in electronic format.

ISBN 978-0-307-35958-2
        I. Title. II. Series: Shrier, Howard. Jonah Geller mystery series ; 4.

PS8637.H74M57 2013   C813'.6   C2012-908595-2

Book design by Jennifer Lum

Image credit: Superstock/Getty Images

Printed and bound in the United States of America

2 4 6 8 9 7 5 3 1

In loving memory of my grandmother,
Jean Wolfson Seidman (1911-2012)

MISS MONTREAL

CHAPTER 01

It was me who gave him the nickname Slammin' Sammy. At Camp Arrowhead, the summer we were twelve—what turned out to be my last summer there. The next year our family went to Israel for my bar mitzvah, and the year after that my father died unexpectedly and uninsured, and we fell out of the middle class like skydivers. We moved from our house to a cramped apartment, and there was no more summer camp for the Geller boys, at least not out of the city.

Sammy Adler was without doubt the least coordinated, least athletic person, male or female, in the camp. Tall, gangly, flat-assed, he ran like Frankenstein's monster, knees knocking together, ankles weak, his feet slapping the ground like a bird headed for extinction. His height made him of occasional use in basketball or volleyball, but on the softball diamond he was what we then called a spaz. And still would. A glove on his hand was like a metal pan ready to clank. Balls hit or thrown to him caromed off his shins or bounced through his legs cleanly. To say he threw like a girl would be an insult to most girls in the camp. There was nowhere to hide him in the field, unless you needed a guy to turn and watch a ball sail over his head while everyone else yelled, "Go!" And at the plate, he'd stand flat-footed, with the bat on his shoulder, and swipe at the ball, stiff as a turnstile, usually

after it had crossed the plate. His strikeouts or accidental ground-
ers elicited groans, forehead slaps and sometimes thrown hats. If
he came to the plate with two out, his teammates went to find
their gloves. The rally killer was up. The automatic out.

The counsellors, who were supposed to be our coaches,
were no help. Natural athletes themselves, they didn't have the
patience or know-how to break his swing down and rebuild it.
They just barked a stream of the usual stuff at him: *Bend your
knees. Draw that bat back. Keep an eye on it. Don't be afraid to swing
away. A walk's as good as a hit. Swing! Not at that. That's eye level.
There—why didn't you swing at that one?*

Sammy needed someone else to help him, and he needed
it soon. Colour War had just been announced: an intense three-
day competition when the campers split into two teams, Blue
and White, and took each other on in all sports, land and water.
The winner was always declared by means of fireworks set off
on a floating dock in the lake, a burst of either blue stars launch-
ing and slowly showering down, or of white. Cheers from the
winning side, cries from the other. Hugs here; over there a few
boys trying to over-console teary-eyed girls.

I was on the Blue team, as was Sammy. Going into the
third and final day, the teams were neck and neck. White was
killing us in land sports but we were winning everything on the
lake, mainly because we had Victor Blum, the future Olympic
qualifier, and he could do everything in water but walk on it
juggling. There was a good chance it would all come down to
Sunday's final event—softball—and our age group, twelve and
up, would play last.

After dinner Saturday, I grabbed Sammy by the elbow and
steered him out to the ball field. The piney smell of the woods
crowded in on us; the mosquitoes came out for blood. The
equipment was all locked away in a shed behind the backstop
but one kid, Teddy Packer, had his own eighteen-ounce alumi-
num bat that he kept under his bed. I'd brought it with us and

as the sky drew darker, more bruised around us, I stood Sammy at the plate and worked with him for a solid hour.

I was all about sports then. It was the one area where I was much better than my brother, the scholar and future lawyer. I couldn't out-study him, outperform him at school or outdo him at potential fulfilled, but I was a natural athlete—and baseball was my game. *Our* game, my dad's and mine. The mid-eighties was a great time to be a Blue Jays fan. They were a rising power in the American League East, sudden contenders with their great core of young players: Bell, Moseby, Barfield, Stieb, Fernandez. My dad and I would go to games when they still played at Exhibition Stadium, sitting in the cheap seats in left, on soft August nights with the lights of the midway flashing over the centre-field wall, the two of us screaming ourselves hoarse as the Jays kept pace with the Yankees, Tigers and Orioles—then the beasts of the East. He was proud, my dad, of what I could do with a glove and a bat. I wasn't big but I could drive the ball on a line to any field and catch anything hit my way.

For an hour that night, until darkness was full and the mosquitoes had bled us dry, I worked with Sammy on his swing, drawing on my extremely limited knowledge of physics to explain weight shifts. I wasn't expecting miracles. I didn't think I'd suddenly unleash a swing like George Bell's. But good things happened when you made contact in softball. Defences were suspect. Balls got over-thrown.

I started by standing at home plate with the bat, swinging easily through imaginary pitches, moving my weight back foot to front, thinking of how I could explain it to him.

"Have you ever played tennis?" I asked.

"My mother got me lessons a couple of years ago."

"So it's like that," I said. "Just like a backhand. You're meeting the ball as it crosses the plate. Your front arm moves through the ball and ends up behind you."

"Jonah," he said, "it's not like I got it then either."

"You'll get it."

I showed him where to stand: a foot away from the plate, feet square and shoulder width apart. Then I stood just in front of him, my back to the mound, my glove held straight out.

"Use your front arm only," I said. "Move from your back foot to your front and use one hand to swing through like a tennis backhand. Here comes the pitch," I said. "Are you ready? Is your weight on your back foot? Okay, it's coming."

I moved my glove closer. "Start the bat slowly. Come on, bring it through."

As it crossed the plate I moved my glove in to meet it and said, "Stop." No yelling at him like the counsellors did, always barking everything twice. *Swing away, Sammy. Swing away.* Or *Walk's as good as a run, Sam. Waaaaalk's as good as a run.* Softly I spoke, the Sammy Whisperer. I had him bend his knees, draw the bat back and step through his swing again, letting it smack my glove.

"Back foot to front foot. Back foot to front. That's it, Sammy. That's where you hit the ball. You watch it come in and only start your swing when it's here. Got it?"

He smiled for the first time. "I actually think I do." He stood square to the plate, at my prompting, and swung through with some perceptible level of coordination.

I had him choke up, shorten his swing. Got him to keep his head down. I tried to break that stiffness in his body with a hand here, a touch there, make his swing less mechanical and more fluid. He listened well. With no one shouting at him, no pressure heaped on his bony shoulders, he started striding into his swing more, looking better with each try. Finally I took a ball to the mound and lobbed him an easy one. He put a pretty good swing on it, shifting his weight, head down, driving the bat head through the zone. And missed it by a good foot.

I had an idea, watching him swing late on the pitch.

"Sammy," I said, "what I told you before about stepping straight ahead with your front foot? Forget that."

I knew that if he made contact, a ball up the right side could get through. As long as it got past the pitcher, there'd be no play at first. Even Sammy, with his awkward gait, could beat one out—if he made contact.

"When you swing, Sammy, step toward first. Not the pitcher, 'kay? First base."

"How?"

"Like this." I took the bat, got into the box and got him to walk in on me with the glove, like I had for him.

"You've watched me hit, right?"

"Sure."

"What do I do?"

"Hit it a mile to left. Most of the time, anyway. Which is funny 'cause you're way smaller than a lot of the kids, but I guess it's physics, not size."

"How I do it," I said, "is I wait until a pitch comes inside and I step toward third. I hit it early, and all my weight answers the pitch."

"And changes its direction at a greater velocity."

"That too. But you swing late. You can't come around on an inside pitch. So what you're going to do, Sammy, is look for a pitch on the outside part of the plate and put that late swing on it right . . . here." I put the glove on the outer part of the strike zone near the back of the plate.

"You put a late swing on that, you won't miss it." Not by a foot anyway.

Sammy always batted ninth. His first time up Sunday was in the second inning, no one on and two out. Most of our team got their gloves on. *Surprise them, Sammy,* I thought. Show them what we did last night. Because by the time we left, sticky with sweat and bloody bites, Sammy had found a swing.

I won't say *his* swing, because he didn't own it yet; that would take months of practice. But if he choked up and watched the ball come in on him like we practised, he could push the ball up the right side between second and first. It was limited but effective. The last ten pitches I lobbed him, at least four would have been base hits.

Hall of Fame average, right?

But nowhere to be seen that first time up. He watched two good pitches come right in for strikes, the bat on his shoulder, then swung stiffly at an eye-high pitch for strike three.

He did no better in the fourth or fifth. Not the end of the world: each time up the bases were empty. No runners for him to strand. But he was leaving me wondering why we'd worked so hard last night, given all that blood, if he wasn't going to do what I'd showed him.

Camp softball games went seven innings. When Sammy came up in the seventh, there was an actual rally for him to kill. We were down a run but had men on first and third, one out. I was the runner on third after a lead-off double.

He came to the plate and squared up to the plate with the bat on his shoulder. His knees weren't bent like they should have been. He looked stiff as a flamingo. Luckily the first pitch was inside for a ball, so his inaction did no harm. But the second was a strike and he watched that too. I clapped my hands and yelled, "Come on, Sammy!" These were underhand lobs, not country fastballs. They weren't that hard to hit. Another came in for a strike, maybe inside but the ump called it anyway. Sammy's bat stayed inert and silent.

It was only when he had two strikes on him that he made eye contact with me and raised the corners of his lips in the slightest grin. He bent his knees, shortened his grip on the bat and shifted his weight back and forth. With two outs and two strikes I got ready to run, wishing for a wild pitch or hit batter, even though neither ever happened in lob ball.

I can still see that last pitch coming in fat as a harvest moon, Sammy waiting, his front foot shifting toward first base and the bat moving off his shoulder late. As I toe the bag at third I see his head staying down and the sweet part of the red metal bat moving across the plate, meeting the ball, lashing it up the right side just as we'd planned. Better. It doesn't even hit the ground. It's a true line drive, a frozen rope—both us runners take off—and it goes straight into the first baseman's glove. He makes sure he has it, then steps on first to double off the runner there.

Ball game over. In a flash of leather.

Colour war over. White fireworks will dazzle the sky tonight.

It was all over so fast, it took me a minute to process what Sammy had done. He had played the other team all game, coming up in meaningless situations and letting them think he still had nothing going. Then with two strikes, all the pressure on, he had delivered. He'd hit what should have been the game winner. I started clapping my hands and chanting, "Sam-my! Sam-my!" until the others joined in and everyone high-fived him, even the counsellors, all of us chanting his name. By the end of the night, I had them all calling him Slammin' Sammy and it stuck through the end of the summer.

That was the last time I had seen him, probably the last time I'd heard his name until yesterday, when his grandfather had called to say he was dead. Murdered. Beaten to death in Montreal three weeks ago. A Star of David carved in his chest.

CHAPTER 02

I've been to too many strange places lately. Places completely foreign to me. New geography, new depth of feelings exposed. The Don River at night, rushing over rocks that look pink in the moonlight. An unfinished tower in Chicago, a thousand feet above concrete, where I'd make a sickening noise if I fell. A panelled hallway in Boston where gun smoke hung in gauzy blue sheets, where shotguns had boomed and automatic weapons had clattered and not one soul had called the cops.

Strange dark places with too many guns. Shots fired in Buffalo, Chicago, Boston. I'd had to use a gun again myself, the first time since my last fucked day in the Israeli army. It got so bad I hid my passport behind a kitchen drawer that has to be disassembled before you can remove it. Sliding it down there was a measure of how badly I need to stay out of the States for all kinds of reasons, including legal.

At least this new case was in Montreal, a place I know fairly well. There's a branch of the Geller family tree there that never made the move to Toronto, cousins I used to spend holidays with. After high school, a number of friends went there for university, where my own presence had not been required. I made many a weekend drive, slept off more than a few youthful adventures in the flats of the McGill ghetto, places rambling in size but still crowded, kids coming and going down halls where they'd crashed, up and down those wrought-iron outside stairs.

It was a straight six-hour drive east down the 401.

With Dante Ryan driving his new hemi powered Charger, maybe five.

My partner, Jenn Raudsepp, had been on leave since we got back from Boston, so the office had been both crazy busy and strangely quiet. There had been more work than I could handle alone but no one to talk to, share info with, complain to when things went wrong, laugh with when they went even worse. No one to hector, needle and otherwise abuse me. Our office manager, Colin MacAdam, who was supremely capable in many respects, was still a rural cop at heart, if not in body. Very down-to-earth. No one would ever mistake Colin for an imp. Especially not a six-foot blonde one.

On a humid morning in late June, dark grey clouds boiling up in the north, the threat of rain in the air, I walked into the office to the smell of a good dark roast and a similarly dark look across Colin's face.

I said, "What?"

"Mr. Ryan is in your office," Colin said. "And not in the best of moods. I asked him to wait out here and he looked like he wanted to slash the tires on my wheelchair."

Given how big Colin's shoulders have become since he started playing wheelchair basketball, I wasn't sure even Dante Ryan could pull that off. In which case he'd probably shoot holes in them.

"Cut him some slack," I said. "He's going through a hard time."

Ryan's wife, Cara, had thrown him out after Boston. Probably for good this time. He had been trying to stay clear of his old ways, for the sake of his marriage and his young son Carlo. He'd given up contract killing and opened an Italian restaurant on John Street in the entertainment district. Now he was getting out, selling his interest to one of his old connections who needed a business to account for some of his income.

As I poured myself a coffee, it occurred to me it was almost a year to the day since Ryan had first walked into my apartment—broken in, actually—and thrown into my lap the case that would end my career at Beacon Security and lead to the launch of my own agency, World Repairs.

And oh what hilarity had ensued ever since. All year long, in and out of scrapes I needed Ryan's help getting out of, to the point where my best friend and partner barely left her house. My long road back from post-concussion syndrome would be a jaunt compared to what she was facing now.

I opened the door to the office she and I shared and saw Ryan at Jenn's desk, his feet up on its empty surface, his shoes, as always, worth more than everything I wore all week. He was drinking coffee out of a mug with the logo of a design firm down the hall. His face had the grim cast I associate with calls to the coroner.

I said, "Thanks for coming."

"It's not like I had anything else to do," he said. "But on the bright side, I'm not the one running down to the Food Terminal at six a.m. to buy fucking romaine."

"You doing okay?"

"If you define okay as having your balls in a bear trap."

"Could you use a little distraction?"

"Fuck, yeah," he said. "You got something in mind?"

"A new case I might need help with. My first murder."

"Well, you know it wouldn't be mine," he said, his clouded look clearing a little, a tight grin appearing.

"You never had to solve one."

"No, but I had to anticipate what the person trying to solve it would see. Trust me, you want me on this. Do not doubt my usefulness."

Who in their right mind would?

"I just need to speak to the client," I said. "Make sure he'll authorize expenses for two."

"I'm not going to charge you, you dick."

"I'm talking about travel costs."

"Why? Where is this one?"

"Montreal."

"For how long?"

"Maybe a week."

"Cool," he said. "I like Montreal. Used to do business with the Cotronis back in the day. So who got killed?"

"A guy I went to summer camp with. His grandfather is hiring me."

"Summer camp? Christ, how old were you?"

"Twelve."

"I was that age, I was stealing, smoking and running from my stepfather. Summer and winter. So when was he killed, this camper?"

"A few weeks ago. His grandfather said the police are getting nowhere."

"Forget what they say on TV. A few weeks can still be early days."

"Not to a dying man."

Arthur Moscoe lived in a condo on top of a seven-storey building on Bedford, overlooking Varsity Stadium and the exploding crystal wing of the Royal Ontario Museum. A small Filipina let me in and led me to a closed room filled with light, even on a grey morning, and soft classical music playing from hidden speakers.

The man himself must have been big at one time. Even now, wasted by illness, he took up most of the king-size bed on which he lay, propped up by three pillows. The rest was taken up by assorted medical equipment, including a small tank providing oxygen through a tube up his nose. The feet thrust up beneath the bedspread like two sharp hills, the hands at the end of his bony grey wrists wide in their spread. If he played piano, an octave and a half would have been child's play. His head was also of great size and dominated by a nose that might once have been Roman but now drooped into a hook. His ears were like ferns, the lobes flopping down below the point of his jaw.

He was eighty-three now and dying of cancer. It was the first thing he told me once his attendant had left the room. "I've got both leukemia and lymphoma. It's a race to see which takes me first. That's one of the reasons you're dealing with me and not Sammy's mother," he said. "I might have months to live, but it could easily be weeks. So I don't have time to waste. The police have had three weeks to find exactly nothing. And I'm more of a take-charge type than my daughter. You want to talk to her, my advice is call before noon. She's a *schmecker*, that one."

"A what?"

"A smoker. Dope, grass, whatever they call it these days. Started back in the sixties and never stopped."

"What about his father?"

"Gone. Has to be three, four years now. A kind of liver cancer and he didn't even drink, that's the kind of luck he had. She's remarried now, my daughter, living in Florida, and the next time her husband is of any help will be the first."

"Siblings?"

"One sister, Sherry. Only she got religion and lives in Jerusalem. Calls herself Shira. Also not likely to be of any help to you. She and Sammy weren't very close. So I'm the man you deal with. I have all the money you'll need. Better than that,

I have lawyers. Good ones. You need anything at all, you call Henry Geniele. I have his direct number."

Jesus. Henry Geniele, senior partner at Geniele, Driscoll, Ross. Finding out he was at your disposal was like finding out Tom Brady just joined your pick-up football team.

"Bill whatever you have to but get results," he said. "It's terrible what they did to him. Beaten so badly. And—did I tell you already what else they did?

"No."

"They mutilated him. Carved a Magen David in his chest. The police said they did it after he was already dead, but still. His mother knows. I know. I can't get it out of my mind, the bastards."

"I'm sorry, Mr. Moscoe—"

"Everyone's sorry. It doesn't change what happened."

"What else have the police told you?"

"He was kicked to death, they think. Probably with steel-toed boots. They broke his head open, that beautiful head of his, full of stories. You ever heard the expression, Jonah, God invented man because he loves stories? If that's true, he would have invented Sammy over and over. There was nothing he couldn't turn into a story, even when he was a kid. And his columns—every week something caught his eye, his funny bone, his high horse. My girl prints them out for me from the computer. But then they kicked his head to pieces. Broke his neck too. Put an end to the stories."

Hearing that he'd died of blunt-force trauma to the head sent a chill over me. I had suffered my own brain injury seven months earlier, and I was still leery of anything remotely close to that. "I'm sorry," I said again.

"I don't need your sympathies. I need your professional help."

"What else did the police tell you?"

"I dictated a letter to my lawyer after I spoke to the detective there, while it was still fresh. I have a copy for you.

Otherwise, it's probably best you speak to them yourself. Get it first-hand. You speak French?"

"Some."

"Some may not get you far enough. They're all French, the Montreal cops, always have been."

"Who did you speak to?

"A Detective Paquette. Reynald Paquette."

"In French?"

"Ha. I'm the first to admit, Jonah, my generation didn't learn much French in Montreal. We were part of the problem, looking back. But Paquette's English is fine. It's his judgment I question."

"Why?"

"They found Sammy in Ville St-Laurent, out by Côte-Vertu. You know Montreal?"

"Parts of it."

"Not this part, I bet. It's all Arab now. It wasn't in my day, but you drive past there now, it's halal this, Islamic that."

"You think Muslims attacked him?"

"They're Jew haters, aren't they? Who else would kick a Jew to death and do what they did after? I told this to Paquette. Connect the dots, I told him. You don't have to be a genius. He said they had to consider all leads. I don't know if he was really clueless or being politically correct. Since then, I haven't heard much that's new. No suspects they've identified, certainly no arrests."

"When was he found?"

"May 29th. Early, just after seven. Guy opening his restaurant found him in the laneway behind. Also some kind of Arab. The address is in that envelope on the side table."

"Any idea what Sammy was doing there?"

"What did I know of his day-to-day life? He was my grandson, living in another city. There was some kind of call to the police that night, I know that much. They went to his place, but Paquette says it was a mistake. Maybe a prank call."

"I'll check into it. Anything else?"

He opened his mouth, about to speak, then closed it and looked out the window.

"Mr. Moscoe?"

He looked back at me: "We spoke maybe once a month, saw each other a few times a year. If it wasn't the Arabs, then maybe it had to do with his work."

"Why do you say that?"

"Because he wasn't a wild man, Sammy. Didn't run around. He was very devoted to his little girl, my first great-granddaughter. He got along with his ex-wife. He loved what he did. And he worked hard at it." He sighed deeply and said, "The little girl. Sophie. She'll be raised completely in French now. Not that it matters to me, I'll be gone soon. But she'll be lost to the family. Maybe there's one or two cousins she'll stay in touch with, but that's it."

"Do you have Paquette's email or phone line?" I asked.

"In that envelope. It has his direct line and cell, your retainer, Sammy's address, his ex-wife's number, the key to his flat . . ." He looked away and I could see teardrops pooling in the deep sockets of his sunken eyes.

I didn't force eye contact. I gave him the time he needed.

"There's a picture too," he finally said. "Take it out and look at it."

I picked up the envelope and slid out a five-by-seven print of a young man with light brown hair, thinning above the temples into an inadvertent pompadour, warm brown eyes behind glasses, a thin nose and a slightly weak chin.

Sammy? Is that you? Remembering the gawky kid I had tried to turn into a hitter.

Could someone look at a picture of me when I was twelve and see the man I was today? Were there hints, even then, of any of the darkness to come?

"You know," Mr. Moscoe said, breathing as deeply as his weak old lungs would allow, "I wish I'd never opened my mouth to him. About Montreal, I mean. He went there for school, I know, to the writing program at Concordia, but if it wasn't for me, maybe he would have come back here to live."

"Why do you say that?"

The old man's lips spread into a smile that moved from his dry lips to his eyes, still some brightness in them. "He's the one I told all my stories to. My Montreal stories. He ate them up. Of all my grandchildren, he was the one who took an interest. Always asking about the streets we came from, the characters, the fights, me and my exploits. You see me here now, running out of gas, but Montreal was my town for a long time. From the early fifties until the separatists came in, that's twenty-five years. And in those twenty-five years I went from nothing, less than nothing, to the owner of a company that set this family up pretty good. You've read Mordecai Richler? His books about St. Urbain Street?"

"Sure."

"Well, they were rich compared with us, that's all I can say. More than one step above. They were west of the Main, for one thing. You know St. Lawrence Boulevard?"

"Yes."

"We were east of there on De Bullion, probably the worst street in the whole area. And I had stories too. Who didn't? Montreal was a special town in those years. It had everything Toronto didn't have. The clubs, the nightlife, the colour. It was Havana North. All the great entertainers, strippers, boxers and wrestlers, hockey players, gangsters. Sammy loved those stories. He even moved to my old neighbourhood. He was paying thirteen hundred a month for a flat on Laval. I'd kid him—I'd say, 'Sammy, when we lived in that neighbourhood, we paid thirty-five dollars a month, and the first bucket of coal was free.' I'd tell him, 'Write a book about those old days when Sammy

Davis was dancing across the street from where Lili St. Cyr was stripping—and there was no question, Lili was the bigger star.' Ah, the poor kid," he sighed. "Poor, poor Sammy. No one should die like that, set upon by animals."

"No."

"You knew him, my daughter tells me."

"From summer camp," I said. "For a few years."

"You liked him?"

"I did."

"Because he was a quiet kid, you know. Loved to read, that one. Always with his nose in a book. You really remember him or you just saying you do?"

"I really do." I told him the story about the softball game, giving Sammy the nickname he used to the day he died. He was in tears when it ended, wiping them away with the backs of his hands.

"I am so glad to hear that," he heaved. "So glad. The better you knew him, the more connected you feel, the harder you'll work to catch the bastards who killed him. It won't just be a job for you."

"It never is," I said.

From *Montreal Moment* magazine, Montreal, March 31

Say a prayer for PQ critic

Slammin' Sammy Adler
Urban Affairs Columnist

Okay, this one might be too weird even for me, and if you're a regular reader, you know that must put it seriously beyond the fringe. And it is, nestled there comfortably in the lap of PQ agriculture critic André Simard, who is shocked and appalled by the fact that some Quebec consumers are unknowingly being sold halal meat that is not labelled as such.

Oh no! Not that! Eating meat that is otherwise safe and humanely slaughtered, but over which an Arabic prayer has been said. And without being told. Rise up, people! Get on your feet and march!

It's one thing to avoid kosher products because you hate Jews, or boycott certain east-end shoe stores that openly sell Israeli sandals, but how can you show your bias against Muslims without a label?

Mr. Simard, who is a veterinarian, said he would not knowingly buy halal meat because it doesn't correspond to his values and convictions.

Personally, I think a vet could better show his convictions by avoiding meat altogether, but I'm a carnivore too, so I won't fire that barb.

Look, I was raised in a kosher home where the only meat we ate came from animals that had had a two-thousand-year-old blessing said over them before their throats were cut. It didn't seem to harm them—at least not the blessing part. And kosher chickens tasted better than their non-kosher counterparts, whether it was the blessing or the way they were raised and killed.

Those words were muttered in Hebrew, these in Arabic. If there is a difference linguistically, it's minute. Both spring from the same Semitic roots. If it's cultural—well, most things are with the PQ, even agriculture, it would seem.

Maybe it's Mr. Simard who needs a prayer said over him as the fall election looms. Because I don't think he has one.

No one knows where this one is going, least of all me. The winds of change are blowing in Quebec, with new parties surging in the polls while older ones like the PQ—perhaps because their august members have time to waste on fringe protests like this—risk being left behind.

My view? Let Mr. Simard go down in the fall and return to life as a meat-eating veterinarian. Let the rest of us go on being subverted. Of all the threats to life as we know it, this is one I can live with.

TUESDAY, JUNE 21

CHAPTER 03

A warm summer rain was falling at seven the next morning. Not on me, though. I was smart enough to wait under the overhang outside 10 Hogarth. It was June 21st, the longest day of the year, but the whole landscape was dark, wet and grey, as it had been for days. Summer was starting somewhere but not here. At that hour it was quiet except for a crow boasting about something on a high wire and a streetcar grinding up Broadview.

I shuddered slightly when I saw Ryan's new car coming south. It was the same car we had rented in Boston three months ago, a midnight-blue Charger, only this one had the hemi-powered V8 engine he had wanted at the time. A few drops of rain hit my face as I loaded my suitcase and knapsack into the trunk. My leather shoulder bag, which had my laptop and tablet, went behind the front seat. I got into the front with a new silver Halliburton case very much like the one Ryan used to transport the tools of his dark trade. His had foam cut-outs that matched his .22 target pistol and its suppressor; the favourite of his Glocks, a G22 that carried only fifteen rounds, as opposed to the usual seventeen, but fired .40-calibre bullets that blew bigger holes in its target; the compact version of the Baby Eagle; an army-issue Beretta that's his throwaway if needed; and the one I think of as his persuader, a chrome Smith & Wesson revolver with an eight-and-three-eighths barrel, long enough to churn butter or a man's insides.

Mine had different cut-outs, things I wanted to show Ryan on the long drive.

He eyed the case on my lap and said, "I know you didn't suddenly go gun crazy."

"Nope. Just some new toys." Yes, they were legitimate investigative tools, but hoo boy, they were toys right out of a kid's spy tale.

He pulled out of the driveway and we headed up Broadview toward O'Connor and the turnoff to the Don Valley Parkway. "You have my interest," he said.

"With Jenn on leave," I said, "I've had to do more work on my own. Pretty much all of it. No one to spell me off on surveillance."

"Colin can sit," he said. "It's what he does best."

"Nice." Colin was in a wheelchair only because he'd been shot coming to my aid fifteen months ago. Being a colder specimen than me, Ryan never understands the guilt I live with.

"He spells me from time to time, and he's actually better at peeing in a car than I am. But I'm still on my own in most situations."

"So what's in the case?"

"Surveillance equipment. Some of the things they have now . . . I mean, why sit outside a guy's house for twelve hours in the cold when you can plant one of these in his house or car?"

I reached around for the case, set it on my lap and snapped open the latches. I took out my new sphere cam, barely the size of a Ping-Pong ball. "Records picture and sound. Motion activated, records thirty frames a second and has a two-gig memory card."

"Yeah? How many rounds does it fire? None? Then I'll still take my toys over yours."

"Look at this. This one I love." I slipped a gold-and-black pen out of a thin vinyl case. "I can record a hundred and forty hours of voice with this and when I'm done"—I pulled the top half of the pen out of the bottom—"there's a USB key that fits right into my computer."

"Didn't I see that on *Modern Family*? The kid with the curly hair has a spy pen? What?"

I guess I was giving him my "You watch *Modern Family*?" look.

"I was still living at home then," he said.

"This is the real thing. You are recorded and downloaded before you know it. Or . . . here. Remember the transponder they planted on me in Boston? The size of a deck of cards?"

I took a small square unit out of a cardboard box and nestled it in my palm. Just half an inch thick, about the size of a book of matches. "See how much smaller they got in just a few months? Water resistant, shock resistant and motion activated. This not only traces a car. It locks into its GPS system and tells you every-thing—I mean, everything—about where it went, where it stopped, how long it stopped. Everything but what you pay for gas."

We turned left off O'Connor onto the ramp that fed onto the Don Valley northbound. So did a lot of other cars, at least one of them so close to our rear, he almost nudged Ryan's new bumper. I pitied the first person who damaged the new car. Gunplay would likely ensue.

"What else you got in there?" he asked. "Looks like a big magnet."

I reached in and pulled out what indeed looked like a ten-inch magnet, shaped like half an oval. Only it came with a range of coloured springs I could mount between the two handles, each offering varying resistance. "Something else I've been using since Jenn's been off."

I gripped the device and squeezed the springs until they were too tightly coiled to move further.

"Grip strength," he said. "How much you got on there?"

"Up to ninety-seven pounds left-handed, ninety-five right."

"Is that any good?"

"Average is sixty or seventy. The highest I've seen recorded anywhere was just over two hundred. So I'm above average but not threatening anyone's record."

"What's this got to do with Jenn being gone?"

"Pressure points," I said. "*Shotokan* karate teaches a lot of them and Krav Maga throws in a few more. I'm working on places in the neck, under the arm, the forearm—if I squeeze them hard enough, I can take a man down myself with minimal effort."

"So can I," Ryan said. "Only mine don't get up."

"Yeah, yeah. The guns. I know. Anyway, my neurologist told me I should still avoid blows to the head. Anything that could help me subdue someone without getting hit is a bonus."

"Just give them the old Mr. Spock neck pinch and they drop?"

"They might not drop," I said, "but the pain would make it hard for them to think straight."

"Must make you a better strangler. In theory."

"Yes, it would."

"Maybe I'll try it at the hotel."

After a period of silence, he looked over at me and said, "So how's Jenn doing? Any idea when she's coming back?"

"It might be more a question of if than when."

"Seriously?"

"Neither of us really knows what she went through," I said. "It's not like getting cut or bruised or breaking a bone."

"You did all that the first week I knew you."

Jesus, he was right. And plenty more had happened to me since then. But I was still doing what I had to do. "What I'm saying is, those injuries, you know how long you're going to need to heal. You get stitches, a cast, a brace, a crutch. What does she get? How long will this take to heal? Like with my concussion, it might be weeks, maybe months before she's back. If she comes back."

"Are you keeping in touch?"

"Sort of. We've had to talk about insurance claims and medical expenses. We email each other maybe once a week."

"She ever mention me?" he asked.

"No. Sorry."

"It's cool. I was just wondering. Anyway, you ain't got her, but you got me."

"Montreal may never be the same," I said.

It took a little over an hour to get past the eastern suburbs and bedroom communities, out in front of most of the big rattling semis. With little traffic and an open road, Ryan took the car up to his usual cruising speed. He never drove over the limit the cops tolerated, other than to pass—especially when he had guns in the car.

We weren't constant chatterers, either of us, and it was easy to stretch out the time in the capsule of his new car, just going with the rain and shitty driving conditions, the delays here and there when one truck lumbered into the left lane to slowly pass another.

I had mixed feelings about being on the road with Ryan. If things got rough, there was no one I'd rather have watching my back. I just didn't want them to get that rough again, not so soon. My head was still healing. My body was still purging the residues of the violence we'd encountered—and engineered—in Boston.

"It was funny watching you pull up this morning," I said. "In this car, this colour."

"Made you think of Boston?"

"It did."

"I didn't pick it to freak you out. But now I'm on my own, I wanted something new. A little muscle, a little style."

"Is this really it for you guys?" I asked.

"It wasn't me that walked out or even wanted to break up," he said. "I told you, she gave me the boot. And the worst part? I seriously fucking tried. That's what is so wrong with it. I understood her concerns about Carlo and his safety. I disassociated myself from the old life. Did I throw myself into the restaurant one hundred per cent? Maybe not, but you couldn't tell it from the outside. I challenge anyone to say different. I challenge *her* to contradict it. I played the part, I acted it day and night. That's what makes me so mad."

"Would you go back if you could?"

He stared out the windshield, as the wipers cleared away the streaking rain.

"I don't know," he said. "I'd rather be with them than not, that's the truth. But at a certain point it's got to be better for Carlo if it settles one way or the other. If she's gonna keep kicking me out every time shit happens, I should just stay out, support them the best I can and let us all get the fuck on with our lives. I'll live close by, she'll give me plenty of access to Carlo. And I won't murder the guys she dates, long as they behave themselves around my kid."

"Did she ask you to leave because of the things you've done for me?"

"First of all, she didn't ask. She told. Second, while I'd love to blame you and not me, it would be a little too handy. It all came down to who we are right now, me and her. Who we grew up into. Who I was when I did what I did for a living. How that translates into who I am now."

I heard what he said, took it in, pondered a few different replies that could prove helpful, one or two that could get me shot if taken the wrong way, and finally leapt for the safety of a male refuge: "So what's the car like with the hemi engine?"

He seemed relieved I'd veered back to car talk.

"The one we had in Boston," he said, "was the basic SE model, had about 300 horsepower. This one has 470. That's fucking ridiculous, it's only thirty less than the turbo Porsche Cayenne, which I also tested. And quite liked. Power and luxury, what's not to? But you know me, I don't like to stand out too much, and a Porsche insignia in a rearview mirror? Fuck it. There's way more Chargers on the road."

"What's the top speed?"

"I tried it one night on the 400, middle of the night, hit one-thirty—miles, not kilometres—but I had to ease off because I wasn't alone on the road. If I was on the Autobahn, on a straightaway, no one else around me? I think it could top one-forty-five."

We were doing maybe a third of that now. But it was good to know we had speed to burn, in case we had to burn it.

About halfway to Montreal, as you get to Kingston, walls of rust coloured stone rise up ten or fifteen feet in the air, once light pink but now darkened by years of seepage and exhaust. This is where crews had to blast through granite hillocks, part of the Canadian Shield, to make way for the road. In winter dazzling ice formations burst through the rock, forming long spouting cones like wizards' white beards. Now it was just wet with the rain that was following us east.

As the rocky walls fell away, and the roadside view returned to the usual flat green fields and poplars trembling in the rain. I told Ryan what I knew about Sammy: the uncoordinated lonely kid I remembered from Camp Arrowhead, and the more self-assured writer he had apparently become.

"According to his grandfather," I said, "plus his obituary and some other things I read about him, he was something of a local treasure in Montreal."

"Based on what?"

"He had a weekly column in a magazine called *Montreal Moment*, which looks like their version of *NOW*. He wrote under the name Slammin' Sammy."

"The one you gave him."

"Yeah. I cracked up when I saw that."

"You have a plan? A starting point?"

"We'll look at his place, speak to the investigators."

"You'll speak to them. I'm taking no part in that."

"Fine. Then there's the editor of the magazine he wrote for, his ex-wife, neighbours. Something will catch our eye. A path will open and we'll walk down it."

"You with your spy tools and hand-grip."

"And you with enough firepower to outfit a Western."

"You're welcome. You buy this idea he was killed by Muslims?"

"Getting the story filtered through the grandfather might or might not match what the cops actually have. But there is a lot of anti-Semitism in Muslim communities," I said. "And more so in Quebec than Ontario. Firebombings of Jewish schools, that sort of thing."

"Well, Muslims, not Muslims, I don't care either way," he said. "You know me."

"You'll abuse anyone."

"Only as needed. But here's my take on them."

"Uh-oh."

"No uh-oh needed, it's very straight on. My people were immigrants, same as them. Or you, for that matter. My mother's parents came here in the fifties, my father's, the Irish side, back in the eighteen-eighties. And they had their problems fitting in but did they try to make everyone do everything their way and fucking gripe about the country that took them in? No. They tried to fit in, shut up and took their lumps, and tried to do better by their kids."

"When exactly did you ever shut up and take your lumps?"

"I said them, not me. And I took plenty of lumps from my stepfather."

His late stepfather, he meant. The one who had supposedly taken his own life by shooting himself in the head. Twice.

"What I'm saying," he went on, "is it worked for my people, it worked for yours, and it would work for them if they'd shut the fuck up about religion and just fit in."

"They should make you ambassador."

"They fucking well should."

The first landmark I made out in the rain was the dome of St. Joseph's Oratory, built on Mount Royal's northwestern slope, where the crippled came in hope of leaving their crutches behind.

"I meant to ask you," I said, "how's your French?"

"I grew up speaking both English and Italian, so French in school wasn't hard for me. A lot of root words are the same, them both being Romance languages, and you know there's no one more romantic than me."

"God, no."

"So I don't speak that much French, mostly since I don't get the chance, but I understand more than I let on."

"Good."

"And you?"

"Same sort of story. I learned English and Hebrew as a kid, plus enough Yiddish phrases to get through a family dinner, so a third language also came more easily. Unfortunately, Hebrew and French share nothing, so I don't have that advantage. I can speak enough to get by but I don't think I'm going to master all the subtleties. Fortunately, I have someone who can."

"Who's that?"

"Beacon Security belonged to a national association of agencies. You helped investigators in other provinces when cases spilled over the borders and they did the same for you. When I was still on staff there, I worked with a guy from Montreal, Bobby Ducharme, and we clicked. Kept in touch. I called him last night and he's going to try to get a read on the detectives working the case. I'll call him once we're settled at the hotel, see what he's got."

"What's he like?"

"Bobby? Late thirties," I said. "In great shape. He was a hockey player, got as far as the high juniors but never made the pros. Played with a bunch of guys who went to the NHL but he was never a good enough skater. Was mostly a goon his last few years, way more penalty minutes than points. Still built like a brick shithouse."

"Trust him?"

"Yup. He's a good guy and I'm sure he'll do what he can."

The closer we got to the city, the more we were swarmed by smaller, speedier cars darting in and out of lanes like panicked animals dashing through a canyon, uncomfortably close on all sides. I could feel Ryan tense up, take tighter control of the wheel. His eyes moved from mirror to mirror, taking in everything. He was never a man to let things go unnoticed.

"Much as I like the car," he said, "I'll be glad to get off this road."

"I would have driven halfway."

"In the old car, maybe. Not this one. And that's for your own benefit."

"How so?"

"It's a brand new car. I've had it four whole days. And we're on the 401, which they should rename the Highway of Idiots. Say you're driving and one of the many idiots currently around us slams into us. Wrecks my new car while you're driving it. Assuming we survive the crash, what's the first thing I'm going to do?"

"Yell at me?"

"Think harder."

I tried to put myself in his shoes. "Shoot the other driver."

"Making you?"

"A witness."

"If not an accessory. You get a bitchy Crown attorney having a bad hair day and suddenly you're being arraigned.

So not letting you drive now is all for your benefit, Jonah. That's how I like to spend my time, thinking how to make your life better, safer and more stress free."

"I should hire you full time."

The hotel was on Sherbrooke Street west of Boulevard St-Laurent—also known as St. Lawrence, the fabled Main of Arthur Moscoe's youth. A Holiday Inn: nothing conspicuous, just the way Ryan liked it. It was easy to find from the highway. We fed off onto the 720 eastbound, past concrete loops and overpasses, the lower parts coloured with graffiti, the tops parts grey and patchy where repairs had been done. More than a few of Montreal's highways and bridges had shed pieces of concrete rather suddenly of late. At one point, four of the five bridges linking the island to the mainland had to be closed for inspection or repair. I hoped the patchwork held as we drove through. Montreal's construction industry was notoriously corrupt even by the bottomed-out standards of that trade.

We got off the highway at the St-Laurent exit and went north past boarded-up stores, places that looked like hoarding would only improve their curb appeal, and cheap hot dog and French fry stands I remembered visiting late into the night. A Chinese archway marked the entrance to Chinatown, its restaurants brightly coloured and jammed with the lunchtime trade. At Sherbrooke we turned left and found the hotel a few blocks west. Ryan drove underground and parked close to an elevator. We unloaded our gear and went up three levels to the hotel lobby and checked in with my credit card. Arthur Moscoe would cover it all and I'd get the bonus air miles.

Life felt grand.

Until Ryan said, "What the fuck is this? We're sharing a room? I thought this client was loaded."

"It's not him, it's the Fête Nationale."

"The what?"

"What they used to call St-Jean-Baptiste Day. The week of June 24th, all the hotels were full."

"You better not snore," he said. "I sleep with a gun under my pillow."

The room was what we needed it to be. It wasn't some chic Montreal B&B off Rue St-Denis amid the sizzling café scene. It was a room where we would make our phone calls, sleep and work on making ourselves better grippers and stranglers.

Ryan showered when we got in. He said his shoulders were tight from the drive and he wanted to loosen up. I turned on the TV, which was set to a French news station. A guy with combed-back hair and a good baritone was reporting on *les sports*, but with no baseball team and the Canadiens out of the playoffs, he didn't have a lot of *sports* to talk about. Then it was over to *le météo*, which predicted more *pluie*, or rain, throughout the next day. The weather person had a clear accent that was easy to follow, for the most part. She seemed to be holding out hope the low system would clear up by the big night—the Fête Nationale—and an outdoor concert at Parc Maisonneuve.

Behind her, footage rolled of work crews erecting a bandshell in the rain, tarps blowing around like they were trying to flee the scene. Then came an interview with someone at the park that went completely over my head. A sponsor of the event who spoke in a thick *joual* I couldn't make out at all. It might as well have been Navajo. A stout man with a white brush cut, he was pointing at the work crews, probably saying the show would go on no matter what.

I could see my French would have to shake off its rust fast if it was going to do me any good in Montreal. Either that, or I'd need Bobby Ducharme on call night and day. Too bad the two solitudes here weren't English and Hebrew.

The clock on the news channel said it was one-thirty. I called Bobby and got his voice mail. I told him we were in and left him our room number, along with my cell.

When Ryan was done, I showered too, just to loosen my body after six hours of sitting. I let the water hit the base of my neck awhile, then leaned away so the hot spray worked down my back. Aaah. Hot water therapy. Cures most ills. For the rest there's always ice.

"You hungry?" Ryan asked when I got out. "Want to hunt down a famous Montreal smoked meat?"

"We had a huge breakfast three hours ago. Let's go to Sammy's first."

"Which is where?"

"East and north of here. On Laval Street. Not far from St-Denis."

"Where all the cafés are?"

"Yes."

"So we could go to that joint on the way back, the famous one on the Main everyone talks about."

"Schwartz's."

"Right."

"Let's see what we find at Sam's."

CHAPTER 04

Driving to the hotel from the highway had been easy. Going north from there was insane, especially on St-Laurent. Trucks and cars stopped without warning on either side of the street to disgorge their goods and passengers, prompting the usual blast of horns that changed the usual nothing. We turned east and tried going north on St-Denis; it was a little more orderly, less abrupt than the Main, but no faster. Pedestrians were a lot like New Yorkers, crossing against lights, daring you to hit them.

Would they do it if they knew who was driving? Ryan leaned the heel of his hand on the horn a couple of times, muttering, "I am not hosing gristle out of my new grille. I am not even paying someone else to do it. It is just not happening. Move, people!" he shouted. "Does a green light mean something different here?"

"Apparently."

"Perhaps they don't know I'm armed?"

"Thought all your guns were packed away,"

He said, "Ahem," and hitched up his right pant leg. His Baby Eagle was nestled there. "Ankle holster, Jonah. Ankle holster. Christ, sometimes you don't think right."

We found parking on Laval half a block south of Sammy's flat. The buildings were all attached brick or stone duplexes with Montreal's signature curving wrought-iron staircases on the outside. Most of these flats had been renovated, linoleum peeled away and the old wide oak planks sanded and polished. Years of plaster and wallpaper torn away to expose brick walls, where people could hang their old guitars and pieces of splashy art under warm pot lights. Some were single-family dwellings, both floors used by one couple. Some, like Sammy's, were still separate units.

His was the ground-floor flat in a stone building with an iron railing that needed repainting: blisters of black had peeled away to show patches of rust. I got out the key Arthur Moscoe had provided. I also had a letter to the building management company, explaining my permission to access the place.

"Hmmm."

"Wrong key?" Ryan asked.

"Right key," I said. "Wrong seal over the lock."

"Whose seal?"

"The Service de police de la Ville de Montréal."

"Nicely pronounced. What else does it say?"

"*Défense d'entrer.*"

I put the key into the lock anyway, breaking the seal, and turned it.

I had the feeling there wasn't going to be much to find in Sammy's flat. Detective Paquette and his team had probably already taken everything worth taking—phone records, bills— to comb through at their discretion. And neither Ryan nor I had any special gift for or experience at searching places. A first-year police detective would have searched more crime scenes in six months than I have in all my cases combined. Any forensic evidence would have been gathered by pros, sorted and sealed for analysis. Most of Ryan's stalking as a killer, from what he'd told me, was done outdoors. He followed victims to learn their habits and routes, note their vulnerabilities. Pick his spot. He rarely broke into someone's house, before or after the job.

But we had to go through it. Forget what the cops took and take in the rest, see what was left, get a sense of Sammy the man, not the twelve-year-old camper I remembered.

Putting a key through a police seal wasn't going to trigger an alarm and we had an official letter and a school of lawyers one call away. Still, we wanted to be quick. Bringing Dante Ryan together with the Montreal police had no upside either of us could see. He flat out does not like law enforcement, not of any stripe.

The rain was keeping most people off their sidewalks and balconies. Those who were out were hurrying along. I opened the front door and we walked into a foyer with scuffed walls, their plaster cracked here and there from the heave and sigh of Montreal winters. There were two hockey sticks by the door, both well used, the tape on them scraped and curled at the bottom. The entry hall was narrow and dark but showed a long railroad flat with two large front rooms on one side of the hall, a living room and parlour separated by an archway with elaborate moulding, and on the other side a small study. The ceilings were high by Toronto standards—ten feet to our usual eight—and the original hammered tin, painted over many times but not enough to hide the floral patterns. The rooms would be filled with light on a less gloomy day. Today wasn't that day. It felt humid and close in there with the windows having been closed all this time, but we didn't want to open any or turn on the lights.

We decided I would take the study, he would take the two front rooms. Then we'd trade and swap notes. Then move to the back and do the same with the kitchen and bedroom. We didn't expect any clues to leap out and declare themselves. There'd be nothing luminous beckoning from dark corners. I figured the best thing a search could do was give us a list of questions to ask and people to ask them of. I'd go to the cops later, speak to Paquette without Ryan's glowering presence, and see if what he told us matched up with what we found. Or didn't find.

The study appeared to have been stripped of most things. I found empty hanging folders in his desk drawer where I imagined recent bills and statements had been. It's what I would have wanted to see first. They would also have his laptop, tablet, phone. An agenda if he kept one. Actual paper notebooks if he still used those. Dusty gaps on his desk showed where a large blotter had been. They'd taken the whole thing. Other clean rectangles showed where things that had been there a long time had been removed.

So what didn't they take that would help me catch a glimpse of him? A hell of a lot of reference books and dictionaries. An entire shelf devoted to books about Quebec's roller coaster ride from the Quiet Revolution of the sixties through two referendums on sovereignty. Collections of columns by great newspaper writers and books on Muslim culture and its accommodation in Quebec. There were cardboard magazine folders exploding with sheaves of used paper, drafts he'd printed and marked with red ink, the pages looking old, years old. Old versions of stories he must have eventually finished. The brick wall of the study had more than a few awards for his writing. Nothing national, but plenty of local and regional ones for best story, best feature, best column, all published in *Montreal Moment* magazine.

On the masthead of a back issue, I found the address of its office, which was close by on Milton Street, right in the heart of the McGill ghetto where I used to crash while missing out on education. The editor-in-chief was Holly Napier, whose direct number was listed.

Another ten minutes looking through the fringes of his writing life didn't tell me more than I already knew, except that he'd also won an award for writing an annual report for CN Rail, but hadn't put it up on the wall. It was down in the drawer that had held his missing financial statements, along with a copy of the report itself, a glossy hundred-page testimonial to the achievements of the company during the fiscal year in question.

I scanned the walls and hutch of the desk for photos of Sammy and anyone else in his life. There was a series of shots taken of him on Mount Royal, up near the summit, the east end of the city sprawling out behind him. One of Sammy with his arm around an older woman who must have been his mother, outside his flat. No clue as to who had taken them.

What if his grandfather was right, and he'd simply been in the wrong part of town, for whatever reason, and had been set upon by an anti-Semitic mob? My chances of adding much to the police investigation of a crime like that were slim. Mr. Moscoe would be better off putting up a reward. I had no entry into the Muslim world, and I doubted the Montreal police had much of one either. But they had to have collected some evidence: beating or kicking a man to death is messy business, and traces would be left. Enough to send someone to prison for life, if someone were ever caught.

I hailed Ryan and we switched rooms. It felt less stuffy in the parlour than in the closer confines of the study. There was a red brocade divan backed against the window, and a couple of mismatched club chairs facing it across a glass-topped table. Every available bit of wall space was taken up with bookshelves. His tastes ran to modern fiction, abrasive comedy, Jewish abrasive comedy—every novel and essay collection by Mordecai Richler, in line with his grandfather's love for that era—more non-fiction collections and memoirs, books on film and music. Plenty of world history and more than a few books on Israel and its recent agonies. I liked the man Sammy had become. I became curious about his music and went in search of his collection. He was old enough to still have CDs—hundreds of them—rather than an all-electronic collection. There was a little bit of classical, a lot of jazz and world music, a lot of it West African. There was a great assortment of roots artists, going back to the Band, and enough local bands, including Arcade Fire, to show his support for the Quebec scene.

More photos: Sammy in this very room, playing a mandolin, someone else partly visible playing a guitar. No face. Just an elbow in mid-strum. Another of Sammy around age five, walking with his small hand in the much larger hand of his grandfather.

"So?"

I turned to see Ryan outside the study.

"What do you think after two rooms?"

"I think I'm sad he was murdered," I said. "I feel like I would have liked him again. Well-read guy, a lot of different music."

"Good at his job," Ryan said. "All the awards on his wall. Plus one I guess he wasn't so proud of. Something for a railroad, down in a drawer."

"Yeah, I saw that. Anything move you in any direction?"

"Not yet."

"Me neither. Let's try the back."

The floors leading toward the rear were hardwood, the high ceilings hammered tin in floral patterns. Halfway down we found a bathroom and linen closet and pawed through the contents of both. Nothing interesting in the bathroom—not even a condom—and no guns, cash or looted Nazi art in the closet.

The kitchen showed plenty of regular use. It was open concept with cupboards made by Ikea or one of its competitors. The doors were all slightly off-kilter, either hanging too low or not closing all the way. The pots and pans were blackened from use, and there were dozens of spices in a tall shelving unit and a lot of different cooking sauces, mostly Asian, in the fridge. The front of the fridge was half covered with photos, slips for medical appointments, a pharmacy receipt for a steroid cream, a parking ticket. There was a sheet of paper with a list of thirty or so names and phone numbers. The names were all French, all prefaced by the initial M., which in French stands for Monsieur. There was also a photo of Sammy in a jacket and tie, accepting one of his awards. With him was a beautiful young woman with a great mess of curly red hair she wasn't trying too hard to tame. For some reason—the chaste way she held his arm as she leaned in for the photo—I felt their relationship was professional, not personal.

"Oh, Christ," I heard Ryan say from the bedroom.

"Found something?"

"Bet your ass I found something."

"Coming."

He was squatting in the small closet of the bedroom, a dusty box at his feet. He was holding a long panoramic photograph in a wood-and-glass frame. I knew exactly what it was because I had one just like it, also stuck away in a box in a closet at home. It was the group photo they took every summer at Camp Arrowhead. All the campers lined up in three rows, all in white Arrowhead T-shirts, no hats, squinting as the photographer took long exposures with his special camera.

"Tell me this isn't you," Ryan said, his thumb on one camper in the first row.

I took the frame and looked at the boy he meant and, yes, he was me. Twelve years old. Smallish, my hair shorn of its usual curls for the summer, very dark and close to the skull.

"Not much size on you," Ryan said. "Except maybe the ears."

"I know. I grew more at fifteen and again at seventeen."

"Aw, and look at those eyelashes. I bet the girls just curled their toes when you batted them."

"Bat this."

I scanned over the rows looking at faces I hadn't seen for years. Mitchell Stroll. Phil Mittleman. Stevie Garber. Irwin Resnick.

And Sammy Adler. There in the back row with the tall ones. Not up to his full height, slouching an inch or two. Age twelve, like me. Now dead for three weeks. I needed to leave his place with more than we knew going in.

And we did, thanks to Ryan. He found the hair in the bed, the long, dark curly one that couldn't have been Sammy's. The cops had probably removed samples for their own analysis and missed this one in the folds of the sheets. Assuming Sammy did his laundry once in a while—and the general tidiness of the place didn't suggest otherwise—someone else had slept in the bed in the last days or weeks of Sammy's life. Which gave us something to start with, ask Detective Paquette or the neighbours about.

"We done?" Ryan asked.

"Here, yes. Let's try the upstairs neighbours. And then the magazine. It's just a few blocks away."

We closed up Sammy's place. I thumbed the seal back over the lock, smoothing the broken halves together. Then I knocked on the door to the main-floor flat. No one answered. I slipped a card with my cell number circled in red through the mail slot and a note saying, "Please call. *Appelez-moi s'il vous plaît.*"

The rain was coming down harder. I heard a heavy drumming across the street. I looked up and saw the balcony on the top floor of a building there had been covered over by light green corrugated plastic that was magnifying the noise. Someone was sitting under it, protected from the rain, watching the street. Looking right at me. An old woman with wiry grey hair pulled back into a bun, loose strands of it flying out away from her ears.

A watcher.

"Wait a second," I said to Ryan.

I tilted my head up and made eye contact with the woman. I pointed to myself and then to her porch. "May I come up and speak to you a moment?" I called. Then tried it in French. "*Madame? Est-ce que je peux monter une minute vous parler?*"

The woman nodded, not giving a hint as to which language she spoke, and got up out of her chair. I crossed the street and went up three concrete steps, then one flight of a wrought-iron staircase. When I reached for the door I heard the click of the lock disengaging.

She had not acknowledged my English or French because she spoke neither to any great extent. She was Greek, about five feet tall and almost as wide, dressed entirely in black. Mrs. Iiamos, no first name offered. We conversed in broken English, with a few hand gestures, first acknowledging how sad it was that Sammy was dead—"Nice boy, very nice. No trouble. Only now."

Of course, she remembered the police coming that night, almost three o'clock. She had heard the rapping on his door—she didn't sleep so well anymore. But they didn't stay long, maybe ten minutes, and then it was quiet.

"That's it?" I said? "Nothing else?"

She breathed in and frowned lightly. "One more time, somebody knocking again. Maybe three o'clock. I look out the window but nobody there. I go back to sleep."

I filed that away and asked about visitors.

"He have a little girl," she said, holding out her hand at shoulder height to indicate her height. "She come every week. Nice girl," she said, sighing and putting a hand to her cheek, shaking her head to show her concern for the nice little girl whose nice-boy father had been killed.

"What about a woman?" I asked. "Long hair?" I brushed my hands down my jacket, turning them to indicate long and curly.

Mrs. Iiamos smiled. "Since one month, maybe. She come at night only, never day. Come late, one, one-thirty. Go home four o'clock, five o'clock." She shook her head, acknowledging the scandalousness of the hours, then said, "It's okay I tell you. If he's alive, I don't say one word against no one, but now . . ."

"Yes, thank you. He was my friend, so it's good to help me. How many times did you see her?"

She thought about it and said, "Five, six times."

"What days of the week?"

"Three, four times Saturday night. The other times Thursday. No Friday, No Sunday. No other day, I don't think."

"You have a good memory."

"My husband pass away. My kids move. And I don't sleep good. Sleep, um, very light. I hear doors open, I hear them close. And when is hot, if I no can sleep, I sit outside. I watch. Watch out for neighbours."

I mimicked the motion of a steering wheel. "She drive?"

"No. She walk away. That way. To Carré St-Louis."

"How old is she?"

"Maybe thirty," which Mrs. Iiamos pronounced as *tooty*. I didn't care how she pronounced it, everything she told me was something I didn't know before. A thirty-year-old woman, with long dark hair, coming to Sammy's late, leaving early. A married woman?

"He's a Jew?" she asked.

"Yes."

"I think maybe she's a Jew." She rolled her hands down her shoulders as I had to indicate the long curly hair.

Thursdays and Saturdays, she had said: A Jewish woman, I wondered, unable to come on Friday?

"So you think he was banging someone else's woman?" Ryan said.

"A possibility."

"An Orthodox Jew."

"A theory."

"That narrow it down enough to reward ourselves with a smoked meat?"

"The magazine first."

"All right. I was just saying we're getting traction."

"Then let's keep going."

CHAPTER 05

The *Montreal Moment* office was in a three-storey stone house on Milton, which runs east of the McGill campus toward St-Laurent. The sales and marketing staff took up the ground floor, editorial was on the second, design was at the very top. As in Sammy's place, the ceilings were high, the rooms generously sized.

A woman at a ground-floor reception desk told us Holly Napier's office was one flight up, rear corner. Up we went, past bulletin boards jammed with notices of upcoming city council meetings, union meetings, protests, cultural openings and some events that no doubt combined elements of all. The newsroom itself was open concept along the right side, with three white pillars spaced evenly from front to back. Along the left side were closed offices with glass fronts.

The closest person to the front was a man in the visible quarter of a cubicle. He looked to be in his late twenties and was staring intently at a stand-alone widescreen monitor, a white Mac at his fingertips. His face was bony and hollow looking, as if he were drawing in his cheeks, and he had two weeks' growth of dark hair and beard. He looked up as I got close to his desk and said, "*Bonjour.*"

I said, "*Bonjour.*"

He said, "What can I do for you?" My French obviously had not fooled him into thinking I was a native.

"Is Holly Napier in?" I asked.

He pointed behind him at two women, one sitting at a desk, the other leaning in over her shoulder, pointing at a monitor. The seated woman was young, Asian, early twenties with long dark hair—but not a match to the hair we'd found at Sammy's flat: perfectly straight, not a curl in it. The woman standing over her had glorious curls, red ones tumbling past her shoulders, the right length but the wrong colour for Sammy's mystery woman. But very right on her. It was the woman from the photo on Sammy's fridge, the one who'd been with him when he collected his award, holding his arm so loosely.

She sensed our presence, looked up, smiled a little. "Can I help you?"

"Are you Holly?"

"Yes."

"Can we talk a minute?"

"If you're looking for freelance work, the short answer is we can't use any right now."

I said, "I want to talk about Sammy Adler."

The smile went away. She said something to the younger woman and walked up to me. She appeared to be about my age, trim in jeans and a sleeveless blue top. Her eyes were pale green and brilliantly clear.

She asked what my interest in Sammy was.

"Can we talk privately?"

She looked at the seated young woman and said, "Can you keep going on your own?"

"I think so," the woman said.

"Go back to your notes and find another quote or two," Holly Napier said. "I'm still not getting who this person is and why she's running for office."

"Okay."

"Keep it to a thousand words. I don't want her picture to be a thumbnail." She said to me, "We're on deadline so I'm gonna need to make it quick."

"That's fine."

"Come on. My office is the one at the back."

Only when I moved did she see Ryan behind me and start a little.

There were a lot of plants in Holly Napier's office. Spider plants hanging in baskets hooked into the ceiling near the window, something large and rubbery in a plastic pot meant to look like clay, a tall, leafy ficus with a lot of new growth, glossy leaves free of dust. They all looked well taken care of.

Ryan and I were sitting in matching chairs with inoffensive beige padding. He was closest to the wall and angled so he could see the door. Holly sat behind a light beech desk with a Mac notebook networked wirelessly to a mouse, keyboard and flat-screen monitor. She had a much better chair than we did, with levers that angled it this way and that. Editions of at least three or four newspapers in English and French covered whatever surface didn't have files, mail and the remains of a salad.

"So you're private detectives," she said.

"I am," I said.

"And you?" she asked Ryan.

"I'm his . . ." He trailed off.

I tried: "He's my . . ."

"Don't say apprentice," Ryan cut in. "Don't say trainee. And do *not* say assistant."

"He's my friend," I said.

"He seems to be more than that," she said.

"He's my shadow. He's learning the PI trade. In his own way."

"I get the feeling that's how he does everything," Holly said. "So how can I help you?"

"We're investigating what happened to Sammy," I said. "How long did you know him?"

"I knew *of* him before I ever met him. I first noticed his byline in the Concordia student paper. I always skim it looking for budding young writers who might work cheap. Sammy was covering the faculty meetings and already skewering people with their own words. When he got out of school, he interned at the *Gazette* and stayed on maybe three years, then left to go on his own. He freelanced pretty much everywhere in English Montreal, including here. Then our urban affairs writer quit—what is it now, five years ago—and I offered Sammy the gig. Did you know his work?"

"Not well. I read his last few columns online last night."

"Read more," she said. "Everyone should. They should be required reading at journalism schools. The way he combined humour with a social conscience, moral fury with wit and compassion. We didn't call him Slammin' Sammy for nothing." Her eyes glazed over with a film of tears. I thought of telling her the nickname story, make her smile, but that's not in my job description. It's when people are in tears that most truth is told.

"Who did he slam?" Ryan asked.

"Who didn't he? He took a lot of things personally. Hated bullies. Couldn't stand hypocrites. People who dip into public money while voting to cut breakfast programs. People who preach family values and get caught with their foot under the bathroom stall. The small-minded bureaucrats who nickel-and-dime people out of benefits, then expense Château Petrus at lunch. City councillors and the provincial government were his favourites, I guess. The more local, the better. But he went after anyone who in his opinion was lowering the quality of life in Montreal."

"No one person stands out?" I asked

"No. The police said he . . . he was beaten to death. Really viciously. I can't imagine anything he ever wrote, not in all the years I knew him, that would provoke that kind of reaction. He got his share of crank mail, and he shared the weirdest of the weird with me. People wrote to complain, to challenge him, God forbid correct him—because he never had his facts wrong. They tried to break him down with logic, but not threats. He was never hateful and people weren't with him."

"He never raked anyone's muck? Exposed their dirty secrets?"

"To be honest, he left that to others. He wasn't the one poring through files to uncover wrongdoing. There's an old newspaper saying about columnists," she said with a sad smile. "They come out on the field when the battle is over and shoot the survivors. Sammy waited for the reporters to dig the dirt, do battle, then he commented. Put it into his perspective. He did call people out. Held them to account. Dared them to justify their actions. Sometimes showed them the high road, what they could have done instead, what could have been. But he did it with such humour—you could get mad at him, but how could you stay mad?"

Now her eyes really watered and she first brushed them with one sleeve, then reached for a box of tissues. "Shit. I keep these there for the people I interview, not me."

We waited while she blew her way through two tissues, wiped her eyes and cleared her throat.

"Anyway," she said, "his columns weren't all negative. People would have tuned him out the first year if they were. He also liked to find diamonds in the rough, people doing things to brighten the town in some way and celebrate them. He wrote about the good things he saw that make Montreal unique. How more Anglos than ever are bilingual, for example. How more Montrealers are intermarrying and raising kids who are fluent in both languages from birth. This one series he wrote about Franglais—the mix of English and French some people speak when they intermarry—it was so popular, it became the basis of a cabaret, which was quite the little hit."

"I saw he also wrote feature stories," I said. "I haven't had time to read any yet."

"Make time. Writing his column was very demanding. He had to work himself up to a very high pitch, his state of high dudgeon, I used to call it. And every week he did it: topical, on time, precise word count, beginning-middle-end, a personal connection, an opinion, a conviction. The features gave him time to come down, work at a different pace. They were long but still tightly written, very well thought out."

"What kind of subjects?"

"Profiles, mostly. Or inevitably, I should say. For Sammy, it was always the person at the heart of the story. Whether it was a political leader or an ordinary person who was making a difference, it was personal with him, like I said. Christ, when he lost his dog to cancer a couple years ago, he had half the town in tears. Or at least half the Anglos."

"Not one piece of hate mail?"

"No. The police spoke to me after it happened and I told them the same thing. Gave them access to his inbox."

"Any chance he owed anyone money?" Ryan asked. "Beating up deadbeats is their specialty."

"Who could he have owed? He owned his flat outright and he didn't have a car. He biked or walked here every day. And if he spent money on anything like clothes, he kept it a big secret."

"He ever talk about gambling?"

"He played poker once a month with some guys for twenty bucks. Same guys he's known since college."

"How did he get along with people here?" I asked.

"Great. He was not only good at what he did, he pitched in on other things if he was around—copy-editing, fact checking, proofing, layout even. When he didn't have his daughter, he was basically here. And he was funny. Oh, God, he was funny. I mean we have totally different senses of humour. Mine is dry as dust—all those generations of English—and his was more . . . generous? Compassionate? Something like that."

"No one was jealous?"

"Of his talent, sure. He was an award winner, and plenty of people in the English media wish they could write like him. But would that inspire enough envy in anyone to kill him that way? He wasn't living the big life, like I said. He was a divorced single dad who got lucky he bought his flat in a down market. Which was the extent of his holdings."

"Any women in his life that you know of?" I asked.

"No one recent. Sammy was better on paper than he was with the ladies. He used to say he was going to try a computer dating service, but he was kidding. I think."

"You ever see him with a woman with long dark hair? Not as curly as yours but not straight either."

"Not in the office."

"Did you see him outside of work?"

"This is a small paper. We put in a lot of hours together. Six days a week, sometimes seven. I know far too much already about some of the people I work with and if I spend time with them outside work, I don't get to vent about the things they do that drive me nuts. So when we finally get out of here, we tend to go our separate ways."

"There's a picture of you on his fridge," Ryan said.

"You're kidding. From what?"

"An award presentation."

"Oh, the night he won the Nicky."

"What's that?"

"Best writing on city life in an English Montreal publication. Named after Nick Auf der Maur. A local hero, man about town, long-time city columnist."

"Who was he profiling now?" I asked.

. "He was working on two. Which wound up connecting even though they didn't start out that way. The first was an Afghan family and how they and other Muslims are adjusting to life in Quebec."

She probably didn't notice Ryan shift slightly in his seat.

"What drew Sammy to that story? What was his take on it?"

"His great-grandparents came to Montreal exactly one hundred years ago. They had to adapt to life here like the Muslims do today. They endured a lot of anti-Semitism, especially in the thirties and forties, when fascism was rampant in Quebec. Some pretty shameful things happened. But his family went on to thrive in the city. His grandfather got rich, at any rate. Sammy wanted to write something that brought the two experiences together: the Muslim struggle to assimilate while remaining true to Islam, as written by a descendant of Jews who had to do it before. He also wanted to show not all Afghans are like the Habib family. You know who I mean?"

"The guy who burned his house with the daughters in it because they wouldn't wear that fucking scarf," Ryan said.

"That's the one."

"The whole world heard about him," I said. "The Canadian honour killer."

"If he isn't killed in prison," Ryan muttered, "there's something wrong with the system."

"They actually did want to wear the hijab," Holly said quietly. "Both girls." Her voice was soft, but there was no mistaking she was just as angry as Ryan—and me. "But their soccer league wouldn't let them play if they did. That's partly what Sammy was writing about."

"And making enemies?"

"He wasn't focusing on Marcel Habib. He was profiling a very different Afghan family, to show this asshole didn't represent the entire community."

"What family?"

"Their name is Aziz. A father who came here with his son and daughter when the Taliban took over Afghanistan. An educated man, a physician and diplomat in Kabul before it fell. He brought his children to Montreal alone after his wife was killed in a bombing. He had a cousin here. Raised them both to do whatever they wanted, son and daughter. They run his rug business now."

"I thought the father was a physician."

"In Kabul, yes. His credentials weren't recognized here and he had to feed two small kids, so he went into his cousin's rug business, and when the cousin passed away he took it over. Now he's retired and the kids run it."

"You have their contact info?"

"I'll link you up."

"What's the other profile?"

"Laurent Lortie."

Neither Ryan nor I reacted.

"Sure, you hear of the honour killer but not the aspiring politician. Lortie is the leader of a new party in Quebec. *Another* new party, I should say. There's been a lot of splintering on the provincial scene."

"What's his called?"

"Québec aux Québécois. Also known as the QAQ. Either he didn't realize the English pronunciation would be *cack* or *quack*, or he didn't care. He does speak English fluently. He studied at the London School of Economics and can put on quite the mid-Atlantic accent when he deigns to speak it."

"Which way does the party lean?"

"Right," she said. "As right as you'd ever see in Quebec. We only ever elect social democrats; it's usually just a question of whether they're also sovereigntist. But Lortie is convinced the people are ready for a change. He says real Québécois don't need a nanny state. They need to rediscover some of that pioneer swing of theirs. I'm paraphrasing but that's the message. He's not big on immigration, which is where this one intersects with the Aziz profile. His daughter Lucienne, who is his second-in-command, is also very vocal on this issue. I wouldn't walk into a Muslim neighbourhood if I were her."

Someone should have told that to Sammy. If he had walked into that neighbourhood on his own.

"How far along on that story was he?"

"He interviewed both Laurent and Lucienne," Holly said. "There's also a son, Luc, by the way, but he isn't part of the political dynasty."

"Not interested?"

"Not capable. Sammy said he seemed slow. I don't know if he meant developmentally delayed—"

"You can say retarded," Ryan muttered.

"Sammy wouldn't have, so I won't either. Anyway, if he ever interviewed Luc, he left no notes."

"Who else did he interview?" I asked.

"Pundits, pollsters, observers who had something to say about the Lorties' policies and electability. The head of the local Muslim congress, who was suitably outraged. One thing I know, Sammy was going to see Laurent again the day he was found. They were supposed to meet at four o'clock that afternoon."

"I don't like it when meetings don't happen," I said. "Any other stories?"

"There was one other folder he created right before he died, but it was empty. No documents in it at all. So if it was a new story, he must have just been starting. He never mentioned it to me."

"Did it have a name?"

"'Miss Montreal.'"

"That mean anything to you?"

"The only thing anyone could tell me was there used to be a restaurant by that name on Décarie near Ruby Foo's. But it's been gone for years."

"Did he ever cover construction?" Ryan asked. "There's a business where people get hurt a lot. And not on the job."

"If you mean corruption, you're in the right place. It's a national sport here. The Charbonneau Commission hearings were the most fun we'd had in months. But it's been over and on to the next thing for ages. The only other thing that came up recently . . .".

"What?"

"Was Sammy adopted?" she asked.

"Not to my knowledge. Why?"

"He asked me a little while ago if I knew any social workers who handled adoption reconciliations."

"Did you find someone?"

"Yes," she said. "One of my girlfriends has a friend who works in that field. I called her and asked if it was okay to pass on her name to Sammy. She told me she wouldn't be able to tell him anything more than general procedures, unless it had to do with him personally. I passed on her name and email to Sammy, but whatever he did with it he kept private."

"Would she speak to us?" I asked.

"She might," she said. "But she won't be able to tell you any more than she could tell Sammy. Maybe less."

CHAPTER 06

Bobby Ducharme told us he'd meet us at six o'clock at a deli called the Main, right across the street from Schwartz's. The Main was the overflow place, Bobby explained. "You get the same food there as across the street, more or less," he said. "But there won't be a lineup and we can get some privacy at the back."

"Tell you one thing," Ryan said as we drove up St-Laurent. "The women alone are a reason to love it here. Check that out."

He pointed at a tall slender woman in a tight gold dress, bare legs tanned, hips swinging side to side. "You walk in downtown Toronto, King and Yonge, say, all the women are in business suits with sneakers, they got a purse, briefcase and gym bag, looking like if you stuck a dime in the crack of their ass, it would still be there when they die. These women here—they're alive, man. They put some effort in."

"Sounds like you're getting over Cara," I said.

He turned to me, scowling, the scar on his jaw a dark red line. "I'm not over her now and I never will be. I been with that girl since I was twenty years old. But I'm not *dead*. I can still appreciate a woman who walks down the street like she owns it."

There was indeed a line outside Schwartz's when we got there, about five storefronts long—in the rain. We found parking around the corner a block north, just past a fenced yard that looked abandoned except for a stack of unmarked gravestones.

We had no trouble finding a table at the back of the Main, next to a wall covered with caricatures of employees that looked so old half the people in them were probably dead. Ryan would normally have taken a seat facing the door, but we were close to the kitchen door too, through which people were moving quickly in both directions. I know Ryan: he doesn't like people making sudden moves around him. So he sat across from me but turned his chair sideways, its back against the wall so he could see all traffic, and seemed satisfied.

Bobby strode in a few minutes later, brushing rain off the sleeves of a cream linen jacket. We shook hands and I introduced him to Ryan. He hung his jacket on the chair next to Ryan and sat down facing me, wearing a short-sleeve white dress shirt that showed off his arms, which were big and well defined. He had jet-black hair cut short and gelled up in front, and his eyes were dark too, like many Québécois whose ancestors married Cree and other Natives. I could see him taking in Ryan, about whom I'd told him nothing. I could sense Ryan doing the same. Bobby pressed his palms together, which bulged his arms bigger. Ryan didn't have to do anything like that in return. Steel was his element, not muscle.

"So you left Beacon Security, eh?" Bobby said. "Set up your own shop?"

"A year ago."

"*Christ*," Bobby said, pronouncing it *Kriss*. "One of these days, I'll do the same thing, start my own place. Maybe with one or two guys from Investigations Globales. It's working out okay for you?"

"I'm not making a fortune. But I wasn't seeking one, so it's a wash."

"What do you do, mostly?"

"Background checks, missing persons, the kind of things a big shop would assign to a team. Only we're the whole team."

"The two of you?"

"No. My partner is a woman named Jenn. Ryan's filling in for her on this one."

"Well, look for me to open up next year," Bobby said.

A waitress long past middle age took our order. On Bobby's advice, we chose the combo platter, a smoked meat on rye, with fries, coleslaw, dill pickle spear and Cokes.

When the waitress left, I asked Bobby about the homicide detectives working Sammy's case.

He said, "You did okay with Reynald Paquette. He's a pretty good cop. I got that from two sources. The first is a guy I know who worked with him before he made Crimes Majeurs, when he was still a uniform in St-Léonard. Not the easiest turf to come up in."

"Why?"

"It's mostly Italian. And it's heavily populated, or at least frequented, by the Mob. A lot of coffee shops the cops would love to put a wire in. My friend said Paquette was smart, worked hard, gave a shit and kept his nose clean, even in that environment. What more could you ask?"

"That he be good at homicide."

"He is, he is. I checked that too. He has one of the best solution rates in the squad and a solid reputation. Not the fastest guy, maybe, but thorough. If there's something to find, he'll find it. Eventually. Unless it was a random attack, a swarming. Then all bets are off, unless someone panics, blabs or gives themselves up."

"Someone always blabs," Ryan said. "Especially if they didn't have the balls to do it alone."

"So what is Paquette thinking?" I asked. "Random attack or targeted?"

"Well, you know the area where he was found. Or maybe you don't."

"His grandfather told me it's an Arab neighbourhood."

"Right. So it could have happened that way."

"Or someone dumped him there to throw people off," Ryan said. "Marked him up with that star."

"You got to keep that open," Bobby said.

"How bad is the blood here between Jews and Muslims?"

"I don't know what it's like in Toronto, but some of the Arabs here, especially the North Africans, they don't like the Jews so much. There have been firebombings in schools, threats, beatings of kids who wear the skullcap. Our firm does executive protection and uniformed security, and all the synagogues need it on their holidays."

"The question would still be what he was doing there in the middle of the night. We know the police answered a call at his house at two forty-five in the morning."

"About what?"

"Supposedly a domestic disturbance. Only there wasn't any."

"And a few hours later," Bobby said, "he's found dead in Ville St-Laurent."

"Yes."

"You don't think it's a coincidence."

"No."

"The call prompted him to leave his house?"

"Could be."

"Maybe he knew who was behind it and went to see them."

"The Afghan family he was interviewing," I said. "Their store is in that area."

"Yeah, but at a quarter to three in the morning?"

"It could also have been a cry-wolf routine," Ryan said. "Someone calls in a false alarm so a second call gets a slower response."

"There was no second call," I said.

"The old Greek lady said she heard something a few minutes later," Ryan said.

"Yes. But she looked out and didn't see anyone."

"Not at the front. But he had a back door too. So maybe the call was meant to give someone the opportunity to snatch him."

"How?"

"Cops show up at your door, you open up, right? You turn off your alarm system. Then the cops go away. There's a knock on the back door. It's late, he's disoriented—three, four in the morning, that's the magic hour, the time cops love to raid a place because you're at your most vulnerable. He answers it without thinking—boom, he's abducted."

The waitress picked that moment to arrive with three platters. The sandwiches were stacked high with steaming meat and I had to sneak a quick bite before we could continue, get that first mouthful of clove and other spices. Both of them followed suit. No one looked unhappy.

"Paquette might be able to tell you where the call came from," Bobby said.

"And whether he was killed in the apartment," Ryan said, "or where the body was found."

"You'll find out tomorrow. Speaking of which," Bobby said, "there is a little bad news. Paquette's partner, René Chênevert. Apparently he's a miserable pain in the ass, what we'd call in French a *trou de cul*."

"Which means?" Ryan asked.

"Asshole. From what I heard, he's arrogant as hell and the kind of political animal who hates everybody equally, including most of his colleagues, sees them all as rungs on the ladder to the sky. Oh, my God, this is good," Bobby said, after finishing the first half of his sandwich and wiping his hands and the corner of his lips with a thin paper napkin. "I haven't had one in a while. I got to keep the waistline trim."

There was enough fat in the sandwich to light an Inuit lamp, but I was savouring every bite too. There's something about the marriage of brisket, smoke and spices that enthralls Montreal, thrills Jews and Gentiles alike. Finally, our plates were clean, except for balled-up greasy napkins and the last burnt fries.

"Is this asshole any good at his job?" I asked.

"If he made Homicide, he's not stupid, and if he's working with someone like Paquette, he has to contribute something. Maybe he's the paperwork fiend or the background checker. The bad cop in interrogations. Just don't expect cooperation from him. Not in English and not in your French."

"Sorry I'm going to miss it," Ryan said.

"You're not going?" Bobby asked him.

"He doesn't do police," I said.

"I haven't been in a police station in over twenty years," Ryan said. "I'm not starting tomorrow, not even for him."

"You want me to come?" Bobby asked. "Translate or something?"

"My French isn't bad," I said.

He responded by ripping off a fast line of *joual* at me. I caught the word *français*, but that's it.

"Sorry?"

He repeated it just as fast.

"Okay, what?"

"I asked you how your French was, more or less, the same way they're gonna speak to you."

"Arthur Moscoe told me Paquette speaks good English."

"To Arthur Moscoe he does. Or his lawyers. That's no guarantee he will to you. And Chênevert for sure won't."

"You free tomorrow?"

"I could be. But we'd have to go first thing, before their day in Homicide goes from bad to worse. I'll pick you up at eight, we'll hit them around eight-thirty. My office isn't far from there."

"I don't want to make you late."

"The amount of time they're likely to spare you, I won't be."

"Okay. Eight o'clock, our hotel."

"'Ey, anyone want another sandwich?" he said. "Since we're here?"

Ryan and I just looked at him.

"No?" Bobby said. "Nobody wants to split one?"

"What happened to the trim waistline?" I asked.

"It stayed outside," Bobby said.

We got back to the hotel around seven-thirty. With the cloud cover still heavy, it seemed darker than it should have on the longest day of the year. It was time for summer to show itself, step out from behind that heavy curtain, splash a few rays our way. But the curtain wasn't moving. All the light did was fade.

When we got to the room, I drew up a list of people we needed to speak to:

Sammy's ex-wife, Camille.
Aziz—son and daughter.
Lortie—father and daughter.
Marie-Josée Boily—adoption worker.
Arthur Moscoe—anyone in Sammy's family adopted?

"You need me for any of this?" Ryan asked.

I was a more adept researcher and reader than he. A glance around the room showed there were no legs to break, threats to utter or shots to fire. "I'm good."

"Then I'll see you later."

"Where you going?"

"I'm antsy. Can't just sit here. Either I start cleaning my guns or I go out for a drive."

"Drive safely," I said.

I started with Camille, figuring a single mother would need the most notice to arrange a meeting. She answered after two rings:

"Oui, allô?"

I had too many calls to struggle through each one in French, so I told her who I was and asked if I could continue in English.

She said, "Okay by me," with a light accent.

I said I was helping the family with the investigation, looking for something that might have been overlooked so far.

"You mean the Moscoe family?"

"Yes."

"How is Arthur?"

"He's dying."

"Oh. I see."

"You didn't get along with him?"

"I had nothing against him. I'm not sure the reverse was true. He didn't really like Montreal anymore. It wasn't the city he used to rule over and I always felt he blamed me in a way. But you want to talk about Sammy, yes? I have a few minutes now while Sophie watches animations. Is that the right word?"

"I think you mean cartoons. Look, I'd rather meet you in person, if we can."

"Ah. You want to read my face, eh? My body language, see if I'm telling the truth?"

"Why wouldn't you?"

"*Oh, mon Dieu*, I'm in trouble already."

I liked her voice. It was husky, earthy, but still had a comic lilt.

"I pick Sophie up at school at three-thirty and if it's nice we go to Parc Laurier. You know where that is?"

"Give me an intersection."

"St-Gregoire and Brebeuf. Near the climbing structure. But don't come right away. Give Sophie time to settle in, find some friends, otherwise it'll be *Maman* this, *Maman* that, the entire time. I also don't want you talking to her."

I hadn't planned to involve Sophie. Upsetting grown-ups was one thing, the victim's child another.

We traded cell numbers and agreed to meet around four.

Next, I called Marie-Josée Boily's office and left a brief voice mail explaining why I needed to talk to her. Left my cell number there too.

Arthur Moscoe would be at home, so I dialled his number. It went to voice mail. I asked him to call my cell at his first opportunity.

The only contact Holly had for the Afghan family was at their rug business, which would be closed now. They'd have to wait until tomorrow.

So would the Lorties. Since they were politicians in pre-election mode, I knew I might have to go through a personal assistant or press secretary. I sent an email to the address Sammy had for Laurent Lortie, requesting a meeting. I copied his daughter Lucienne, in case she was more plugged in than her father.

Getting nowhere fast. Actually, not even that fast. Just nowhere. I thought of taking a walk but a look at the rain through the hotel window put that to rest.

I propped up some pillows on the bed and stretched out with my laptop, intending to read the work files Holly Napier had copied onto a memory stick.

As soon as I thought of her, I veered off course, wondering what she was doing right now. Probably still at the office, angled over a monitor. An attractive woman. A bit like Jenn, in that she was tall—no six-footer but five-eight or -nine—and strong looking. I liked her high cheekbones and fair skin and her great red tangle of curls. Very bright eyes. Smart enough to know she was smart, relaxed enough not to have to prove it. Nice smile.

When it started to shape up like a duel between research and a cold shower, I plugged in the USB stick that contained Sammy's notes on the stories he was working on. The folders came up alphabetically: *Aziz, Lorties, Miss Montreal.*

I started with the Aziz file. The father, Abdul, had been born in 1947 in Kabul to a Tajik family—a minority in a Pashtun-majority country. He excelled in school and was accepted to the school of medicine at University of Kabul in 1968. When the Soviets invaded in 1979, he became known as an anti-Russian speaker and pamphleteer, likening the president, Babrak Karmal, to Joseph Stalin. Accurate or not, it landed him in prison. He was married by then to a nurse, a woman who had attended university when maybe one percent of Afghan women did so. They had a son, Mehrdad, and an infant daughter named Mehri. He was beaten and tortured in custody until a sizable bribe secured his release. He emerged determined to flee at the earliest opportunity via Pakistan and India. A cousin in Canada would help him get started.

Papers, however, were expensive and scarce and the bribe had depleted the family's resources. They stayed in Kabul as resistance to the Soviets grew, as religious fervour began to grip the city in ways it hadn't before. People shouting "*Allahu akhbar*" in the night, all night, in defiance of the ten-o'clock curfew and army patrols. Men growing out their beards and criticizing those who drank liquor or dressed in Western style. Veils, once scarce, became more common. Taliban rocket attacks became a daily event, targeting the bus station, markets and other crowded places. Everyone had a story about a friend, neighbour, classmate or kinsman killed.

Caught between the oppression of the Soviet occupation and the Islamism that had taken over the rural areas and was encircling Kabul, Abdul kept at it, pleading with contacts, scraping together funds, selling off jewels. The desperate government was conscripting boys as young as fourteen or fifteen and sending them to the front to fight the mujahedeen. Poorly trained, illequipped, many were killed within weeks. When he finally had their documents in hand, Abdul's wife insisted on a last visit to the grave of her brother, who had been murdered while the plotter Mohammad Daoud Khan had been in power. On a day in late March, right after the solstice that marks the Afghan new year, she was placing fresh daisies on the grave when a rocket shattered the peace of the graveyard and buried most of her while disinterring her brother.

The family arrived in Montreal two years later.

CHAPTER 07

fell asleep before Ryan got back to the room, so it wasn't until the next morning that I found out where he had gone.

"Point St. Charles," he told me over breakfast in the hotel coffee shop. The Point is a poor neighbourhood south of the Ville-Marie Expressway, even further south than St-Henri, also poor and working-class. Churches abound in the Point, their domes and spires once brass, now green and streaked with pigeon shit.

"Why there?" I asked.

"Ancestral home of the Ryans," he said. "It's where my father was born and raised. And his father and grandfather. Right off the main drag, Centre Street. All the times I been here, I never had the urge to go. This time—maybe because of what happened with Cara—I needed to see it."

"And?"

He reached into the pocket of his black linen jacket and pulled out an old photo of a strapping young man in a white T-shirt, a pack of cigarettes folded into one short sleeve, his hair combed up like a young James Dean. "That's him," he said. "Early or mid-sixties, I'm guessing. A few years before he came to Hamilton and got himself killed."

His father, Sid Ryan, a member of an Irish gang in Montreal, had met an untimely end trying to muscle in on the drug trade in Ontario, over which Johnny Papalia's outfit then ruled.

"You know I never knew him," Ryan said. "I was a month old when he was killed. The only family I ever knew was her side. I thought maybe if I saw where he grew up I'd feel some kind of connection."

"Did you?"

He mopped up some egg yolk with a piece of toast and chewed it before answering. "Nothing. Whatever it was back then, it ain't now. The address I had for him, the building burned down ten, fifteen years ago, one of the neighbours said."

"I'm sorry."

"Don't be. It was a stupid idea to begin with."

"Why?"

"Because I got to get it through my thick fucking skull that I'm alone now. I got no wife anymore. I got a mother I'm not close to. And whatever I thought I was gonna find last night . . . I'm not. I got no roots here. No history. Wherever the Ryans are, whoever they are, it's all smoke."

"You have a son."

"Who I'll be lucky to see a couple times a month."

"You said Cara would give you access."

"That's what she says now. Wait until the first time I piss her off."

"You have me," I said.

"Shut up."

"I mean it."

"So do I."

———

Bobby Ducharme was right on time, outside the hotel entrance at eight in a black Jetta.

"Sleep okay?" he asked.

"Sure."

"Good. Buckle up, 'cause I heard the traffic is bad going east."

It wasn't as bad as open warfare, but it wasn't much better. Bobby took no prisoners in his conquest of Boulevard René-Lévesque. Tailgating, honking, swerving in and out of his lane, anything to gain a car-length's advantage and beat an amber light before it turned red. We went past a giant Molson brewery and an equally big CBC complex.

"How do you want to handle this?" he asked. "If you're more comfortable in English, you can ask me the questions and I can translate for you."

"Let's see how it goes. Maybe Paquette will speak English to me."

"And if not?"

"I passed high school French."

"Great. And if you have to ask for more than directions?"

Here's the thing about learning French in Canada.

If you don't live in Quebec, the main reason you learn it is so you can speak to your countrymen there, and they can speak to you. In this you are likely to fail miserably because they teach a neutral, international French in Ontario schools. My teachers were from France, Belgium, Switzerland and the francophone parts of Ontario. None came from Quebec. They spoke the kind of French that would help you get around Paris just fine. A lilting, musical French that enunciated every syllable like it was the last arcane wisp of the secret to eternal life. The French spoken in Quebec is rougher, faster, with its own pronunciation, rhythm and slang. The street version, *joual*, even more so. Never having learned it, never having lived there, I can pose a question to a Québécois, but can't always follow the answer. It's like taking your Queen's English to the East End of London, the heart of Texas or the outports of Newfoundland.

Detective Reynald Paquette's French wasn't as hard to follow, perhaps because he knew he was speaking to an outsider. He was around forty, with dark hair neatly trimmed and precisely parted on the left, in a crisp white shirt, blue striped tie and dark slacks. I couldn't tell his size because he was sitting behind a desk, a matching jacket hanging on the back of his chair. He wore a wedding ring and a slim gold watch, which he looked at—it was eight-forty—and then he turned to me.

"*Alors,*" he said, "*vous êtes Monsieur Geller? L'enquêteur privé?*"

"*Oui.*"

"*Vos papiers?*"

We were in a small office in the Crime Majeurs bureau on Sherbrooke Street East, probably as far east as I'd ever been in Montreal, far past the Olympic Stadium and the Botanical Garden. The room felt crowded with four men in it, none of us particularly small.

I gave Paquette my licence. He looked it over, made a note of the number, and handed it back to me. His partner, René Chênevert, showed no interest in it. I made him around thirty-seven or eight, six-two and a solid two hundred pounds. He wore a light grey suit with a faint white line through it, a dark grey shirt and matching tie. He leaned against the wall with one knee bent, arms crossed, either to bulk up his shoulders or just to show some general hostility. He squinted some, also attitudinal, I suppose, but I could still see he had blue eyes. No rings of any kind. A clunky chrome watch that could probably tell you twelve time zones while you stood on the ocean floor.

Paquette turned to Bobby and said, "*Toi là, t'es avec Globales?*"

That was the firm Bobby worked for, about the size of my former employer in Toronto, Beacon Security. He said, "*Oui,*" but pronounced it closer to *why*.

"*Bon*." Paquette had a black binder, thick with documents that had been punched and placed inside. He flipped it open and said, "Adler. Samuel Jo-*seph*. *Victime d'un homicide le 29 mai par une personne ou des personnes inconnues*." He looked at his watch again and said, "*Nous sommes très occupés ici. Vous avez dix minutes. Posez vos questions.*"

I wasn't sure about the first part—probably that they were busy—but I got the second. Ten minutes. I had to think about how to phrase the question in French. "*Pouvez-vous confirmer que le location où le . . . le*"—couldn't remember the word for body—"*où la victime a été trouvée n'est pas le même où il a été tué*." All right. Not bad.

"*Oui.*"

"*Est-ce que vous savez où il était tué?*"

"*Non.*"

"*Aucune . . . scène du crime?*"

Chênevert snorted from his wall spot.

Okay, I'd pronounced something wrong there. Maybe said "scene of the cream." But Paquette was civilized enough to answer. "*Non.*"

"*Vous avez pris toutes ses papiers importants et les autres choses de son appartement. Est-ce qu'il y a quelque chose là, un, un —*"

"All right, Mr. Geller," Paquette said. "You've suffered enough. And so has the French language. Ask your questions in English."

Chênevert came off the wall, his arms unfolded, his face reddening. "'*Xcuse*," he said, "*j'travaille ici moi et le français est la langue officielle ici*." Then he pointed at me and let out a stream of words that went over my head like a hail of bullets. The only words I was sure of were *maudit juif*, which is French for damned Jew. That much I remembered from Mordecai Richler.

Bobby said something so fast I didn't get it—it wasn't *trou de cul* but sounded almost like "on fire"—but Chênevert clearly did and he turned even redder. He said something back and they both went on throwing the bait back and forth, their voices rising with each volley until Paquette bounced out of his chair, slashed the air with his arm and cut them both off, the word *Assez*—enough—ringing out above their snarls and insults. Both men were bigger than he was but they stopped their rutting-stag thing and broke eye contact. Paquette told Chênevert to go get a coffee. Bobby got back in his seat.

"Now you better get on with your questions," Paquette said to me. "You have about seven minutes left."

"After three weeks, there has to be something," I said. "A man who lives in the Plateau doesn't just wander out in the middle of the night and go all the way to Côte-Vertu to be happened upon by a random Muslim mob eager to kick a Jew to death. It had nothing to do with his daughter or ex-wife. So it has to do with his work. Would you agree?"

"I am not in a position to agree or disagree, at this point. We don't know everything about his private life."

"You've been through his finances, talked to his friends and family. You must be able to rule out some things."

"What type of things should I rule out, Mr. Geller?"

"Gambling. Drugs. Reckless affairs."

"Gambling and drugs do not fit the profile we have assembled. There are no fluctuations in his income and spending, other than some spikes related to his daughter. A trip to Orlando one year. California another. As for reckless affairs?" He shrugged. "Who can truly say?"

"A person who might have found a hair in the victim's bed, one that did not fit its usual occupant."

"We left one behind?"

"You did."

"If we find someone who matches it, we'll take the necessary steps. What else?"

"You have his phone records."

"We do."

"Anything unusual?"

"What would you consider unusual in a man's phone habits?"

"Late-night calls."

"They're not unusual in my line of work."

"If you're going to hold me to ten minutes, can't you just tell me something I can help with instead of volleying?"

"Ah, there we come to the point of the matter, which is the assumption that I am looking for your help here, which I am not. You have been given ten minutes—now five—for me to help you, which I think you'll both agree I have been going out of my way to do, even doing so in English when I did not have to. Continue with your questions, if you still have any."

"I want a copy of his phone records."

"That would be a waste of our time and resources."

"Fighting with Arthur Moscoe's lawyers would waste a lot more."

"All right. Fine. You'll get your copy."

"What have your forensics shown?"

"Be specific, please. Running down the full report would take you past your allotted time."

"What was he hit with?"

"We don't know, exactly."

"Why not? Doesn't every contact leave a trace?"

"You know Locard's Theory? How reassuring. Well, it still holds true in this case. What left a trace, however, is the kind of material used in a duffel bag."

"They put a bag over his head, then beat him?"

"So it seems."

"So you have no splinters, fragments, to help identify the weapon."

"No. They still left imprints on his skull, so we have working theories on what might have been used, including boots, but it has made the job more difficult."

"Any nasal fractures?"

Paquette sat up and leaned his elbows on the desk. "Why would you ask me that?"

"Getting a bag over someone's head and holding it there while he's struggling and someone else is taking a swing with something? Not that easy, Detective. If it was me, the second the bag is over his head, boom, I'd break his nose, get him down on the ground and go to work with the boots and bats."

"Really? That is how you would do it?"

"Yes."

"I suppose you were in Toronto May twenty-ninth?"

"Yes."

"Too bad. All right, Mr. Geller, you earned this one. There were fractures to the nose and left orbital bone. Someone hit him very hard indeed, almost certainly right-handed. Probably knocked him out, but there were so many different brain injuries, it's hard to tell."

"Any idea how many assailants?"

"Only that there was more than one. There were two different types of shoe or boot involved."

"Ask him about the police call," Bobby said.

"Right. Do you know why the police were called to his apartment that night?"

Paquette thumbed through his binder until he found what looked—at least upside down—like an incident report.

"Apparently a misunderstanding. Perhaps a joke of some sort played on him."

"You don't think there's any connection to what happened later?"

His lower lip moved out past the upper and his eyebrows went up and down: "What sort of connection would you suggest?"

"I don't know," I said. "It just seems like an unlikely coincidence."

"Most coincidences are unlikely," he said. "That's why a word for them had to be invented."

Just my luck: I had a cop who was probably trained in rhetoric by Jesuits.

"All right. Have you talked to the people he was interviewing for his stories?"

Paquette looked at his watch, held up three fingers, then leafed through the black binder again. After spending at least one of my remaining minutes, he looked up and said, "We have to date interviewed twenty-three individuals in person, including family, friends, neighbours, colleagues and, yes, people he was interviewing for his work. We also checked through his email archives to see if his writing had prompted anything our profilers would consider a death threat. We found nothing. I am told he was a humorist, although for me it would be hard to tell in English. Most of the email he got was funny or trying to be. Sometimes sarcastic. Occasionally angry. Nothing that set off alarm bells."

"What about the current stories?"

"In your final minute, Mr. Geller, what about them?"

"You said you questioned the people involved."

"Some of the principals, yes."

"On the story about the Afghan community, who did you interview?"

"Whom, Mr. Geller. I'm surprised I have to correct you in English too."

"Whom?"

"The story focused on a family that is very much the opposite of the one involved in that so-called honour killing of ours. I'm sorry, I saw no honour of any type in that crime and I resist calling it that. It was what it was. I spoke to the brother and sister Mr. Adler was profiling. They struck me as well-educated people. Not at all closed or limiting to their women."

"No extremist connections?"

"Ask them yourself."

"I will. What about the other family?"

"Which other one?"

"The Lorties. Did you interview them?"

"Of course. Quite an interesting family. Well, father and daughter, anyway. They're sure to spice up the election quite nicely this fall."

"Was there anything to indicate animosity toward the victim?"

"From what we read of his notes and his previous work, his profiles tended to be pretty balanced. They weren't—what do you say, hatchet work? Hatchet jobs, that's it. He didn't do those. We saw some emails back and forth between him and both the Lorties, and there was nothing heated in them."

"What's your feeling about the Lorties?"

"About their political fortunes?"

"As people."

Paquette laughed, genuinely so, I thought. "Why on earth would I share my feelings with you, Mr. Geller? You're not a friend, relative, colleague, therapist or priest. You'll have to meet with them yourself and see what *you* feel."

"You don't think Sammy could have been a threat to them somehow?"

He looked at his watch. "That will have to remain unanswered, Mr. Geller. Your ten minutes are up. Do you want to wait for the phone records or come back for them when they're ready?"

"How long will it take?"

He shrugged. "I agreed to do it, not to give it the highest priority. If you like bad coffee, you can wait. Otherwise, I will try to send it by the end of the day. You are at the Holiday Inn on Sherbrooke, *non*?"

"Yes," I said. And wondered how he knew.

We saw Chênevert on our way out of the building, having a cigarette with two other men in suits. I waved to him. He gave us the finger, then ground his cigarette out on the concrete, even though he was standing next to an ashtray.

CHAPTER 08

Not everyone walks into their hotel room to see a man sitting at the small desk they provide, cleaning a field-stripped Glock. But when you are rooming with Dante Ryan, anything's possible.

It was the pistol he'd bought from a dealer in Boston, enough to stop any human who wasn't full of crank or angel dust. It was broken down into four pieces: the frame, barrel, recoil spring and slide. The magazine and the round from the chamber—and he always had one in the chamber—were set off far to the side, out of reach. He had a can of CLP solvent, a bore brush, a soft rag, a few Q-tips and a toothbrush, which I hoped wasn't mine, and the kind of compressed-air cleaner people use on keyboards.

"You've only had that three months," I said. "I'm surprised it needs cleaning."

"It doesn't," he said, pushing a nylon bore brush through the barrel. "But I told you last night this relaxes me when I'm bored. No pun intended," he added, waving the brush at me.

Not many guys I know can make gun jokes like that.

He sprayed some CLP on the spring and guide rod assembly and used the toothbrush to work it in. Without looking up, he asked how the meeting with the detectives had gone.

"Unproductive," I said. "If they know anything, they're not telling."

"Typical."

"They are going to send copies of Sammy's phone records, so that'll give us something to look at."

"How was his partner? He come as advertised?"

"Completely. If there was a Hall of Fame for assholes, he'd have his own wing."

"Now I'm really sorry I wasn't there."

"One interesting thing they did know."

"What?"

"Where we're staying."

"Already? Who knows we're here?"

"Besides the client? I told Holly Napier, the adoption worker, Sammy's ex, the Afghans he was interviewing, the Lorties . . ."

"When'd you do all that?"

"I sent out emails last night. Left some voice mails."

"My money's on the Lorties."

"Why?"

"What we heard about them, they sound the most con-nected. The Afghans, if they're like most immigrants, want fuck all to do with the cops. The editor, the ex-wife, the adoption lady—they don't seem likely."

He put the barrel and recoil spring back in place, used the air spray to blow out any remaining dust, fit the slide back in and dry-fired once to make sure the reassembly was complete. Then he put the magazine back in place and thumbed the single round into the chamber. Glocks have no safety, so I'd have left out that last part, but I've learned not to question Ryan when it comes to guns. I've already been shot once and don't want to repeat the experience.

He was reaching for the Baby Eagle in his case when the phone rang. It was Marie-Josée Boily, the caseworker Sammy had spoken to about adoption.

"Thanks for calling back," I said.

"You are welcome," she said, in heavily accented English. "But I am not likely to be of 'elp to you. We try to be open in Québec about the adoption, to 'elp families come together and, um, see themselves as normal, yes? But there is also very strict rules regarding *confidentialité*."

"You know Mr. Adler was murdered."

"Yes. It's the only reason I call you back. Are you family? You did not say on your message."

"I'm working for his family," I said. "Trying to find out what happened to him."

"But that has nothing to do with me."

"Maybe not. Did you ever meet with him or just speak on the phone?"

"We met," she said. "Twice."

"About his own family?"

A few moments of silence passed. I said, "Hello?"

"Yes, I am still here. I am thinking what I can disclose to you."

"Let me put it this way: if it wasn't about his own family, if it was for a story he was working on, would you have spoken to him?"

"Only in generalities. About the process, the regulations of the adoption act, that sort of thing."

Then they probably would not have met twice, I thought. He'd have done one interview and then followed up by phone or email if he needed more information.

I said, "Why don't we meet for a coffee? Talk about this in person?" Man, I wished Jenn were here. I might have boatloads of personal charm and dazzling interrogative techniques, but she can get information out of people like a farmer milking a bloated teat.

"I don't know if that will be possible."

"Please," I said. "His family is desperate." Thinking that a social worker would give in to help a family in trouble.

I heard a deep sigh on the other end of the line. "Do you know where is the Centre Jeunesse? The youth centre of Québec?"

"No."

"It's on de Maisonneuve, at the corner of St-Timothée. Just a few streets east of St-Hubert, maybe six past St-Denis if you know that better. Our bureau is across the street from there. Next to that is a café called Romarin where I will be taking my lunch. Is a quarter to one okay for you?"

"It's fine," I said.

"We won't need a lot of time," she said.

I wondered if it would be more than the ten minutes Detective Paquette had offered.

"What now?" Ryan asked when I'd hung up.

"Ville St-Laurent," I said.

"The rug store?"

"And the place where his body was found."

I've been on some bad roads in my life. In Israel, for example, where you are more likely to die in a road accident than in any war or act of terrorism. In France where passing on blind curves is a sudden-death national sport. Even in Ontario, where winter whiteouts make the tamest straightaways deadly.

Give me any of those anytime, day or night, over Montreal's elevated highway: the Metropolitan. Narrow lanes, potholes the size of bomb craters, tailgaters, cars crossing double solid lines as if they weren't there. Ryan was snarling like a Rottweiler by the time we exited onto Boulevard Marcel-Laurin and headed north into Ville St-Laurent. "If the GPS tells me to take this road again," he said, "I'm going to empty a fucking clip into it."

"Save the last bullet for me," I said.

The traffic got lighter as we headed north and the rain had all but stopped. We made it to Côte-Vertu without further mayhem and headed west until we came to the strip mall that housed Les Tapis Kabul, along with a market called Medina that advertised halal products, both next to a travel agency with posters of sun-kissed beauties in bikinis, framed by palm trees and white sand. Walking past were two women in full black niqabs, nothing visible but their eyes. Whatever they thought about the women in bikinis would remain a mystery.

The selection inside Les Tapis Kabul was dazzling. Dozens of carpets hung from the ceiling, many in vibrant shades of red. Some were clearly handmade, their surfaces rough and nappy, their edges not quite straight. Others must have been machined, with a smooth, almost glossy surface and perfectly straight edges. Behind the hanging rugs were deep pigeonholes where more rugs were rolled up, some inside brown paper.

A man around thirty was behind the counter at the back, guiding a woman through a catalogue, nodding enthusiastically when she stopped him and placed her finger on one image, apparently complimenting her on her taste. He wore a crisp white shirt and dark slacks, and had coarse black hair and a five-o'clock shadow hours ahead of schedule. Ryan and I walked around, looking at carpets like we were just two other customers, waiting for the man to finish serving the woman.

"Nice stuff," he said, running his hand over a nine-by-twelve tribal rug from Pakistan. Then he looked at the price tag and whistled. "A grand for this? Are they serious?"

"Don't you have gym bags full of cash?"

"Not after buying the Charger."

"Can I help you gentlemen?" a woman said.

We turned to face a beautiful young woman in her mid to late twenties. She wore a bright green long-sleeved silk blouse and black slacks that flared widely enough at the bottom to cover her shoes. Her eyes were a shade of green that very nearly matched her blouse. Her headscarf was a shade in between. "I see you were looking at the tribal rugs. We have quite a few excellent samples here and many more in our storeroom."

"We're actually here on other business," I said.

"I don't understand."

"Are you Mehri Aziz?"

"Yes."

"We're here about Sammy Adler," I said.

She looked away quickly, craning her neck around to the counter where the young man was still leafing through the catalogue, head down, unaware of the ripple we'd just caused.

She looked back at me, swallowing hard like something was going down the wrong pipe. "What about him?"

I handed her a business card. "My name is Jonah Geller. This is my associate, Mr. Ryan. We've been hired by Sammy's family to help find his killer."

She looked the card over, carefully examining both sides. Buying a little time. "I—I don't see how I can be of any help."

"He interviewed you for a story he was writing."

"Yes. Very briefly," she added quickly. "But he was finding out about me, not me about him."

She turned to look at the man behind the counter and I saw, clinging to the silk of her blouse, a long dark hair that had escaped her hijab.

I said, "Can we speak privately somewhere? There is a personal question I'd like to ask."

Her shallow breaths reminded me of old Mr. Moscoe trying to fill his lungs in his deathbed. "That would not be possible," she said. "We are very busy here."

"One whole customer," Ryan said.

She glared at him and said, "I manage the inventory. I only came out because I thought you were shopping."

"Don't you want justice for him?"

"I value justice like anyone else," she said. "I answered the questions the police asked me, and I am sure they will find out what happened. Now please excuse me."

She turned to walk away. Now or never, I thought. "Was he your lover?"

She spun on her heel, a panicked look on her face. "That is outrageous," she hissed, her voice much lower than before. "A terrible, reckless thing to say. Not just in my place of business but in public at all."

"A witness told us about a woman who visited Sammy late at night. She matched your description."

"Then your witness was wrong."

"Don't tell me the police didn't ask the same thing."

"What they asked is private. As were my answers."

As she said it, the woman at the counter shouldered her purse and walked toward the door. Now the man behind it looked over at us. "Mehri?" he called, followed by words that were neither English or French. Pashto, I guessed. Or Dari.

She responded and he came around the counter fast, striding toward us in a way that probably wasn't in the customer service manual.

He stopped just short of us, hands on his hips, and said, "What do you want? Why are you bothering her?"

"No one is bothering anyone," I said.

"She says you are."

"Are you Mehrdad?"

"If you are not buying a carpet, it does not matter who I am. Leave our store. Now."

"Sammy Adler interviewed both of you for a story he was writing, didn't he?"

"What if he did?"

"We're trying to find out who killed him."

"We have spoken to the police already. Are you more police?"

"No. Private investigators."

"Then we don't have to speak to you."

"Maybe you want to," Ryan said.

"Look," I said. "Sammy was trying to help you, wasn't he? He wanted to show the Afghan community was about more than honour killings."

"Good for him. Now that he is dead, the story is finished and our part is over. Are you going to leave or must I throw you out?"

He reached out with his right hand and grabbed my shoulder, trying to turn me toward the door. From the corner of my eye I saw Ryan step forward and reach into his coat. I didn't want him to pull a gun; maybe I also wanted to prove to him what I could do with a pressure point. I took hold of Mehrdad's wrist, put my thumb against the vein in the soft underpart and squeezed the top muscles hard with three fingers. He gasped and his hand opened and I moved back, free of his grip.

See? I wanted to say.

"Stop it," Mehri said. "Both of you. This is a place of business, not an alley."

Mehrdad ignored her. He turned and shouted something short and gruff. A few seconds later, a door behind the counter opened. Two men came out of a storage area, both about his age, one a good deal bigger than the other. Or me, for that matter. The big man held a flat blade about ten inches long, thick layers of masking tape forming a makeshift handle. The other was brandishing a long pole with a hook on the end.

"Now there is three of us and two of you," Mehrdad said. "And we will hurt you badly if you don't go."

"There's three of us too," Ryan said, opening his jacket to show his holstered Glock. "Tell those morons to back the fuck off."

"Call the police," Mehrdad said to Mehri. "Tell them a man with a gun is—"

"No," she said. "That won't be necessary. They will leave of their own accord." She looked at me, beseeching me with her eyes, glassy now with tears. "Won't you?"

I shrugged. "Sure."

Ryan said, "What?"

"It's cool," I said to him.

And it was. Because I had seen her slip my business card into the front right pocket of her slacks.

No alley looks good in the rain. The wetness, the grey sky, the puddles forming in dips and potholes, the spattering of drops on weeds. And when you know a man was found there dead, his body battered and mutilated, the empty coldness is only magnified.

We were a few blocks west of the carpet store, behind a Lebanese restaurant called Byblos. There were no physical signs that a body had been dumped there. If there had been blood, it had been washed away by hoses or rain. Anything else would have been collected by the crime scene investigators. We had no real reason to be there, but there we stood.

"Why'd they dump him here?" I wondered aloud.

"Let's ask inside," Ryan said.

We drove around to the front and parked in one of the restaurant's designated spaces. The door was locked. Next to it was a sign with the daily hours of operation: 12:00 Noon – 3:00 a.m.

It was eleven thirty. Half an hour until opening. Through the glass I could see a heavy-set man with a few strands of hair pasted across his shiny dome flapping a tablecloth out to its full size, then laying it out across a table. I knocked twice and waved when he turned.

He looked up, checked his watch, then mouthed what looked like "*Fermé*," waving his hands like an umpire calling a runner safe.

I got out another business card and held it up to the glass. He came over and looked at it, scanning the details, and cocked his head at me.

"Can we speak to you for a minute?" I asked.

"We are not yet open," he said. "Only at noon."

"Please," I said. "We just need a minute of your time. About the man who was found here three weeks ago."

He looked undecided, then sighed and unlocked the lock and let himself out. He relocked the door behind him, as if letting us in would bring more corpses into his life.

"May I see that card?" he asked.

I handed it to him.

"Not police," he said.

"No. Private investigators hired by the victim's family."

"Quickly, please," he said. "I get many people for lunch here."

"Was it you who found the body?"

"Yes," he said. "When I come in at seven. But more like seven-thirty, when I go out back the first time to put out garbage."

"Would you show me where?"

"I don't have time."

"Please, *monsieur* . . . For his family."

"Khoury. Rafiq Khoury. Fine. Go around back. I will meet you there."

He locked the front door and walked into the darkness of the rear.

"Funny," I said. "He took the family bait and the social worker didn't."

Ryan said, "He could have let us walk through with him."

"Maybe you make him nervous."

"I haven't said a word."

"Maybe that's why."

It was faster to drive around to the alley than walk. When we pulled up behind the restaurant, Khoury was waiting outside the back door.

"Right there," he said, pointing to a gravel patch near large waste bins on wheels. "Like he was trash."

"How was he positioned?"

"On his back. One arm stretched to me, where I am standing now. The other one folded across his chest."

"What was he wearing?"

"Blue pants. Jeans. A T-shirt."

"What else?"

"Nothing else."

"No jacket?"

"No. And it was still cold for May."

"What kind of shoes?"

"No shoes."

I looked over at Ryan. He was frowning, just as I was. "No shoes at all?"

"Or, um, *chaussettes*."

"Sorry?"

"Oh, what are they in English? Hose?"

Hose? Hosiery? "Socks?"

"Thank you, yes. No socks or shoes."

Which could only mean one of two things: the people who had killed him had stripped his feet bare, or he hadn't been wearing any in the first place. Which meant he'd been taken from his house and not off the street.

"He was clearly dead by then?" I asked.

"Yes. I saw many bad things in Lebanon before we came here, believe me. So I am not afraid to look at the dead. I stood over him to make sure he did not need an ambulance. All what I saw was the blood on his head and the, um, bruises on his face. A lot of them. Someone beat him a lot."

"Yes, they did."

"Something else you need? People will start arriving soon. I still have preparations to make."

"Why do you think he was put here?"

Khoury shook his head. "I wish I knew. I have no enemies in this country. I left Lebanon to get away from enemies, war, invasions. Almost twenty-five years I have been here—and in all these years not one enemy I have made. Many, many friends. Zero enemies."

"No one has zero enemies," Ryan said.

"The police ask me this same question. They say, no one wants to make trouble for you? I say if we were back in Beirut during the civil war, maybe. But here, in Montreal, there is no hate."

Tell that to Sammy, I thought.

To get back to the East End in time to meet Marie-Josée Boily meant getting back on the Metropolitan. "Anything else will take you more than one hour," Khoury told us. So we gritted our teeth—Ryan in particular—as the Charger bounced from pothole to pothole.

"No socks or shoes," I said.

"I didn't like that either. Were his feet scraped in any way, do you know? Burned or cut?"

"Paquette didn't say."

"If they weren't, then he left the house without shoes, which means he didn't go under his own steam."

"Same thing I was thinking." Which was better than thinking about him having gone in shoes, which had been removed so he could be tortured.

"Would he give you a straight answer if you ask?"

"Let's see."

I called Paquette from my cell. As I waited for the call to go through, I saw the exit for Boulevard St-Laurent and pointed at it. Ryan signalled and moved from the middle lane to the right, just missing the back bumper of a car that had pulled out behind him and sped up to cut us off and take our lane.

He was muttering something about hood-mounted machine guns when I heard Paquette answer. I started to say hello before I realized it was his voice mail. The outgoing message was in French; at least the beep at the end was universal.

"This is Jonah Geller calling," I said. "I have a question regarding the conditions of Mr. Adler's body. I'll be back at the

Holiday Inn around one-thirty—you know the one—or you can try the cell number on the business card I left."

After hanging up, I said to Ryan, "You're thinking the same thing I was. Someone set him up with that phony call to the cops, got him to answer the back door and abducted him from there. Barefoot, in the jeans and T-shirt he was found in."

"That's how I'd have done it."

"Don't tell that to Paquette. He's fishing for any kind of suspect."

"They always fish for my kind," Ryan said.

We were driving south on Clark Street, the street looking dreary and grey. People sometimes call Toronto a forest with buildings—even streets close to the downtown core are lined with huge maples, elms and oaks. Not here. Just grey streets, brown brick buildings, black wrought iron. If there were any trees, they were artfully hidden.

And while I mused about trees, dumb-ass that I sometimes am, it was Ryan who picked up the tail.

"Two cars back," he said. "Silver Lexus. Think it's the goons from the carpet store?"

I undid my seat belt and turned around, trying to see past the dark green Golf that was right behind us. I couldn't see the driver of the Lexus, but I was pretty sure the passenger seat was empty. "I think there's only one person in it. You sure he's following us?"

"You ever know me to be wrong about shit like this?"

I couldn't say I had.

"Can you see the plate number?" he asked.

"No."

"Then belt up or hang on to something."

As soon as I was facing front he sped up, moving from the left lane to the right and back again, putting more cars between the Lexus and us. The light ahead of us turned amber and he would have blazed through it, but a taxi in front of us saw a fare waving from the curb and jammed on its brakes. Ryan had no choice but to stop.

The Lexus was right behind us. Ryan slipped his Glock out of his shoulder holster and handed it to me butt first, then powered his window down. "There's a round in the chamber, so keep your finger outside the trigger guard unless you need to fire. And if you do, you lean forward, I lean back. Got it?"

I had it. "Me forward, you back."

"Okay. Let's see if the fucker wants some."

When the light turned green, the car on our left hit the gas heavy and bolted straight ahead. Ryan stayed where he was. Someone behind us hit their horn, but it wasn't the Lexus. I held the gun down by my leg and turned as far as I could with my belt on. I could see the driver now—and he was alone. A man in his forties with dark hair and a moustache, wearing a grey suit over a black shirt, the collar open, no tie.

Now more horns sounded. Ryan eased slowly through the intersection. The car behind the Lexus veered into the left lane and made a big show of passing us, honking and giving Ryan the finger. On any other day he might have signed his own death warrant but Ryan ignored him and drove slowly along. More cars changed lanes. Not the Lexus. Ryan put his hand out the window and waved to the driver, telling him to pass. He stayed where he was.

"Your finger outside the guard?" he said.

"Yes."

He floored it, throwing me back against the seat and putting half a dozen car lengths between us and our companion. The Lexus sped up too. "Too bad we're not on the highway," Ryan said. "Me and my hemi would lose his asshole fast."

The speedometer climbed past sixty kilometres an hour—too fast for the street we were on—and was approaching seventy when I saw a truck parked in the right curb lane, its four-way flashers on.

"Here we go," Ryan said. He glanced at his side mirror and pulled into the left lane. As soon as we were clear of the parked truck, he wrenched the wheel to put us back on the right and hit his brakes. The Lexus had also moved left and now had no way to get back behind us. We were driving side by side. The driver looked over at us and smiled, then made a pistol of his thumb and forefinger and dropped the imaginary hammer.

"Gimme the gun," Ryan said.

"Don't," I said.

"I won't, fuck, okay? Just gimme."

I handed it back to him, glad to get it out of my hands, hoping he'd stay true to his word. And he did. He pointed it at the driver of the Lexus who lost his smile in a hurry and eased off the gas, both hands on the wheel now.

Ryan tucked the gun back in its holster and said, "See? Very few situations a Glock won't solve. You get the plate number?"

"I got it."

The question was what to do with it: I had no contacts at the Quebec motor vehicle department.

But Bobby Ducharme probably did.

CHAPTER 09

We drove east on Sherbrooke past St-Laurent, St-Denis, St-Hubert, St-Christophe and St-André before arriving at St-Timothée. I figured we'd have to drive a lot longer before we came to Rue Moses or Boulevard Rabbi Akiva.

Ryan dropped me at the café where I was meeting Marie-Josée Boily. I gave him Bobby's cell number and the licence plate I'd memorized.

"How long you think you'll be?" he asked.

"Fifteen, twenty minutes. I hope. If it's much less than that, it means she has nothing to say."

"All right. I'll wait in that park over there," he said, pointing up the street at Parc Lafontaine. "Call my cell when you're done or look for me on a bench if it ain't raining."

Café Romarin was a small place that served crêpes, omelettes and sandwiches, and most of the tables were full. I looked for a woman with a copy of *Prochain épisode* by Hubert Aquin, which she told me she'd be reading. I saw women of the right age reading newspapers, checking cellphones and tablets, scanning menus.

No one reading a book.

I took a table for two near the window, looked the menu over while keeping watch on the front door. More people were leaving than coming in as they finished their lunches and headed back to work. The only language I heard was French, albeit with English words and phrases dropped in here and there.

Ten to one.

A waitress in her twenties, jet-black hair cropped short, a loop through one nostril and small metal bars through both eyebrows, asked me if I was ready to order. "*Juste un café pour le moment*," I said.

"*D'accord.*"

The coffee arrived at five to one. It took five minutes to drink. No one came in with Aquin's book.

At one o'clock, I phoned her office. The woman who answered said something about a *réunion*, which I didn't quite get.

"A meeting," she said. "She left for a lunchtime meeting."

"At Café Romarin?"

"I am not permitted to tell you that."

"Please," I said. "I'm the person she was supposed to meet and she hasn't arrived."

"But she left twenty minutes ago and we are right across the street."

I felt a flutter in my sternum, the kind I get when my gut intuits something faster than my brain can process it.

"Does she have a cellphone number I can try?"

"I cannot give that out," she said. "You must understand, not everyone we work with is satisfied with our efforts. They sometimes get angry with us."

"Can you call her and tell her I'm waiting here? Or better yet, give her my cell number and ask her to call me?"

"Okay," she said. "Please wait."

She put me on hold long enough to listen to half a French rock song; all I could tell was that it was about love, possibly lost forever.

"I'm sorry," the woman said when she came back on the line. "There is no answer on her cell. I left her a message so maybe she will call you, but that is all I can do."

I thanked her, paid for my coffee, loitered outside the café for five more minutes, then walked to Parc Lafontaine to find Ryan.

He was on a bench, jacket off, watching kids play on the swings and jungle gym. Maybe thinking of the son he wasn't seeing very often. I made sure I came around from the front; surprising him from behind was not the secret to longevity.

"You get hold of Bobby?" I asked.

"Yeah. He has someone's gonna run the plate for us. Probably won't have it before tomorrow though. What about your meeting? She tell you anything?"

"She didn't show."

"She call?"

"No. Her office told me she left to meet someone, which I assume was me."

"You think she got held up somewhere, or just decided she had nothing to say?"

"She could have told me that yesterday."

"Maybe someone told her she had nothing to say."

"I didn't tell anyone we were meeting."

"She might have. Or . . . When you set up the meeting," he said, "did you call from the hotel room or your cell?"

"The room."

"That's it, then. We book the fuck out of there. Now."

We called around to half a dozen downtown hotels on our cell-phones before finding a room at the Delta. We were fortunate, the booking agent told me, that there had been a cancellation. "Otherwise . . ." he said, leaving unsaid whatever unfortunate circumstances he had in mind.

We packed up in record time and checked out of the Holiday Inn.

"Was something wrong?" the concierge asked.

"No, just a change of plans. But I am expecting a package to arrive at the end of the day. Would you put it aside for me?"

"Normally, *monsieur*, once a guest has checked out, our obligation to him has ended."

"I understand," I said. "But you would be doing me a great service."

"I see."

And he did, once he took the twenty-dollar bill I palmed him.

We drove the short distance to our new lodgings without maiming any jaywalkers. This time Ryan checked us in, using a credit card in the name of Alessandro Spezza.

"I don't suppose I want to know where you got that," I said.

"I don't suppose you do."

The room was a little larger than the Holiday Inn, with a TV a foot or so larger, and mini-bar prices that would have embarrassed most black marketers. But at least we could do our business privately.

I used my cell to call Marie-Josée's office again. She had not returned from lunch, or wherever she had gone at noon. The only thing we knew for sure was that she had not gone to Café Romarin as scheduled.

I called Arthur Moscoe in Toronto. It went straight to voice mail again. I left another message asking him to call as soon as he could.

Nurses and waitresses. Every man I know has fallen in love with one or the other at least once in his life.

In Sammy Adler's case, it was a nurse.

"He was riding his bike home from work," his ex-wife, Camille, told me. She was in her early thirties, with short dark hair and milk white skin: a Goth effect without makeup. We were on the south side of the park, away from the dog run and playing fields. Her daughter, Sophie, was climbing a plastic structure that had tubular slides curving gently down to the ground, discharging one child after another into the sand.

"He was not paying attention," she said, "which I found later was him in a nutshell, and someone opened a car door and knocked him over. He wasn't hurt too badly, mostly scrapes and bruises, but I was walking past, also on my way home, and I stopped to check on him, make sure he was okay. He said he was in a lot of pain and could I help him around the corner to his flat. Later on, he admitted he was faking it a bit because he wanted to get my phone number and ask me out."

"And you said yes."

"Of course not. I told him nurses cannot go out with patients. He said he was not my patient. He told me his name and asked me mine. Again, I said no. What did I know about this man? So then he said this was all frustrating to him because he had actually paid a friend to open the car door at that exact moment so he could get knocked down and meet me, which made me laugh so hard. Which I needed very bad at the time, because I had split up with my guy of a long time, and finally I was charmed enough, or flattered, and I gave him my number."

"How long until you got married?"

"Two years. I was already pregnant with Sophie. I had not planned on getting married ever—most Québécois don't bother with that anymore. But he said he was old-fashioned and wanted a wedding—plus we would get nice gifts from his family and their friends. So we went ahead. Had the big wedding, my God, almost two hundred persons. For all the good it did."

"What happened?"

She didn't answer right away. Kept an eye on her daughter as she came laughing down one of the chutes—a small girl with light brown hair held back with a bright yellow clip—picking herself up and running back to the ladder that would take her up again.

"When you first meet someone who is different from you, different from all the guys you have been with, you think how

fresh it is. Here is someone who is not full of anger, resent-
ments, who isn't wasting his life being a student forever, or plotting the next revolution on Rue St-Denis. Here is someone who
is funny and real and free of all the history we carry in Québec."

"But . . ."

"At the same time, he was a little too different. Sam didn't
have family here or many friends when we met. They were all
back in Toronto. So he was absorbed into my circles and didn't
always fit. My parents, my sister, my brothers, most of my friends,
they support sovereignty. They voted yes in both referendums.
They want Québec to be its own country. It is already its own
nation, the distinct society, I think it's called in English. Sam was
sympathetic to that, as much as any English-Canadian could be,
but in the end he could not support it. His attitude was—*Christ,
c'est quoi le mot en anglais?* Condescending? Patronizing?"

"Either one."

"Okay. In his view, Québec should stay in Canada because
of what separation would do to the rest of the country. He didn't
see what it would do for us, make us *maîtres chez nous*—masters of
our own fate, you would say. So there were arguments. Not
between me and him, I am not so political. But between him and
everyone else. And it wasn't really his fault. He would ask honest
questions and expect to get honest answers but instead he got
emotion. Grievances. Two hundred years' worth. As if he were
the occupying power and we were still so downtrodden."

"Did anyone ever get really angry?"

"To kill him over, you mean? Christ, no. Arguing about
federalism, sovereignty, is a bit like hockey here. People are passionate about it, but no one would murder him for his opinion.
Besides, we were separated more than a year before he died."

"Is that what ended your marriage? Political differences?"

Camille smiled. "No, of course not. That's just where the
cracks first showed. What it really came down to? Sam was an
observer of life. And a good one. He could be at the most

fantastic party in the world, the greatest concert, the biggest gathering—like a Woodstock—and he'd be off to the side making notes, taking down the details, planning how he would write it in his magazine. Me, I'm a doer. I go right to the centre of things. Like I did the day I met him. I saw someone fall, I went over to help. That's me. If I'm at a party, I'm dancing. At a concert, I'm singing along. Painting my face blue and white for the Fête Nationale, lighting a lighter, hugging strangers. I am nowhere else but where I am. Sam was always somewhere else. Always in his head. His perfect night would be to eat dinner at home and watch a movie, or hockey. Even before we had Sophie. After she was born, to get him out for something besides work, forget it. To be honest, I got very bored in our marriage. I started going out with my sister, sometimes dancing, sometimes to a show. I have to experience life by doing, not watching."

She looked at her watch, then her eyes trailed Sophie as she moved around the playground.

"The first summer we were together," she said, "I took him camping in the Gaspésie. Me, I love camping. I went every summer with my family because we had no money to stay in hotels or resorts. I took him to a park where I'd been a dozen times, and I couldn't wait to show him everything. The river where my dad taught me fishing, the trails you could walk and see the tracks of wolves. And all he did was complain. Too many bugs. Too much he's allergic to. Too much work cooking and cleaning. No electricity for his computer. Too hard to understand the local accent. We were supposed to stay a week but he was so miserable, I broke down after three days and we drove to Quebec City and stayed in a bed and breakfast. I should have seen then how different we were, but his complaining was funny in a way. Like his big hero, Woody Allen. He wrote a great column about it. One of his best, I think. But life isn't a column. Or the movies. After two hours, you're still there and the complaining isn't funny anymore. Sophie!" she called. "*Fais attention!*"

The girl had come down the slide and landed on the feet of a boy her age who was still picking himself up out of the dirt. She looked at her mother, took me in and called out, "*C'est qui, lui?*"

"*Un ami de Maman, Sophie. Ça va.*"

That satisfied her and off she went to continue the ups and downs of her four-year-old life.

"How is she doing?" I asked.

Camille shrugged. "She's four. She doesn't quite understand what has happened. She knows her father is gone but . . . whether she understands he is not coming back, who knows? She asked last week if she could still sleep at his apartment and she cried when I said no. But I don't know honestly what she was crying about. The change in the routine, or the things of hers I haven't yet collected from there."

"What about you?"

"It's a loss for me too. I'm not grieving as if he was still my husband but we had good years together. We parted as friends, I think. I will have to raise Sophie alone and when she is old enough to know how he died, that will be hard, I think."

"At least she'll know why he died, and who killed him."

"It's you who will find this out?"

"It's me."

It had to be. You don't take someone like Sammy out of the world, take him away from a four-year-old girl, rob his city of a unique voice, without having to answer for it. And if Paquette were making progress, he was keeping it well hidden.

"Do you know if he was seeing anyone?" I asked.

She cocked her head slightly and smiled for the first time. "Sam?"

"Why did you say it like that?"

"He wasn't exactly a, um, *un homme à femmes?*"

"A ladies' man."

"Yes."

"But he got you."

The smile vanished as quickly as it had appeared. "Yes, he did. He did. So I suppose it's possible. But he said nothing to me about that. We always told each other that if we met some-one serious—if someone was going to be part of Sophie's life—then we would talk about it. And we didn't, so that is as much as I know."

"Did he ever talk about enemies?" I asked. "People threatening him?"

"Not to me, never."

"Money problems?"

"Everyone in Montreal has money problems. Or at least everyone I know. But his grandfather has so much and he won't live to spend it. I'm sure if Sam had troubles that way, Arthur would have helped."

"Did he ever talk about adoption issues?"

She frowned. "No. Why would he?"

"He recently contacted a woman who works on adoption reunification. I was supposed to meet her today but she didn't show up."

"It must have been for his work, then. He never talked about anything like that when we were married."

"Did he usually tell you what he was working on?"

"When we were together, sure. All the time."

"Nothing lately?"

Camille looked away and up to the right as if searching her memory: "There was something about an Arab family. I know that because he asked me to keep Sophie one Saturday night when she was supposed to be with him. He had to go out to Ville St-Laurent."

"To a carpet store?"

"He didn't say."

"Was it near where he was killed?"

"All he said was Ville St-Laurent."

"Anything about Laurent or Lucienne Lortie?"

"The ones running for election?"

"Yes."

"He was writing about them?"

"Apparently."

She laughed. "*Mon Dieu*, that would be funny. They are so, so out there on the right. He would have made hamburger of them."

"His editor told me he was usually fair to his subjects."

"Yes, but the Lorties—Sam was very liberal, very left on most things. Christ, I would love to see what he would have written about them."

A raindrop hit the bridge of my nose. One must have hit Camille as well because she looked up and took one in the centre of her forehead.

"*Merde*," she said. "I think I'm going to have to go."

"Can I give you a lift?"

She thought about it as more raindrops started to fall, spattering against the dirt of the playground, leaving dark pockmarks. "You know, that would be good, because there is something I have of Sam's at my place. A box of things I took from the flat by mistake when I moved out. I was meaning to give it back to him."

"Do you know what's in it?"

"Memorabilia Arthur wanted him to have. Old photographs, mostly. Images of Montreal the way it was in Arthur's day. When the English ruled and all was well and the east end was the place you escaped from."

CHAPTER 10

I stopped at the Holiday Inn to see if Detective Paquette had sent Sam's phone records and bank statements as promised. The concierge said no, nothing had arrived. I was wondering if it was going to take another twenty to jog his memory when someone behind me said, "Mr. Geller?"

I turned to see Paquette, holding a thick manila envelope, which he handed to me. "The material you asked for. Hand delivered, no less." He didn't look as fresh as he had earlier that morning. His tie was loosened, the collar unbuttoned. His eyes were bloodshot. Only his hair had escaped the rigours of another day in Homicide, still neatly parted with nothing amiss.

I said, "Thanks. You have a minute to talk?"

He made a show of looking at his watch and said, "I suppose."

I pointed to a seating area where club chairs were arranged around a glass-topped coffee table. We sat at diagonal corners. He hiked up his slacks and crossed his legs. I kept both feet on the floor and leaned forward. "Did you get my message?"

"Something about Mr. Adler's body?"

"Yes. He was found barefoot, wasn't he?"

"I believe he was, yes."

"Which suggests he was abducted from his home, shortly after the phony call to the police."

"We all arrive at conclusions in our own way and at our own speed. I must remind myself you are not as experienced at this as we are."

"'We' being you and Detective Chênevert."

"And our investigative team. So you think he was assaulted near the rear door, is that it? And then spirited away from there?"

"That's what I think."

"And your friend, does he agree?"

"My friend?" Wondering if he knew about Ryan. There was no reason for him to, unless he was the one having us followed.

"Monsieur Ducharme."

Ah. Bobby. "I haven't discussed it with him."

"I see. Well, since I wish not to have lawyers from Geniele et al. receiving complaints that I'm being uncooperative, I will disclose the following: having looked through the reports filed by the scene of crime experts, I can say there was indeed a small amount of blood in a crack between two floorboards near the rear of the flat. I repeat, a small amount. We are not prepared to make any firm conclusions from this."

"But it's likely he was first assaulted there and taken elsewhere."

"Between you and me, yes. That's what is likely. Anything else? My workday is not over by any means."

I waited until Paquette stood up and had turned to leave before saying, "Are you having me followed?"

He turned back, an amused look on his face. "Why on earth would I do that? Are you so significant as to warrant surveillance?"

"You tell me."

"No, Mr. Geller."

"No, you're not having me followed?"

"No, I don't think I will tell you."

———

Holly Napier called my cellphone as I was pulling into the entrance of the Delta. I parked off to one side and flipped it open.

"How's it going?" she asked.

"How do you say dead end in French?"

"*Impasse.*"

"That's how it's going."

"Sorry to hear that."

"Did you by any chance tell anyone about our meeting yesterday?"

There was a brief pause before she said, "Just the people in the office. I told you yesterday, we're a very close bunch. I thought they'd want to know someone was trying to find out what happened to Sammy. Plus I thought it was cool—private detectives in my office. Or one anyway, plus your friend Ryan. Why do you ask?"

"The police seemed to know where we were staying before I even met them."

"Well, I certainly didn't tell them."

"What about your employees?"

"I don't think any of them knew where you were staying. That isn't something I shared."

"Did you tell them about Marie-Josée Boily?"

"The social worker? No."

"She was supposed to meet me this afternoon but she never showed up."

"You think there's something sinister about that?"

"It's how my brain works. Like hearing that Sammy missed a meeting with Laurent Lortie."

"You need a drink?"

"I probably do."

"I'm hoping to get out of here around eight tonight. You want to grab one together?"

I thought of her clear green eyes and the mass of red curls

that swirled around her head and said yes before I could think of any reason to say no.

A moment after I ended the call, it rang again. I thought Holly had probably discovered a reason why she couldn't meet after all, but it wasn't her.

It was Mehri Aziz, speaking in a whisper.

"I'm sorry about what happened at the store today," she said. "My brother has a bad humour some times. No, not humour. Temper."

"We might have provoked him a little."

"He thinks you are looking to blame him for what happened to Mr. Adler."

Mr. Adler— keeping up the pretense that she didn't know him better than that.

"The only people I want to blame are the ones who beat him to death."

Silence.

"Hello?"

"If you still want to talk to me," she said, still in a low voice, "I can meet you about five-forty-five. I've told my brother I have errands to run."

"Where?"

"Do you know where is the Marché Jean-Talon? The big market?"

"No."

"Where are you staying?"

At least she didn't know that. And I decided to leave it that way. "At the Holiday Inn on Sherbrooke near St-Laurent."

"Then you take St-Laurent north to Jean-Talon and turn right for a few blocks. It's just before St-Denis. I'll be inside the entrance on the south side, buying flowers. At five-forty-five, but please, no later. The market closes at six and if I am much later than that coming home, there will be questions."

"I thought your family was more liberated than that."

"Not on every subject," she said.

Ryan was on the bed when I got in, watching something on my laptop. In a perfect partnership, he would have been doing research, scouring Sammy's files on the Lortie family, the Kabul carpet trade or something else connected to the case. That's what Jenn would have been doing if she'd been here. Instead, Ryan was watching a compilation of Manny Pacquiao's greatest knockouts.

"Unbelievable fighter," he said. "He's held eight titles in six different weight classes. Ninety-eight pounds his first fight, worked his way up to a hundred and forty-four as a welter-weight. You're what, one-eighty-five?"

"Give or take a pound."

"He'd still kick your ass, I don't care how many black belts you got."

"In the ring, maybe."

"Not in the street?"

"No."

"He hits fucking hard for a little guy."

"But he's never been kicked in the throat."

"True. And what's that you got?" I was carrying the box of memorabilia Camille Fortin had given me, along with Paquette's manila folder.

"Sammy's phone records and bank statements. And some things his ex-wife had."

"You look at it yet?"

"Haven't had a chance."

He moved my laptop aside and said, "Want to spread it out here?"

"Not now. The woman from the rug store just called. She wants to meet me in an hour at a market north of here."

"Which one?"

"Jean-Talon."

"Hell, I know that place. There's a lot of Italian places around there I used to eat with some of the local boys."

He got off the bed and slipped his jacket on, pulling it away from his shoulder holster when it snagged on the butt of his Glock.

"You don't have to come," I said.

"You afraid I'm gonna spook her?"

"You'd spook Manny Pacquiao, why not her?"

"I'm coming anyway. It could be a set-up. Don't forget someone followed us from their place."

"All right. Let me check my email first." I did it on my phone, thumbing through my inbox past messages that had gotten past my filters to promise cheap Alaskan cruises, to an hour-old message from Gabriel Archambault, Lortie campaign press secretary, asking which media outlet I was with. He said Monsieur Lortie was getting so many requests for interviews that he was giving priority to those based in Quebec.

I've posed as a reporter before to get interviews with people who might not otherwise want to grant one, most recently in Boston. This time, I went straight to the point. I wrote back saying I was not a reporter but an investigator looking into the murder of Sam Adler, late of *Montreal Moment* magazine. I would need about fifteen minutes of Monsieur Lortie's time, the sooner the better. I left my number and asked him to reply as soon as he could.

Driving north on St-Laurent, past the east side of Mount Royal, I saw for the first time the great cross perched atop its summit. At night it's lit up so the whole east side of the city can see it, a constant reminder of the Church that utterly dominated Quebec society—as much as if not more so than Ireland's— from its founding to the sixties, when the people finally, and resoundingly, threw off that yoke and started down the road to secularism. But the cross remains, a hundred feet tall, telling the people that even if they have abandoned the Church, it is still there for them. For those who still believe.

We got to the market at five-thirty. There was a large parking lot on the south side but most of it was taken up with stalls selling produce, so we had to hunt for a spot on nearby streets, finally finding one on Henri-Julien. We didn't want to enter together so I told Ryan to wait a minute and then follow me in.

"You hear me whistle," he said, "look alive. It means someone's coming up behind you."

Even with just fifteen minutes left before closing, the market was packed with people. It was a long, wide rectangular space with a peaked roof. Along both sides, vendors stood behind counters calling out their specials, their closing-time deals. As I scanned the different outlets looking for Mehri, I could smell coffee, spices, strong cheeses, fresh meat. Over some of the stalls hung dried chilies, sausages and strings of garlic heads. There were flats with six dozen eggs, baskets brimming with peppers of every colour, stacked cans of homegrown maple syrup, and every fruit and vegetable you could imagine; some were not yet in season in Quebec and some would never be. As I walked down the main aisle, I saw corridors leading off to the left and right with more stalls selling fancy mustards, scented candles and soaps, jam and marmalade, honey, candies—and flowers.

And Mehri, watching as a man in a sailor's cap wrapped bright yellow carnations in cellophane. Even though she was expecting me, she flinched when I called her name. She smiled, sort of, glanced at her watch and said, "You made it."

"Why wouldn't I?"

"I didn't give you much time and the traffic sometimes . . ."

The man behind the counter handed over the flowers and we moved closer to a door that led out the east side of the building.

"Tell me the truth about Sammy," I said. "Was something happening between you beyond the story he was writing?"

"You have to understand," she replied. "This is not easy for me to talk about, especially to a man I don't know."

"You said you wanted justice for him."

"And I do. But how do I know that telling you this will help?"

"Did you tell the police?"

"That we were—no, I didn't."

Those first three words, at least, gave me my answer. "Did they ask?"

"No."

"Of course they did, they found the hair."

"What hair?"

"Like the one we found in Sam's bed. The police found some too. You can't tell me they didn't ask."

"Why would they? I was wearing hijab when I went to be interviewed. They never came to the store."

"But it's true. About you and Sam."

She lowered her eyes. I could see the discomfort. "That we were becoming intimate? To a certain extent, yes. But we were not lovers, not in the way you think."

"We found a hair in his bed that matches yours."

"I lay in his bed with him, one time only, the night before he was killed."

"May twenty-eighth?"

"Yes. But we did not have relations. We held each other and—please, I can't give you details. I am not one of those Western women who divulge every aspect of their lives, who keep cameras going in their apartments night and day."

"Did your brother know about it?"

"What does this have to do with him?"

"He wouldn't have approved, would he?"

Mehri examined her flowers, the bright yellow petals peeking out through the wrap. They'd look beautiful on a dinner table, heartbreaking on a grave. She said, "Of course not.

Any relations outside marriage, to him, would be difficult to accept. And because Sam was a Jew . . . that would have been even harder. Some things are ingrained in us at an early age and they are hard to leave aside."

"You did."

"Because I saw the person, not his faith. When he interviewed us for the story he was writing, I could feel his honesty, his warmth, his compassion for people. He had no prejudice against us because we are Muslim—which is more than I can say for many people in this city—and I felt none toward him."

"Did he interview you and Mehrdad together?"

"At first, yes. But then he came to the store once or twice when Mehrdad was not there. I think he must have figured out when I would be there myself. And then he called and invited me for coffee. I knew I should not accept but I wanted to see him. I was lonely at night. I had tried to find someone in our own community but none wanted me to be what I am. They were like my brother. I think the English phrase is control freak, is that right?"

I couldn't help smiling at that. "Exactly right."

"Sam had no conceptions of how I should be. However I was, it was fine with him. He introduced me to new things, new parts of the city I did not know. New foods. And he made me laugh, so much of the time, with the things he knew, the things he saw in people and their crazy behaviour."

"He made a lot of people laugh." I thought of what his ex-wife had said about him being a homebody and wondered whether a relationship between him and Mehri would have lasted had he lived.

I said, "Mehri, do you know where your brother was when Sam was killed?"

"He wouldn't do that to Sam. Kill him like that."

"You said he would have disapproved if he knew."

"But he didn't know."

"Can you be sure? Isn't it possible Mehrdad saw or heard you sneaking out at night? Coming back in late? Followed you one time?"

She broke off eye contact. When she looked back at me, her jaw was clenched, her lips curled in on themselves. "My brother was home that night. With me. We worked late counting our inventory. Making ready some deliveries. We didn't get home until eleven and we were both exhausted. He went straight to bed. I saw with my own eyes."

"How do you know he didn't leave after you fell asleep?"

A tear rolled down her cheek, taking with it a dark trail of mascara. "I would know if he did something so terrible. He could not keep such a secret from me. Ever."

"You said he doesn't like Jews."

"A lot of Muslims don't. It doesn't mean they commit murder. My God, you are like everyone else, blaming us whatever happens."

There was a lot I could have said to dispute that, but I heard a sharp whistle behind me. I turned to see Ryan standing next to a dairy stand, unbuttoning his jacket. He nodded his head toward the side door, where two men in suits had just entered.

One of them was the driver of the car that had followed us from Les Tapis Kabul.

Mehri turned, following my gaze, and saw them, then turned back to me, a look of panic in her eyes. I pushed her to my right and started backpedalling, watching their hands. The driver, still wearing his grey suit, was reaching inside his jacket. I couldn't tell what the man behind him was doing but assumed he was also going for a gun. I backed up past a display of cans of syrup, grabbed the top one and threw it as hard as I could. The driver sidestepped it but his partner, who didn't see it coming until it was too late, took it in the chest and staggered backwards. I swept the bottom row of cans—the vendor shouting something raw in French—and they toppled to the floor between the driver and me. He had to stop in his tracks, trying to find a path through the cans. As soon as he looked down at the floor, I leapt at him and slammed the palm of my left hand into his nose, which shattered and spouted blood as far up as my elbow. A woman behind me screamed—not Mehri—as I followed up with a right hook to the jaw and an uppercut left that snapped his chin back. He sagged to the floor on top of the syrup cans.

The man behind him—younger and leaner but with a strong resemblance to his partner—had his gun in his hand, bringing it up from waist level. That's as far as it got before he dropped it and put his hands out. I turned and saw Ryan in a shooting stance, his gun aimed squarely at the man's chest. I jumped over the cans, kicked the man's gun aside and grabbed his lapels.

"Who are you?" I hissed.

He answered in a guttural language close enough to Hebrew that I assumed it was Arabic. Or Pashto. I looked at Mehri and said, "What did he say?"

"I don't know," she said. "It is not my language."

"*Qui êtes vous?*" I tried.

I got the same thing again. I grabbed his arm below the elbow and put a hundred pounds of pressure onto the nerve. His eyes rolled and he went pale.

"You speak English?" I said. "*Parle français?*"

He groaned something in neither. The pain he was in, he must have had an incredibly high tolerance or really didn't speak either language. I patted his jacket with my other hand and felt a wallet. I got it out and tossed it to Ryan.

"Get the other guy's too," I said.

He got both wallets into his pockets. Then said, "Shit."

I turned around. At least a dozen people were gathered in a semicircle staring at us. One young man wearing a bicycle helmet was holding out a cellphone, videotaping the scene. Ryan strode over to the cyclist, pointed his gun at him and grabbed the phone out of his hand. "Anyone else want to try?"

he said. "The last thing you'll tape is a bullet coming at you." He walked backwards toward the door, keeping his Glock at waist level, making sure no one tried to film us. I didn't want anyone following us out: I drove an elbow into the base of the partner's neck. His head snapped back and he fell to the floor.

I grabbed Mehri's arm and steered her outside.

"Who were they?" I demanded.

"You have their wallets," she said. "You can look at their names."

"I want to hear it from you."

"Why?"

"Because the guy in grey followed us from your store today."

"Move faster," Ryan said behind me. "There are cameras over the door."

I kept hold of her arm. "If you don't know them, your brother does. Should we go ask him?"

"It won't be nicely," Ryan said.

"Look," she said. "The one in front, I have seen him at the store once or twice. Usually late, sometimes after we close. But Mehrdad never introduced us."

"And the other one?"

"He never came in. One time, he was outside in a car, waiting, but that's all."

"Why did you say you didn't understand him?"

"Because I didn't. I speak Pashto and Dari and he spoke neither. I believe it was Arabic. Where are you taking me? I am going to be very late getting home."

"Tell your brother you were with me."

"Don't joke."

"I wasn't joking. I think he killed Sam, and if he did, I want him to know I'm coming after him."

"He didn't do it. I told you, I would know."

"Then what's with the fucking gunmen, Mehri?"

"There is no need to speak to me that way," she said.

"There fucking well is."

Ryan said, "In here," pointing at the doorway of a small store for rent, its windows covered over with newspapers so old they still had hockey scores. I took out the two wallets and read out the names on their drivers' licences.

The grey suit was Mohammed al-Haddad; the black suit, Faisal al-Haddad.

"Oh, no," she whispered.

"What?"

"He said that he was done with them."

"Done with who?"

"The Syrians."

CHAPTER 11

"Syrians?" "Ryan asked. "I thought we were dealing with Afghans. Who invited Syrians?"

"No clue," I said.

"This from the so-called detective."

We had let Mehri go on her way, flustered, late, in tears again, mascara streaking both cheeks. Then Ryan had put the incriminating cellphone under the front wheel of the Charger, crushing it as we headed south. I didn't think the two men at the market would be cooperating with the police, who no doubt had been called in. If they had regained consciousness, they were probably playing dumb like they had with us, pretending to speak neither English nor French.

I called Bobby Ducharme and asked if he'd had any luck with the licence plate we'd given him to run.

"It's registered to a numbered company," he said. "Which I traced to a group called Les Importations Homs. That's H-o-m-s."

"Like the city in Syria."

"I watch the news. You dealing with Syrians, I'm not sure that's a good thing," Bobby said. "They have a reputation of being fairly badass, at least in Montreal."

"Who owns the company?"

"Don't know yet. There's a lot of layers there. And I also have a day job to work at. Let me see what I can find in the morning."

"Thanks, Bobby."

"If you want to pay me in beer, I like St-Ambroise. The pale ale, not the oatmeal stout. If I want cereal, I'll have it in a bowl."

When we were back in the room, I checked my email. Laurent Lortie's press secretary had replied, asking if I were an early riser. If so, the man and his daughter could meet me at 7:30 at their campaign office on Avenue du Mont-Royal. "He has a great deal to do tomorrow but he is enthused to help you determine the circumstances behind the unfortunate passing of Mr. Samuel Adler."

"He actually wrote that?" Ryan snorted.

"It's not his first language."

"Sounds like bullshit is."

I wrote back saying 7:30 was fine, that I looked forward to meeting Monsieur and Mademoiselle Lortie.

I looked at my watch: quarter to eight. I googled Les Importations Homs but couldn't find anything but an e-mail address, phone number and post-office box. No street address. Nothing to search out in the night. No windows to break, no alarms to trigger, no men in suits to batter.

Nothing more to be done tonight but have the promised drink with Holly Napier.

We met in the hotel's ground floor Café Bar. She wore a light blue silk jacket over a white camisole, jeans and sandals with a modest heel. Her hair was loose, falling past her shoulders, the colour of embers.

Like her much?

Over glasses of wine that cost the price of a bottle each, I told her about the day we'd had, from my visit to Crimes Majeurs to the fight in the market.

"You pack a lot into one day," she said.

"It's not over yet."

"What else is on your agenda?"

We were facing each other across a marble-topped table. Keeping eye contact. Things were stirring inside me, palpably, and I wanted to touch her hand. But didn't. "There are some records of Sammy's I need to look over. And some memorabilia I got from his ex-wife."

"I could help," she said.

"You don't have to."

"I didn't say I had to. I'd like to. I knew Sammy better than you. Maybe something in there will make more sense to me than it would to you."

I said, "Sure." Thinking of a Willie P. Bennett song, "Lace and Pretty Flowers," where a would-be lover uses silks and perfume to get a girl up to his room. With me, it's records and statements and a musty cardboard box. I am smoothness but smoothness is not me.

Up I took her anyway.

Ryan wasn't in the room. He'd left me a note saying he was going to Little Italy to have a drink "in a place that won't hose me." He signed off saying, "Back in 2 hrs. Call if I need to stay out later."

Suddenly the room felt smaller. Warmer. Darker. I opened Paquette's envelope and spread the phone records on my bed—still made from the morning, the bedspread taut—and Holly and I started going through them. She put checkmarks beside all the numbers she knew: the office, her cell, the managing editor's cell, her home number. I noticed he sometimes called her late at night, close to or after midnight.

"Those were probably the nights Sophie stayed with him. He'd wait until she went to bed, then he'd work on that week's column. If he had questions, he'd call. I'm a night owl," she said. "I don't need much sleep."

I checked off numbers for Camille Fortin, the Lortie campaign office and Les Tapis Kabul. Noted calls made to and from his cell, which only confirmed he was speaking to Mehri more often and at odder hours than a strict journalistic relationship would have required.

I also recognized the office number for Marie-Josée Boily. And right below it, dialled just a minute afterward, a number with a 438 area code. Holly thought it was probably a cell. I called it and got a message recorded by a woman who sounded like Marie-Josée. I left a brief message saying I was sorry we had missed each other at the restaurant—no blame assigned—and that I still wanted to speak to her, if only for a moment.

When I hung up, Holly was highlighting a dozen or more calls made to Toronto.

"That's his grandfather's number," I said.

"There's a lot of calls to him. Especially the month before Sammy died."

"Long ones too. Look at this one, forty-four minutes."

"And this one was more than an hour."

"Arthur told me Sammy liked his old-time stories. But you'd think he'd heard most of them by now. What was he working on then, do you remember?"

"He hadn't started the Lortie profile yet. Or the Afghan one. Let me think a second. There was the one about the halal food . . ."

"The agriculture critic he roasted? I loved that piece. First one of his I read."

"I know, it was great, but I doubt his grandfather knew anything about it. There was another one on the jazz festival, how everyone comes out to that in July but ignores good jazz the rest of the year. Honestly, I can't think of anything his grandfather or his memories would have helped with."

"I've called the old man a couple of times about another thing. I'll ask him."

"Something to do with adoption?"

"Yes."

"You're still wondering why Marie-Josée never showed up?"

"I always wonder why someone doesn't show up. It usually means they're hiding something."

"Good thing I showed up. Otherwise you'd be investigating me."

We set the phone records aside and I used my thumbnail to split the tape with which the box had been sealed. I pulled the flaps open.

"Phew," she said, waving her hand over the top. "That's been sealed a long time. Maybe we should do it on the floor."

There were a few ways I could have responded to that. I wisely chose none. We sat opposite each other, cross-legged, and I started pulling out envelopes full of photos and negatives, the kind everyone got from labs before cameras went digital. Each pack commemorated an event in the family's life: weddings, graduations, reunions, bar and bat mitzvahs. I saw Sammy at different stages in his life, from childhood through the years I knew him at Camp Arrowhead to his university graduation. I saw him with his parents in some, with his grandparents in others, Arthur Moscoe easy to spot with his great height and prominent ears.

"Look at him," Holly Napier said, pointing at an image of Sammy in a suit, maybe sixteen or seventeen, smiling for the camera at some formal event. "So young. So skinny."

I saw her eyes turning glassy with tears and asked if she was okay.

"Fine. It's just the dust on these things. Keep going."

I pulled out more photos, a set of silver candlesticks with blackened tops, a Crown Royal bag filled with old silver dollars. Letters Sammy had written to his grandfather from camp, from Europe—those thin blue airmail letters that became their own envelope when you licked the sides. The deeper we went into the box, the older the materials looked. There were photos of older generations, sepia-toned images of people looking stiffly into cameras. Men with thick moustaches and trimmed beards, children in sailor outfits, women in dresses that blossomed out at the hips. Images of old Europe, of communities that had been wiped from the map in this war or that. None of it told us a thing about Sammy or why he died.

When we thought the box was empty, I found one more photo that wasn't in an envelope. It was stuck to the top flap of the box. I'd missed when I'd opened it. A small image, three inches by two, black-and-white with scalloped edges. At the bottom, stamped in fading ink, was the date it was taken: July 18, 1950.

There were two figures in the photo: a tall young man of about twenty who had to be Arthur. Dapper looking in a light-coloured suit and a straw fedora on his head, his arm around a lovely young woman who in no way resembled the woman he married later that year. We had seen his bride in photos. And this woman had a small cross dangling from a chain around her neck.

Holly was gone when Ryan got back, home to her place to get some sleep before another long day at *Montreal Moment*. I had told her I'd keep her posted on any new developments, especially anything Arthur Moscoe told me about the photo once I reached him.

"Any luck with the files?" Ryan said.

"Some. I got Marie-Josée's cell number, which might help pin her down. And there's this." I showed him the long list of calls between Arthur Moscoe and Sammy Adler.

"An old man, dying," Ryan said. "Might just have been reminiscing."

"Maybe. But such a cluster of them, all at once. I'm wondering if there's more to it."

"Get hold of him."

"I've been trying. I keep getting voice mail. He probably sleeps a lot."

"Next time pass me the phone," he said. "I'll wake him the fuck up."

"I know you would." I looked away, thinking of something, wondering whether it was worth a try.

"What?" Ryan said.

"What time is it now?"

"A little after ten. Why?"

"Just an idea I had."

"Good or bad?"

"Maybe both."

I excused myself and went into the bathroom, where the hotel had thoughtfully placed a phone on the wall next to the toilet. I didn't need the bathroom, just the privacy. I sat on the toilet, took a deep breath, and dialled a number I knew so well, it could have been my own.

I've known Sierra Lyons almost as long as I've known Jenn. They've been together five years, and Jenn introduced us soon after we became friends. They love each other completely and are fiercely protective of each other. I always thought that if anyone harmed Sierra, even spoke rudely to her, Jenn would exact a short, sharp vengeance.

So it was no surprise that Sierra didn't want to call Jenn to the phone. She said Jenn had gone to bed but I knew it wasn't true, not at ten-fifteen. "I just need to ask her one favour," I said.

"Does it have anything to do with work?" Sierra asked. She's always been warm and welcoming, but there was something in her voice now that brought to mind an iron gate clanging shut.

"Yes, but—"

"You can't be serious. You know what she's been going through."

"There's nothing dangerous in it. If there were, I wouldn't ask."

"Everything is dangerous where you're concerned. Look at what happened in Boston."

"There's an old man in Toronto," I said. "He's eighty-three years old and dying and he lost his grandson. I just need Jenn to ask him something. It would only take a few minutes."

"Ask him yourself."

"I've tried. Repeatedly. I can't reach him."

"Ask Colin to do it."

"I would, but . . ."

"But what?"

"Colin was a patrol cop, not an investigator. I don't know that the old man would open up to him."

"Why not?"

"It might be a sensitive topic."

"Sensitive. Kind of the opposite of what you're being now."

"That's not fair."

"Isn't it? She is the love of my life, Jonah. There is no one I've ever loved as much as Jenn and I almost lost her because of you. Do not drag her into this."

She went silent and I thought she was going to hang up on me. Then I heard Jenn's voice in the background, asking who was on the phone. Sierra's reply was distant, muffled. Probably covering the receiver with her hand.

The next thing I heard was Jenn's voice saying hey into the phone and Sierra's heels stomping away.

CHAPTER 12

awoke the next morning to a head buzzing like a beehive busted open by a bear paw. Thinking of so many different things, I couldn't light on any one long enough to make sense of it. An appointment with a social worker that evaporated soon after it was made. A Syrian following us from an Afghan rug store. Two Syrians showing up at the Jean-Talon Market to bust up our meeting with Mehri.

Had she set us up? She'd seemed genuinely shaken by their sudden appearance, by whatever connection they had to her brother.

Then there were thoughts of Sammy and his grandfather, their long conversations over the phone—about what? And that lone black-and-white photo in a box of memorabilia. Thoughts of Holly Napier—I realized I had dreamed about her, that I had come into my hotel room to find her sitting at the desk, her feet up on the polished surface. No shoes on, her feet bare and delicate.

Thoughts of Jenn and the brief conversation we'd had last night. Wondering whether I had been right to ask her to pay

Arthur Moscoe a visit and find out whether there was anything to the adoption angle. If there was, I knew she'd get it. She is so open, so trusting herself, that people have a hard time keeping secrets from her. They pull their cards away from the vest and lay them on the table.

I stood under the shower, adjusting it from steaming hot to cool, then cold, until I could focus on the first meeting of the day, with *la famille* Lortie. Ryan was up when I got out, sitting on the bed in boxers. His muscles were lean and hard-looking and he had more scars than a fighting dog, including one puckered dent above his right hip. I didn't ask about it and he didn't tell.

"You gonna have breakfast before this meeting?"

"Just coffee," I said.

"I'll drive you?"

"I can take a cab. No point in you sitting around."

"Sit around here, sit around there. What difference does it make? At least if you need me, I'll be close."

We took Park Avenue up and around the southern flank of the mountain. Something had changed since the last time I'd been in Montreal and I couldn't put my finger on it right away. Then I realized the ugly old cloverleaf where Park met Pine had been torn down. Everything was open to view now. All that crumbling grey concrete gone and nothing but a wide vista of green—the mountain on the west side, Jeanne-Mance Park on the east. Like someone had come along with a mop and bucket and scrubbed away something grimy.

Better not put the bucket away just yet, I thought. This was Montreal. There was plenty more fixing to do.

We turned onto Mont-Royal, lined on both sides with cafés, pâtisseries, clothing boutiques, small bookstores and sec-ond-hand record shops. Most were still closed, except for the cafés. Near St-Hubert was a storefront papered with posters for Québec aux Québécois, showing Laurent Lortie with his arm around his daughter's shoulder, each waving with one arm to an unseen crowd.

Ryan left me outside the front door and went to find a meter. The door was locked. I rapped on it and waited. After half a minute, I rapped again. Just a few seconds later, a young man opened the door and ushered me in. "I'm Gabriel Archambault," he said, extending a fine bony hand. He was losing his hair and kept it cut very short, little more than a bristle. A neatly trimmed beard of the same length framed his chin.

Both sides of the room were lined with desks that had computers, phones and printouts, where staff or volunteers would spend the day calling voters. "It is quiet now," he said, "but by eight o'clock we will be very busy, so you must keep your interview brief."

"No problem," I said. After dealing with Detective Paquette and Mehrdad Aziz, I was getting used to people having little or no time for me.

"Kindly wait here a moment. Will you take a coffee?"

"Sure," I said. "*Merci.*"

"*De rien,*" he said and off he went.

According to Sammy's notes, Laurent Lortie had been born into an old-stock family, what the Québécois themselves call *pure laine*. The Lorties had been among the first settlers to sail from Brittany—one of the few places in France where French sounds like Québécois. They had originally settled in the north coast of the Gaspé Peninsula, where for generations they farmed, fished for salmon or worked in forestry. His great-grandfather moved to Montreal, where he worked as a customs clerk in a shipping company. His grandfather finished high school and obtained a post in the civil service, eventually becoming assistant to the deputy minister of finance. His father, Lucien, was the first Lortie to graduate from university and outdid his own father by winning a seat in the provincial parliament, the Assemblée

Nationale, serving in the Liberal government of Jean Lesage at the onset of the Quiet Revolution.

Born in 1951, Laurent was educated at Collège Jean-de-Brébeuf. According to Sammy, it was the school where the elite sent their children for a good Jesuit education and grounding in Quebec nationalism. He studied history and political science at the Université de Montréal, graduating with top marks, and went on to the London School of Economics, where he honed his already keen mind and perfected his English.

On his return to Montreal, he'd been expected to follow in his father's footsteps and prepare for a life in politics. He surprised his parents by going into business instead, working for Power Corporation of Canada, a global media and finance giant owned and run by French-Canadians, often cited as one of the powers pulling the federal government's strings. When CEO Paul Desmarais told prime ministers to jump, they grabbed their pogo sticks. At thirty, Laurent married his secretary, Dorothée Rivest. Lucienne was born in 1982, Luc in 1985. At age forty, he was named senior vice-president of Power Corp.'s financial services division. It was only when he took early retirement at sixty that he began taking a direct interest in politics.

After a ten-minute wait, Gabriel returned and led me to an office at the back of the store. There were two desks, both neat as a pin, neat as Gabriel himself. They formed an ell: one desk backed against the rear window, the other at a right angle to it. He pointed to a seat opposite the desk that backed onto the wall. I took it. A moment later, I smelled something light and floral snaking past me in the air. I heard footsteps coming, two sets, one with harder heels than the other, and the fragrance grew stronger as a tall blonde woman came in. Gabriel followed, carrying a tray with two mugs of coffee, both emblazoned with the blue QAQ symbol.

"I forgot to ask how you take yours," he said.

"I am guessing black," the woman said. "Isn't that how detectives like their coffee? Strong and simple?"

"I usually take milk," I said.

"Not even cream but milk?" she smiled. "Now you are shattering all my illusions. I am Lucienne Lortie, by the way."

"Jonah Geller."

"Yes, I know." We shook; her grip was stronger than Gabriel's. I wondered if she used a strengthener like mine. By any reasonable standard she was stunning: about five-nine, slender, wearing a tight cream-coloured pencil skirt and jacket over a pale coral blouse. Her jewellery was simple but expensive looking: a pearl choker and pearl earrings, a slim gold watch. No rings. Her hair was blonde—very blonde—but short, neatly parted and gelled with something to fit her head as tight as a legionnaire's helmet. Beautiful, but not in Holly Napier's natural way. Too highly processed for my taste. Holly struck me as the kind of woman who'd roll out of bed looking great; Lucienne Lortie looked like she'd need a gaggle of stylists.

"My father will join us in a moment," she said. "In the meantime, please sit. Enjoy your coffee."

"Thank you."

She sat behind the desk and told Gabriel in French that he could return to his work. Her accent was easy to understand: not the *joual* of the streets but the clearly enunciated tongue I had learned in school.

"So," she said. "You have come all the way from Toronto to see us."

"Among other people."

"Ah. And how are you liking Montreal so far? Are you familiar with it?"

"Parts," I said.

"West of St-Laurent? The English areas?"

"Mostly."

"If I know my history, that was a largely Jewish area for many years. You are Jewish yourself, of course."

"Of course."

"Now most of our Jewish citizens have moved farther west, to Hampstead, Côte St-Luc, Dollard-des-Ormeaux, except for those ultra-Orthodox in Outremont. And in some cases they have gone all the way to Ontario. Which is a pity. Previous generations viewed the Jews as a necessary evil. To me, those who assimilate make up one of the more successful immigrant groups in Montreal."

"Unlike the Muslims."

"You don't approve of our platform?"

"I don't vote here."

"Nonetheless, there is a note of—what?—disdain in your voice?"

"I don't know enough about it."

"Then let me spell it out for you."

"I'm really here to talk about Sam Adler."

"And this is what we talked about, he and I. And my father, of course."

"Shouldn't we wait for him?"

"I am not sure how long his call will take. But we speak with one voice, he and I."

"Go on then."

"It's rather simple," she said. "There were two founding peoples in Quebec, the French and the English. The English won at the Plains of Abraham and for more than two centuries after, we were strangers in our own land. The workers, never the owners or managers. Yes, the Catholic Church was complicit in keeping things that way, denying us a good education, a greater view of things. But more than that was the contempt, the arrogance, of the English, the Scots and, yes, the Jews, who kept us in the menial and clerical classes."

I had heard this before, dozens of times, through two

referendums that had almost split the country. The laments of French-Canadians, how the English had humiliated them, stymied their ambitions at every turn. Who could forget the second referendum in 1995, which the sovereigntists lost by a whisker, hearing the leader of their camp blame the loss on money and ethnic voters—code for Jews and other immigrants who had voted massively against separation.

"Your family seems to have done all right."

"We were the exception in many ways," Lucienne said, "not the rule. We gained our education. We secured a different future. But for the Quebec masses, it took precisely two hundred and sixteen years, from the loss to the British in 1760 until René Lévesque's historic victory in 1976."

"Up to '76 already?" a gruff voice cut in. "I swear, I was only gone a minute."

I turned to see a man in a dark grey suit, white shirt and blue tie—the same shade of blue as his party's colour. I knew he was over sixty, but he looked fit enough. His hair was grey, so neat he looked like he'd just stepped out of a barber's chair. Maybe he and Lucienne shared a crew. He wore aftershave, which clashed with Lucienne's scent. His chin protruded but his lips were thin and tight, making him look like he had no teeth. But when he smiled, which he did without warmth as we shook, he showed a row of even teeth that looked professionally bleached.

"I'm sorry I missed the beginning," he said. "But I trust my dear daughter has given you a thorough grounding in our politics." His English was flawless, even tinged with a slight British accent.

"We were only up to the historic victory," I said.

"The first one," he said, "but not the last." He threw his head back a little when he laughed—a practised politician's move that let me know he truly appreciated humour. Whoopee.

"Let me take it quickly from there," he said. "I know you have some specific questions regarding the death of your client."

"He was also a friend."

"Then you have our deepest sympathies. Doesn't he, Lucienne?"

"Of course, Papa," she said, with all the warmth of an abandoned igloo.

"Our party," he said, "was born of necessity. The Liberals have always pandered to immigrants. Where else would they get their majority, if not among the English and the others? And the Parti Québécois, in order to increase the French-speaking population, has not taken great enough care when deciding whom to let in."

"Not discriminating enough."

He looked at his daughter, who shrugged, as if to say, *This is what I was dealing with.*

"Have your jokes, Mr. Geller. But the truth is there for all to see. Allowing certain communities to grow without the appropriate checks and balances—"

"By which you mean Muslims?"

All traces of his smile vanished. "If we are to complete this interview in the time we have, you should make fewer such comments and spend more time listening. And yes, since you raise the issue, I speak of Muslims—not all of them, just those who resist our way of life. Who would impose their will if we allow it. If we insist that Quebec will never again be dominated by the Church, we most certainly will not submit to the laws or practices of unassimilated minorities."

"So you would restrict their numbers."

"The federal government has wisely ceded control of immigration to the province of Quebec, and when we form the next government, we will use the powers granted us to ensure a secular future."

"How far did you get with Sam Adler on this?"

"I am surprised you don't know the answer to that? Or do you?"

"I read his notes. Unfortunately, he didn't live long enough to complete the interviews or write his profile."

"Regrettable, indeed."

I noticed Lucienne was sitting back in her chair, watching her father, paying me no attention at all. No question who was in charge.

"Were you concerned about the story he was writing?"

"Why would I be?"

"I doubt he agreed with your platform."

"That is not my concern. As long as he reported it accurately, and his reputation suggested he would, then any publicity would be good publicity. We have nothing to hide, Mr. Geller. We make our views very well known, whether on our website, in our printed material or in speeches. In fact, I was working on a speech when you arrived this morning. I will deliver it Friday night during the festivities of the Fête Nationale. It will be my first major address of the campaign, and I assure you every step of our platform will be clearly and unequivocally put to the people. No hidden agenda. Isn't that true, Lucienne?"

"Yes, Papa."

"We don't expect to gain the support of all English voters," he said. "At the same time, I believe a significant number will appreciate our views on the economy."

"You speak better English than most English-Canadians," I said. "You and Lucienne."

He smiled and said, "In my day, coming of age in the early seventies, I felt it behooved me to speak the best English I could. After all, for the fox to enter the henhouse, it should first learn how to cluck." He paused, as if waiting for laughter from his audience of one. None came, so he went on. "As for Lucienne, when we form the next government, she will need her English to communicate with her counterparts in other provinces. And when she eventually succeeds me, as I hope she will, she will take her place at the table with the other premiers, with the

governors of American states. And she will not be found wanting on any level. Isn't that right, my dear?"

"I appreciate your faith in me, Papa."

What were they reading from, a teleprompter?

"You're so certain you're going to form this dynasty,"
I said. "But everything I've ever read about politics in Quebec
suggests you're out of step."

"Ah," he said. "That myth that our population will only
support a leftist government. Needless to say, we don't agree.
We don't think the government should support its citizens from
cradle to grave, as the saying goes. We would form a less inter-
ventionist government that provides more freedom to the
entrepreneurs, the business class, the ones who want to compete
with the other provinces and even the United States."

"I've been told no right-wing party can win an election here."

"Right wing, left wing—I will leave that to the hockey
enthusiasts."

"Your operation here doesn't suggest a huge swell of
support."

"This office?" he said. "It is only the first of several that will
open as we get closer to the election. On July 1, for example, we
will move into a much larger space with capacity for dozens of
volunteers. And then everyone will see that we are a force to be
reckoned with. A difference maker. Why? Because no existing
party of any stripe has had the answers to the problems we face.
Did you know, Mr. Geller, that Quebec, despite all its vast
resources, is Canada's second-poorest province and on its way
to becoming dead last?"

"I've read something to that effect."

"But do you know why?"

"I think you're about to tell me."

"For more than fifty years, we have been building a welfare
state we can no longer afford. And while I admire France on many
levels, this is one aspect of their society we have been fools to

emulate. Providing everything to everyone at every stage of life. And because of these expenditures, along with declining revenues, our debt now stands at fifty-five per cent of our gross domestic product. Fifty-five per cent! We now get equalization payments from the federal government. We are considered a 'have-not' province, qualifying for handouts from the haves. Nearly ten per cent of our provincial budget comes from Ottawa."

He stood and opened a file cabinet next to his desk, thumbed through the drawer and pulled out a thick sheaf of paper. "This report," he said, "published just this month, shows that we could very quickly become one of the haves, instead of a pathetic have-not, if we just developed more of our natural resources. Offshore oil deposits, natural gas, more electricity and the like. But no government has done much, if anything, about it. Why? Because we would lose our equalization payments. They would rather remain in thrall to the rest of Canada than stand up on their own two feet. Like the person who would rather stay on welfare than seek honest work. All of that will end under a Lortie government. We will be one of the haves, oh yes. And even better than that, who will work these mines, pipelines and hydro projects?"

"Let me guess. You'll need halal markets."

"How astute. Yes, we will require new immigrants to move to regions where they can find honest work, instead of forming these seething little pockets of resentment in Montreal and other cities where true Québécois are afraid to walk. You've seen what happened in France, in the suburbs where North Africans congregate. It is hell on earth, right outside one of the greatest cities in the world."

"You see them as that big a threat?" I asked.

"Lucienne," he said. "Hand me that garbage that arrived yesterday. Look at this," he said to me, holding up a crude leaf-let that showed caricatures of Laurent and Lucienne, badly drawn but easy to identify—both wearing shirts with QAQ arm-bands, meant to draw comparisons with other notorious armbands from history. Under their feet was a woman wearing a headscarf, blood spurting from gaping wounds.

"*Mort aux racistes*" was written below. Death to racists. And in block letters, "*Front de Libération des Musulmans du Québec*." Quebec Muslim Liberation Front.

"That's your precious immigrant right there," he said. "Threatening violence against real Québécois. But we will not be intimidated, will we, my dear?"

"Never," Lucienne said.

"We will win this election," he said, "and form a government that sets this province on the right course, the one that is its true destiny and has been since 1760. Must we separate from Canada to accomplish this? Not in my mind. We must simply be strong, stronger than we have ever been. We must fight to become an economic powerhouse. And we must rid ourselves of medieval forces that would impose their outrageous views on the Québécois majority. That is what I told Mr. Adler and that is what I tell you."

"Is that your only answer? Cut down on immigration?"

"Not all immigration. Only the ones who challenge the collective will. And we have other solutions to offer from an economic and social perspective, but I don't have the time to explain them to you. Nor are they germane to your inquiries."

"So let's stick to what is. Are you sure there was nothing in Mr. Adler's profile that might have put you in a bad light?"

"We'll never know," he said. And the way he said it was utterly devoid of any sympathy. It sounded like gloating to me.

The office door banged open then, and a muscular young man strode in, carrying a heavy carton, the veins of his biceps and forearms bulging with the weight. He set it down loudly. "*Eh, Papa*," he said. "*Y'a une douzaine de ces boîtes-là. Où veux tu que je les place?*"

His French was unlike that of either of the Lorties. Rough and fast, the words *boîtes*—boxes—pronounced *bwytes*. *Place* sounded like *plowce*. Were it not for the fact that he'd addressed Laurent as Papa, I'd never have guessed that this was his son, Luc. He was short, with long dark hair that covered his eyes like a sheepdog's. His T-shirt was stained with sweat and dust from the box he'd carried. His jeans were frayed at the bottom and the lace of one shoe was untied.

"*En avant, Luc*," Laurent said. "*Toujours en avant, comme je te l'ai dit*." With a note of impatience in his voice, even more than he'd shown to me and my lack of understanding of Quebec.

"Okay," Luc said, shaking his hair out of his eyes. He never looked at me or his sister. Laurent made no move to introduce us. Luc picked up the box and backed out of the office, bumping it shut with his hip. His footsteps clumped loudly until they receded into the distance.

It was hard to believe he and Lucienne were brother and sister. One tall, slender and blonde; the other stocky, dark haired. Lucienne articulate in two languages; Luc's gruff French straight off the street.

It came out of my mouth before my brain had fully processed the thought: "Did Sam Adler ever ask you about adoption?"

CHAPTER 13

"So what did the big man say to that?" Ryan asked.

"For the first ten seconds? Not a word," I said. "He looked at his daughter, she looked at him. Then he said it had never come up. Didn't say, 'No, why would it,' which is what I would have said."

"But you're not a born liar."

We were having breakfast in a café on Mont-Royal that made great omelettes and better coffee than the Lorties had offered me.

"So you think the son's adopted?"

"Let me tell you what happened when I left. I knew Luc was at the back, unloading boxes, so I went around to talk to him. He's there with another guy, handing him cartons out of the back of a van. I can tell they're QAQ flyers because there's a sample taped to the outside of each box. He's got earbuds in and he's bobbing his head to something with a thrash kind of beat. I walk up to him and say, '*Allô.*' He looks at me like I just walked down the ramp of a spaceship. Taking me in but not computing. I stick out my hand and say, '*Bonjour.*' He ignores me and goes to get another box. I get in between him and his helper and say, '*Tu est Luc Lortie?*' He shrugs. Says something I don't quite get but his friend laughs. I say, '*Je suis Jonah Geller.*' He says, '*Pis?*'"

"Pec?" Ryan said.

"How he pronounced *puis*, which means 'and,' or in this context, 'What's your point?' I tell him I'm a private investigator and I want to ask him about Sammy Adler. He says, '*Qui?*' Like he's never heard the name. I say, '*Il était journaliste qui écrit un article sur ton père.*' He laughs, his friend laughs. I think *article* was the wrong word or I pronounced it wrong."

"Let me guess," Ryan said, "Your hackles started to rise."

"A little," I admitted. "I mean, I was trying. So I say, '*Est-ce que Monsieur Adler a parlé avec toi?*' He doesn't answer. Just smirks, steps around me and hands the box to his friend."

"And you wanted to lay them both out. Bing bang boom, Jonah Geller strikes again."

"Wanted to, but didn't. So he turns and pulls another box out of the van, and this time I step in close, almost pinning him up against the bumper. And I say to him, '*C'est quoi le problème? J'ai quelques questions très simples pour toi. Ça prendrait deux minutes.*' He tries to step around me and I move with him. I want to say to him, 'This will all go faster if you just answer,' but I can't put the words together. So I say it in English. I figure he has to understand a little at least. And he puts the box back and turns—I think he's going to take a shot at me."

"Tell me he did."

"Sorry. But get this. He strikes the exact same pose his father strikes in their poster. And he does a pitch-perfect impression of Dad's mid-Atlantic accent. Says to me, 'Sorry, old chap, I don't speak English as well as dear old Pà-*paw*.' I'm thunderstruck. He says, 'I never met Mr. Adler and I have nothing further to say.' And he picks up the box and chucks it at his friend."

"Weird."

"It was beyond weird, it was eerie. Except for the fact that Laurent is older and his voice is a little more gravelly, it was like listening to the same person."

"Except he's supposed to be slow on the uptake."

"Exactly."

"Still think he's adopted?"

"Maybe he is, maybe they both are, I don't know. It sounds like Sammy knew something, was asking around, but would it really make any waves? In today's world, if Laurent and his wife couldn't have kids, so what? Adopting is a positive thing, a contribution. Not something they'd have to hide."

"He's a politician," Ryan said. "They all have something to hide."

"But to kill over?"

"No, you're right. Adoption would probably get him on *Oprah*, or whatever the local version is. Have all the daytime ladies weeping in their recliners."

"Still must be hard for Luc," I said. "The sister gets the looks, the brains, the seat at Daddy's right hand, and he's in the back alley humping boxes."

My phone rang and I saw it was Bobby Ducharme.

"You owe me at least three cases of beer," he said. "Twenty-four each."

"For what?"

"First, I got you the unlisted home number of this adoption worker you mentioned. Marie-Josée Boily. And her address. What part of town you in now?"

"Mont-Royal just east of St-Hubert."

"Then you're not far. She's on Chambord, which is maybe six, seven blocks east of St-Hubert, and judging by the street number, right around Laurier, which is only a few blocks north. Less than a five-minute drive."

"Great." I jotted the address down on a napkin.

"The second case is for the address of the import-export company I told you about, Homs. It's on Boulevard de l'Acadie just north of the Metropolitan."

He gave me the address, which I scribbled on the back of the napkin.

"That's two," I said.

"I also reached out to someone I know at the RCMP. He might know a thing or two about your Syrians."

"What branch is he in?"

"Intelligence," he said. "I think maybe Counterterrorism."

It was just past eight-thirty and I thought Marie-Josée Boily might still be at home. As we drove toward her house, I used Ryan's cellphone to call her. I knew she wouldn't answer a call from mine, not with caller ID. Ryan's phone had a blocked number that divulged neither his name nor the Toronto area code.

"*Oui, allô?*"

"Good morning," I said. "This is Jonah Geller."

"*Maudit Christ,*" she said. "How did you get this number?"

"I'll tell you if you tell me why you're ducking me."

"I have no obligation to speak to you. In fact, my obligations are very much against it."

"You were okay with it yesterday."

"You put me in the spot and I didn't want to be rude."

"Standing me up wasn't rude?"

"I had no choice."

"Did anyone tell you not to talk to me?"

"You have no right to bother me like this. Now please excuse me," she said. "I must leave for work."

It was exactly what I was hoping she'd say, because we were just pulling up in front of her brownstone. We only had to wait three or four minutes before the second-floor door opened and a woman in a tan raincoat came down the wrought-iron stairs, holding onto the railing. I got out and said, "Good morning," while she still had her head down.

She jumped back, clutching her purse to her body, then recognized my voice and said, "Oh, for Christ's sake, it's you. Why don't you leave me alone?"

"It's not my nature."

"I will call the police if you keep on harassing me."

"This isn't harassment, trust me."

"Are you threatening me, then?"

"I'm asking you to keep your word. You said you would help. Just tell me what Sam Adler wanted."

"If I do . . ."

"What?"

"You will leave me alone?"

"I promise."

"And you won't tell anyone?"

"No," I said. "Including Laurent Lortie."

Her jaw fell. "But if—"

"If what? If I already know he's involved?"

"I didn't say that."

"You didn't have to."

"Now look," she said. "I never mentioned his name. Or any names. It would be against the law for me to do that. All I am going to tell you is this: Sam Adler asked for my help in a *retrouvaille*—a reunification. He wanted to connect a birth mother with a child who had been adopted and needed help to approach this person."

"What kind of help?"

"You can't just walk up to someone in this province and say, 'I know you are adopted, do you want to meet your first mother?' That is against the law. You have to go through an agency like ours, that has the experience to handle it without causing trauma to the adopted person."

"Sam knew the birth parents?"

"Apparently. I contacted the adopted person in question and as far as I was concerned, the matter was concluded. I did not hear from him again or from anyone connected with it. And that is all I have to say to you, now or at any other time. If you call me again, or wait outside my home like this, I will call the police, I promise."

When I got back in the car, Ryan said, "Get anything out of her?"

"A couple of things. One, I'm sure it was Laurent Lortie who pressured her into missing yesterday's meeting. Which leads to two: Sammy knew something about Lortie's family that Lortie didn't want made public."

"The question being what."

"Yes."

"What next?"

"You won't come."

"Cops?" he said.

"Mounties."

The Royal Canadian Mounted Police local headquarters was in Westmount, far enough west that Boulevard René-Lévesque reverted to its original name, Dorchester Boulevard. Ryan went for coffee around the corner on Ste-Catherine and said he'd wait for my call.

Bobby's contact was an officer named Aubrey Hamilton. Tall, slender, near but not past forty, with fine blond hair in a cut that made me think of a British civil servant. His office had a good-size window facing south; it was so brightly lit from the outside that he needed no lamps or overhead fixture.

"So," he said, "what's your interest in the Haddads?"

"It's more like they took an interest in me."

"Do tell."

I did. I told Hamilton about being followed by Mohammed al-Haddad from Les Tapis Kabul and our subsequent bloody encounter at Marché Jean-Talon. He listened without taking any notes of any kind, which led me to wonder whether we were being recorded.

When I was done, Hamilton grinned and said, "You knocked him out?"

"Cold. Along with someone named Faisal, same last name."

"One of his brothers."

"How many does he have?"

"There's four of them. Mohammed, Faisal, Omar and Sayeed. And knocking two out? That's not going to go unanswered."

"That's why I'm here."

"You want to know who you're up against."

"Always."

"Okay. Before I get to Mohammed, let me go back a generation or two." He stretched his back with his hands pressing in on his spine, then exhaled and sat back again, using the heel of his shoe to open a lower desk drawer so he could rest his foot on it. "Fucking back. I spend way too much time on my butt. Okay. You ever see *Lawrence of Arabia*?"

"Sure."

"Remember the tribal Arabs? The British would bribe them to blow up Ottoman train tracks. They were basically brigands and thieves. Hostage takers. Saboteurs. Badass warlord types who looted what they could and killed when they wanted to. Did very well for themselves as those things went."

"But?"

"They're Sunnis, not Alawites. Even though Sunnis make up three-quarters of the population in what's now Syria, the regime that took power in 1970 is Alawite. Within a year of that, the Haddads took their cue to seek greener pastures elsewhere."

"Why Montreal?"

"They needed an Arab community to exploit and Montreal's was growing. It was mostly Lebanese here at the time, because of the French, but Salah figured he could lean on them."

"Salah?"

"That's the grandfather. Tough bastard. When he passed, his oldest son, Tariq, took over. And Mohammed is the oldest of Tariq's four boys—he also has two daughters but they don't count when it comes to business—so Mohammed's being groomed for the corner office. He's actually not bad for third-generation. No softie, that's for sure. More the bull-in-a-china-shop type. Very built, likes to show it off."

"I still knocked him out."

"Good quote for your tombstone."

I couldn't help liking the guy. "So they're extortionists? That's it?"

He shrugged. "When Salah stepped off the boat here, drugs, prostitution, gambling—they were all spoken for by the Italians. He did better sticking to his own thing, among his own people. Same with Tariq and now Mohammed. He and his brothers work up and down L'Acadie Boulevard, Côte-Vertu, Grande Allée in Brossard, leaning on the small businesses. Shaking down new immigrants. We think he's also pulled a few kidnappings for ransom, usually an Arab businessman liquid with cash, someone he can scare with a hot iron."

"So why is he on my ass?"

Hamilton shrugged. "No idea."

"And what's your interest in him? If all he's doing is shaking down local businesses, the Montreal police would be handling it, not the RCMP."

"You an expert on jurisdiction? Let's just say we run our own gang investigations. Part of our mandate."

"Bobby told me you're Counterterrorism."

"He spoke loosely. I'm just an intelligence officer."

I thought of the crude flyer the Lorties had showed me and asked, "Ever heard of something called the Quebec Muslim Liberation Front?"

"Nope. Who are they?"

"Laurent Lortie—the head of Québec aux Québécois—received a threat from them."

Again, he made no note of it, not on paper. "What kind of threat?"

"Death to racists."

"Hmm. The platform he's putting out there, I'm surprised he hasn't had more. I'll check it out. We done now?"

"One more question. Has Mohammed al-Haddad ever been investigated for murder?"

Hamilton sat forward at his desk and put his elbows on the surface. "Not to my knowledge. Should he?"

"A journalist named Sammy Adler was killed a few weeks ago."

"Slammin' Sammy? The columnist? Hell, I loved his stuff. What would Mohammed want with him?"

"I was hoping you could tell me."

"The way things work here," Hamilton said, "is we gather intelligence. From dispensers just like you."

"I told you what I know."

"Not much that was new. Unless you have something that links Haddad to this murder."

"Sammy was writing a story about the owners of the carpet store. It was supposed to be a fairly sympathetic profile, showing not all Afghans in Montreal are like that lunatic who burned his daughters. If Haddad is linked to them somehow, maybe Sammy found out something he shouldn't have."

"It could also mean nothing. They could be bringing in goods together."

"What kind of goods?"

"Carpets," he said. "What else would someone want from Afghanistan?"

"Heroin," Ryan said. "You make it from poppies and Afghanistan is covered with them."

"Did Mehrdad strike you as a heroin smuggler?"

"He's already bringing in carpets from there. How hard can it be to throw in a few bricks of smack? And it's not like the door ain't open."

"Which door?"

"Look, I'm not in my old life anymore, you know that. But I stay informed. Have you followed what's been happening to the Rizzuto family?"

"Not really."

"They were running the smack trade here. Basically owned it. Only the last few years, almost every last one of them was shot to pieces or grabbed off the street, fate unknown. Nicolo, Nick Junior, Agostino Cuntrera, Paolo Renda. All gone. So if someone was looking to muscle in on that business, like I said, that door's been opened."

"Only one way to find out," I said. "Back to the carpet store."

Ryan checked his GPS, then headed west to the Décarie Expressway, which would take us north to Ville St-Laurent. The clouds were heavy again, promising more rain. I didn't like the big outdoor festival's chances of getting through Friday unscathed.

I'd had my phone turned off while I met with Aubrey Hamilton. I checked it to see if there were any messages: nothing from Jenn yet. Or anyone else. No one called to confess to Sammy's murder, finger the culprits or reveal a previously unknown dark side of his character.

We were on Sherbrooke Street, a bastion of English-speaking shoppers, most of them old enough to count their remaining sunsets, when blue lights flashed behind us. I looked in the side mirror and saw an unmarked car, the lights flashing in the grille. Ryan pulled over and turned off the engine.

"Look who it is," I said.

"Who?"

"René Chênevert. Paquette's partner."

"The asshole?"

"Yup. All the way here in Westmount, making traffic stops."

Chênevert took his time coming up to the driver's side, showing us his swagger. When he got there, Ryan took his time powering down the window.

"*Permis de conduire et les enregistrements du véhicule*," Chênevert said, holding out his hand.

Ryan answered him in the fastest, most guttural Italian I'd ever heard.

Chênevert said, "*Quoi?*"

Ryan said, "*Ma che dice 'sta paparella?*"

"*Votre permis. Vos papiers. Maintenant.*"

Ryan shrugged. "*Non parlo francese. Sugno un turista di Ontario, mangiacake.*"

Chênevert's complexion began to redden. He breathed out loudly through his nostrils—letting us know he was put upon—and said to me, "*Dites-lui de me donner son permis et les enregistrements.*"

"Sorry," I said. "I don't speak Italian."

He brushed back the vents of his sport jacket so we could see the pistol holstered butt first on his left hip. "*Tu penses que c'est une blague, là? Que je suis comédien?*"

Ryan looked at me, all innocence, and said, "*Boh?*"

"I think he said he's just joking with us." Then I leaned across to look at Chênevert and said, "Don't suppose you know how to say that in Italian?"

"I am not joking wit' you," he hissed. "Tell him to give me the fuckin' licence now or I'm gonna have your car towed to the farthest lot I can find."

I said to Ryan, "Ah. *Licencia di conduira.*" Having no clue if that was even close.

"*Patente di guida?*" Ryan said. "*E perchè non l'ha detto a prima vota, chista faccia di minchia?*"

He got out his wallet and handed Chênevert his licence—someone's licence, at any rate. Chênevert snatched it and stomped back to his car.

"What was the last thing you said?" I asked.

"Something along the lines of, 'Why didn't he ask for it in the first place, the prick?'"

"Good thing he didn't understand."

"Like I give a shit."

"What's going to happen when he runs that licence?" I asked.

"You underestimating me?"

"Never."

"The same thing's gonna happen that always happens. It's gonna come up clean and a perfect match for the registration."

"You are Al Spezza and Al Spezza is you."

"*Certamente.*"

Chênevert made us wait a good ten minutes while he ran the licence. When he returned, he came curbside to my window and tossed Ryan's papers in my lap. "You think you are funny guys," he said. "You want to make me look stupid."

The obvious line there was to say he needed no help in this regard. But I swallowed it. No point in making him so mad he'd do something we'd all regret.

"You're a long way from Homicide," I said.

"My work takes me everywhere."

"Your boss said I wasn't important enough to follow."

"My *partner* doesn't tell me what to do, okay?"

"*Qualcuno dovrebbe,*" Ryan said. Which meant, he later told me, "Somebody should."

"Your friend Bobby was right about him," Ryan said. "A *trou de cul.* An asshole. A *stronzo.*"

"But what's he up to? Why follow us around?"

"See what we know."

"Why? Can they be that hard up they need to latch onto us?"

"He could be in someone's pocket," Ryan said. "When I was in the game, we had a dozen like him on the payroll. Hamilton cops, Toronto cops, OPP officers. Didn't matter. They all get paid shit and most of them want to live beyond it."

"The question is, whose pocket? The Lorties?"

"The best possibility. It seems like the old man reached out to the adoption worker, told her not to talk to you. He could also have friends on the force."

"He could. What about the Syrians?"

He shrugged. "I have a harder time picturing them and the *stronzo* together."

"Me too."

"But they did both follow us."

We went through the Décarie Circle and headed north on Marcel-Laurin, past a modest mosque with a brown brick minaret. A knot of men stood outside talking, most wearing traditional dress: skullcaps, white trousers, long white blouses.

"How do you want to handle Mehrdad this time?" Ryan asked. "We gonna make nice or bust in and put a gun on him?"

"Let me ask nicely first."

"We know this Syrian is into some kind of shit with him. Heroin or not, he was on us the minute we left there."

"And again when we met Mehri."

"Maybe your friend Sammy saw something there he shouldn't have. Or heard something. Maybe some pillow talk with the sister."

"Could be. So he finds out something, asks the wrong question and Mohammed muscles him out of his apartment and kills him."

"But not right away. If all he wanted was to kill him, he could have put a bullet in him. A lot less sweat and risk than abducting, transporting and beating him to death."

"Maybe Mohammed was trying to find out if he'd told anyone else."

"That makes more sense. Then he either goes too far, or decides to finish it the way he started."

As we pulled up at the strip mall that housed Les Tapis Kabul, I said, "I'll go in the front. You come in the back."

"You want a gun?"

"No. You have enough for two."

"That I do," he said. "And unresolved marital issues eating my insides. People better listen to me good."

CHAPTER 14

Why aren't more people happy to see me? I'm a nice enough guy, my wit is sharp, my knowledge of world events adequate. My breath unburdened by halitosis.

Even so, Mehrdad Aziz's face turned sour when he saw me come into the store, like someone had mixed lemonade in his toothpaste. He was alone at the counter, not a customer to be seen.

"You have the nerve to come back here?" he said.

"We never finished our talk."

"We certainly did."

"Then let's start a new one," I said. I locked the front door and flipped the Open sign to the side that said Closed.

"You can't do that," he said.

"I just did."

He came around the counter, heading toward the door. I moved into his path and held out my palm. "Unless you want to wake up in a dental chair, I suggest we have a very quiet talk."

"I am calling the police."

"Make it the RCMP. They're already interested in Mohammed al-Haddad."

The mention of Mohammed's name didn't cause him to fall into paroxysms of fear, but it also didn't go over his head.

He called something over his shoulder, then he said to me, "You come here alone, you are one against three now. We'll see what kind of talk we have."

He was expecting his two associates to come out of the back, as they had yesterday. The door remained closed.

He called out again. No one came out of the stock area.

"Keep calling," I said, moving closer. Now he backed away from me and got behind the counter, looking behind him, seeing no one coming to his aid.

"You put your hands on me again," he said, "I will kill you."

"I'm tougher than Sammy Adler. Much harder to kill."

"I did not kill him."

"Why not? He was trying to sleep with your unmarried sister. She might have dishonoured your family."

His dark eyes sparked with anger. "She would do no such thing. Not ever."

"She was getting pretty damn close."

"Liar!"

I reached the counter. He turned and threw open the door and took three steps into the back room. I vaulted the counter and followed him through into an area filled with hundreds of rugs rolled up in pigeonholes, like those in the front showroom. His two helpers were lying on the floor on their stomachs, their hands behind their heads. Ryan had his foot on the big one's back, his Glock pointed at the man's neck. A suppressor was screwed onto the barrel.

"If you were expecting help from these fuck-ups, it ain't forthcoming," he said to Mehrdad.

Mehrdad turned back to me and said, "Only with guns are you tough."

I slapped his face hard, a quick left backhand that turned his head and left a bright red mark on his cheek. Then I dropped my hands to my side. "No guns on me. Take your best shot."

"Why? So your friend can shoot me in the back?"

"The only people I'm shooting in the back are these two," Ryan said. "If they're dumb enough to move."

Mehrdad untucked his shirt, rolled his shoulders, stepped forward and threw a right-handed punch that I could have blocked while reading a menu. Then I slapped him again, dropped my hands by my sides and waited for his next try. He faked a punch and tried to kick me in the groin. I swept his foot aside and he fell to the floor, almost landing on the beefier of his friends.

"I can do this all day, Mehrdad. Tell me what you and Mohammed are up to."

"We are rug sellers, that's all," he said, standing up slowly, head down, resting his palms on his knees. I knew from his body language he was going to rush me, go for a takedown. When he did, I sidestepped him easily. When he turned back, I hit him hard with an open hand on the right ear.

He cried out in pain, but I hadn't hit him hard enough to do any permanent damage, just set it ringing. While he was wondering which telephone to pick up, I dug my right hand into the base of his neck and squeezed. He yelped like a Yorkie.

"You and Mohammed," I said. "What're you doing?"

"Fuck you. Fuck your mother."

I squeezed harder.

"May your mother spend eternity in hell! Fucking the devil, you bastard."

I squeezed harder still and he sank to his knees. "I can do this all day."

"We don't have all day," Ryan said. "Why don't I shoot one of these idiots? See if that speeds things up."

"He'll do it," I told Mehrdad.

"You are bluffing."

"Me, maybe. Him, never."

Ryan knelt down with his knee in the big man's back and put the barrel of the suppressor at the base of his spine. "I can start by putting this one in a wheelchair." Then he drew the gun barrel down a few inches. "Or put a round up his ass and see if it comes out his mouth."

"It's heroin, isn't it?" I said.

"What?"

"Heroin," I said. "The pride of Afghanistan growers. Goes for fifty thousand a kilo. A lot more when you break it into ounces and grams."

"You are crazy. I have nothing to do with this."

"Why not? You're bringing in carpets already. How hard can it be to throw in a few bricks?" I winked at Ryan, acknowledging I was stealing his line.

"All right," Mehrdad said. "Don't hit me again. You are right. I bring heroin into the country and Mohammed knows how to distribute it."

The smaller of the two men on the ground said something and Ryan stepped over and kicked him in the ribs.

"Did Sammy find out?"

"Why do you always ask me about him? I tell you over and over, I had nothing to do with that."

"Maybe Mohammed did."

"He couldn't have!"

"Why not?"

"Because that night," Mehrdad said, "he was with me."

"Your sister said you were at home."

"She lied. To protect me. So I won't go to jail for drugs. But I was with Mohammed, right here. Getting heroin out from the rug shipments and transferring it to him."

"How much?" I asked.

He looked away from me, kept his eyes on the floor. "Fifty kilos. Okay? Enough to go to prison for a long time."

A very long time, I thought. So why was he admitting to it if it weren't true?

———

"Everything in his voice, his body, said he was lying," I said. "The shift in his eyes, the change of pitch."

"So he'd rather admit to trafficking in heroin than what?" Ryan asked.

"Killing Sammy."

"You still think it was him or the Syrians?"

"Him or. Him and. Some combination thereof."

We were parked a block away from Les Tapis Kabul, waiting to see if Mehrdad left and if so, in which car. That would give us something to follow, or at the least, a car on which to slap a transponder if the opportunity presented itself.

Nothing so far.

I had also left my small sphere cam in the back room of the store, tucked in a long cardboard tube inside a rolled-up rug. Its viewing range would be limited but the audio feed would pick up any conversation within those walls. If it was in Dari or Pashto, we'd be out of luck. But if Mehrdad called Mohammed al-Haddad, they'd have to speak a language they both knew, which I hoped would be English. If it was French, I could get Bobby Ducharme to translate.

We waited thirty minutes, ready to receive and record any conversations Mehrdad had. But he wasn't speaking to anyone, not yet. Maybe he was seething inside, plotting my demise. Or leaning forward in a chair, his head in his hands, wondering how his plans had degenerated so badly.

Cars drove up to the plaza. People got out and entered the travel agency, the bank, the halal market. One woman went into the carpet store and came out fifteen minutes later with a brochure. If Mehrdad came out of the laneway behind the store, we'd see him feed out onto Côte-Vertu.

Nothing.

"Too bad you couldn't tap his phone," Ryan said. "Or hack into his email."

"I'd need my guy Karl in Toronto for that," I said. "Or

Jenn, if it wasn't too heavily encrypted. She's a lot better at that than I am."

"You gonna call her, see if she spoke to the old man?"

"I don't want to push her," I said. "I'm just thankful she's involved at all. If I haven't heard anything by tonight, then maybe."

"So what now? I'm getting overheated here."

We had the windows halfway down but the engine was off and without air conditioning, it was stale and humid inside the car. I looked at my watch. Ten-thirty.

At ten-thirty-three, the sphere cam picked up Mehrdad's voice. He was speaking English, as I'd hoped.

"Let me speak to Mohammed," we heard him say. Then a pause of about thirty seconds. "It is me," he said. "Mehrdad. He was here. The one you saw at the market. Him and his gunman." *Pause.* "No, I didn't, not a word. I swear to you. No, he thinks it is something else." *Pause.* "Drugs is what he thinks. Heroin, the idiot." *Pause.* "I didn't say it, he did. He said it was easy to bring in drugs with our carpets and I didn't tell him differently." *Pause.* "I just told you, they had guns. Or one did. What was I supposed to do? Let him shoot me?" *Pause.* "Yes, he would have, believe me. He wanted to. You have to do something about them. Geller said the RCMP is interested in you. And maybe me." *Pause.* "Whatever you decide. Otherwise I cannot meet you tomorrow night. If he finds out the truth, we will have very big problems." *Pause.* "I don't know which hotel. I will try to find out."

Pause. Long pause. End of conversation.

We waited another fifteen minutes to see if Mehrdad made another phone call or left the store. He did neither.

"Let's drive by Mohammed's place," I said. "See what it looks like in daylight."

It was a two-storey building of white brick, part of a small industrial strip on L'Acadie Boulevard north of the elevated highway. We parked in the lot of a large market called Adonis, whose windows advertised a large selection of products from the Middle East, along with posters for upcoming concerts by performers from Lebanon.

Ryan took the Baby Eagle out of his ankle holster and said, "Do me a favour. Stick this in your pocket just in case."

"Does it have a safety?"

"On the slide, not the frame, which is the only thing I don't like about it. But it's a good piece otherwise."

"The safety on now?"

"Pull the trigger and tell me."

"Ryan . . ."

"Yeah, yeah. It's on."

I stuck the gun in the small of my back and pulled my shirttail over it. We got out and walked past the front of Les Importations Homs, the name of the company in gold lettering on the front door. No phone number to go with it. No web address. There was no point in walking in the front door. They knew our faces. Probably our names as well, and whether we liked our hotel bedspreads tucked in or not.

We kept walking past the building, past the next one and the one after that, all three built at the same time: same height, same white brick, same windows in dark brown frames. Same rusty discoloration where eavestroughs had leaked. At the far end of the third building, we turned down a driveway that led to a wide rear lane. We stayed close to the wall in case anyone was at an upper window.

We walked single file past the first building, which housed a clothing manufacturer. Its rear doors were open and two young men were rolling racks of raincoats directly from a loading dock into the back of a half-ton truck. The next building was closed up; nothing going in or out. I looked across the lane at the buildings backing onto the other side. There were fire escapes at their rears. As long as they didn't belong to businesses that sold guard dogs, we might be able to scale one for a better look.

"Hey," Ryan said.

"What?"

"There's his car." He pointed to a silver Lexus parked nose in at the rear door of the building. "Got your tracker with you?"

"Yes." I'd pocketed it, hoping to stick it on Mehrdad's car. But Mohammed's seemed just as good a bet.

I did a Groucho walk alongside the building, then crouched beside the rear door on the left side and stuck the transponder onto the chassis, away from the muffler. I turned to give Ryan the thumbs-up.

Saw him pulling his gun.

I peered through the windows of the car and saw the back door of Homs swinging open; saw Mohammed exiting with his broken nose taped down and behind him his brother Faisal, wearing a neck brace. If he got to the driver's side door, he'd stumble over me.

Ryan's gun spat a bullet that hit the bricks right above Mohammed's head. He jerked back in surprise, swivelling his head around to see where the shot had come from. A second bullet hit the glass of the open door and it shattered, crashing to the pavement in sheets and shards. Both men stumbled backwards into the building. A hand reached out and pulled the door shut. I yanked the Baby Eagle out of my waistband, thumbed off the safety and started backing up away from the car close to the wall, as low as I could get. I saw a hand come through the door where the glass had been, the hand gripping a gun. The muzzle flashed and the sound roared through the empty space around us; no suppressor on it. Ryan fired again. So did I, not trying to hit anyone, just letting them know we had more than one angle on them. The hand withdrew, giving me a chance to sprint for the alcove where Ryan stood.

I heard a door open in the building behind us, then heard it slam shut just as fast. I guess the sight of two men with guns convinced the person to stay out of whatever was going on.

"Time to go," Ryan said.

"Right behind you."

We backed out of the laneway, jogged around to the street and walked quickly up L'Acadie, watching the front of Homs to see if anyone came out that way. No one did. Two minutes later, we were in the car, driving south toward downtown. No one followed us this time. No cop pulled us over.

"When you fired," Ryan said, "you weren't trying to hit anyone, right?"

"No."

"In which case you did good. Now we can follow this douchebag wherever he goes."

"The beauty of it is we don't have to," I said. "We can keep our distance and the tracker will do it for us."

"And take us to the meeting with the rug seller tomorrow."

"Assuming that's still on."

"And that Mohammed takes his own car."

"True."

"So you really don't think it's heroin?"

"No."

"Any other ideas what it might be?"

"I might have one."

"You gonna share?"

"The intelligence officer I spoke to this morning told me something interesting about the Haddad family."

"What?"

"Why they had to leave Syria."

CHAPTER 15

We had a late lunch at a Chinese noodle joint on St-Laurent, just north of Ste-Catherine. I had a large soup with barbecued duck and greens; Ryan went for Singapore noodles. Funny dishes to order with the day growing hotter and more humid, but we both inhaled them like we hadn't eaten in days.

I guess browbeating people and threatening their lives is harder work than it seems.

In between slurps and lip-smacks, I told Ryan what I'd learned from Aubrey Hamilton about the Haddad family, how they'd left their home country to come to Montreal once the Alawite regime had taken hold. "After 1970, they didn't like their chances," I said.

"But Sunnis were still the majority, you said."

"I guess it didn't count for much."

"And you think the situation there now, this uprising or whatever—they're trying to get involved somehow?"

"I'm not sure what I think. Maybe I'm overthinking it, not believing what Mehrdad said about heroin."

"For the record, I didn't believe him either."

"No?"

"It's like, the second you mentioned it, he jumped at it like you'd thrown him a lifeline."

"So I come back to my original question. What else are y hiding? What brings an Afghan and a Syrian together?"

"If it ain't dope, gambling or girls," he said, "my money is ¸n guns. Big ones."

"Which might be why the RCMP is watching them."

"The Afghan could be bringing them in. That fucking country, there's definitely no shortage. I know a guy who served over there, he said guns went missing from the Canadian army bases by the dozens. And not side arms neither. Assault rifles, I'm talking."

"Mehrdad could be importing them with his rugs and selling them to Mohammed, who turns them around and sends them home."

"Wouldn't it be easier to send them direct from Afghanistan to Syria? My geography isn't shit hot, but they're kind of in the same part of the world, no?"

"You'd have to go through Iran," I said. "Which doesn't necessarily support a regime change. And then Iraq, where the Americans would probably intercept them. It might actually be easier for one established company in good old Canada to bring them in and for another to ship them out."

"I don't think they were at the store," Ryan said. "Gun oil has a particular smell."

"Sharing a hotel room with you made that clear."

"So this other warehouse Mehrdad talked about—where is it again?"

"Brossard."

"Which is where?"

"The South Shore. Over the Champlain Bridge."

We were walking back to the car when Holly Napier called. "I was wondering . . . ," she said.

"Yes?"

"If you wanted to meet tomorrow night."

I thought about the meeting that Mehrdad and Mohammed might be keeping, that Ryan and I would be watching. Listening to. Maybe breaking in on.

"I might be working pretty late," I said.

"So will I. I'm covering the concert at Parc Maisonneuve and I'll be there at least until eleven."

It sounded good, assuming I was still in one piece at night's end.

"Did you have somewhere in mind?" I asked.

"My place."

"Where's that?"

"You know Westmount at all?"

"I was at RCMP headquarters today."

"That's what we'd call lower Westmount. Where I am is lowest Westmount, just above the expressway."

"What street?"

"Stayner."

I said, "Shit."

"What?"

Stayner was a name I'd grown to hate in Boston: a world-class surgeon who turned out to be a no-class citizen.

"Nothing. Just a negative association."

"Tell me about it when I see you. Maybe I can turn it positive. Say midnight if it's not too late? Unless you want to find me at the concert."

"Among a hundred thousand people?"

"I'll be near the stage," she said. "There's a holding pen there for journalists. I can put your name on the accredited list."

"That would be great."

"The Fête always is."

More than ever, I wished Jenn were with us. She'd have teased me the minute I hung up, noodged me, provoked me about making a date in the middle of a case. "*Someone's* getting some tonight," she'd have cooed with a crooked grin. She'd have rhymed *Jonah* with *boner* or something equally juvenile because that's what brothers and sisters do, and she is and always will be the sister I never had.

Ryan just looked at me when I got off the phone and said, "What now? Back to the hotel?"

"Let's try Sammy's again," I said. "Ask if anyone saw a silver Lexus that night."

It took us most of the late afternoon and evening to determine that none of Sammy's neighbours whose windows faced onto the laneway at the rear had seen a Lexus the night he was killed, silver or otherwise. Most hadn't seen anything at all; they'd been sleeping at that ungodly hour. His upstairs neighbours had been out of town that night and had nothing to add.

Only one confessed to having been awake, an actor named Eric Thorn who'd been performing that night in Centaur Theatre's revival of *The Threepenny Opera*. He lived in a top-floor flat two buildings over.

"The cast all went out for drinks after the show," he said. "I got home around two, but I was too wired to sleep, so I was going over the opening number. I play the street singer, the one who sings 'Mack the Knife,' and I was still trying to find the right edge. A little before three, I heard knocking out front, and I went to the window. Saw a police car at the curb, a couple of cops at Sammy Adler's door."

"Did you know him?" I asked.

"Sure. He liked theatre, I liked his columns. We'd shoot the shit sometimes coming and going. Two Anglos, talking about how both our audiences were getting older and smaller. So many young people leave Montreal. At least the ones that come to English theatre."

"What else did you see that night?"

"Well, I was a little worried at first, wondering what brought the police to Sammy's door. But they left—I don't know, about ten minutes after they got there and everything got quiet again, so I figured he was okay. But then . . ."

"What?"

"I thought I heard knocking again, maybe five minutes later. Not as loud, though. I went back to the window but there was nothing there. The street was dead quiet. No cop cars or anyone else."

"Don't suppose you looked out the back," Ryan said.

"As a matter of fact, I did. I grow tomatoes and basil on the deck out there and the raccoons and squirrels get into it. Even people's cats. I thought maybe the sound I'd heard was coming from there so I opened the back door and checked. But there were no animals. None I could see."

"No one at Sammy's back door?" I asked.

"I can't see it from my balcony. I mean, not unless I stood at the rail and leaned all the way over. Which I didn't."

"Did you see a car in the laneway? A silver Lexus maybe?"

"No," Eric said. "There was a van parked there, but no cars."

"What kind of van?"

"I don't know what make. Kind of old looking. Light grey or white."

"Anything written on it? A company name?"

"Not that I remember."

"Homs? H-o-m-s?"

"No," he said. "I'm pretty sure it was blank."

"All right," I said. "Thanks for your help."

"No problem," he said. "And if you're around on the weekend, come see the show. You'd bring the average age down by ten years."

"So Mohammed might have more than one vehicle," Ryan said. "Makes perfect sense. A van for his business, with or without the name on it."

"It definitely fits with the theory we have. The phony call to the police, the knock at the back door. Sammy lets his guard down, opens up and bam—he's gone."

We walked around to the laneway and opened the gate that led into a small yard the width of Sammy's kitchen. Shaded by a large maple, there was no grass growing. The surface was flagstone, leading up to a small balcony with weathered paint, just big enough for a barbecue and two lawn chairs. I tried to picture everything that had happened that night: Mohammed al-Haddad, or men working for him, bundling Sammy into a waiting van, taking him to a dark, deserted place where they could beat him at their leisure.

The Homs office? Mehrdad's storeroom? The warehouse in Brossard?

Looking at the back door, I could see small alarm contacts. *But they got you to disarm it, didn't they?*

We walked back into the laneway. The base of the fence was piled with trash: beverage cups, food wrappers, sheets of newspapers blown out of recycling bins, torn envelopes whose contents had been removed, a flyer for a singer called Coeur de Pirate, another for window and eavestrough cleaners, and one with a crude caricature of two figures I recognized: Laurent and Lucienne Lortie, stepping on the bleeding head of a Muslim woman in a headscarf.

There were a dozen good reasons why it could have been in that laneway.

And only one bad one.

CHAPTER 16

At eight o'clock the next morning, we parked at a meter outside the headquarters of Québec aux Québécois. We paid for an hour of parking and walked to the next intersection, turned north and doubled back through the lane behind Avenue du Mont-Royal. The smell of garbage was ripe in the muggy air, especially behind the restaurants. Almost like a body would smell.

Halfway down the lane, I saw the white van Luc had been unloading the day before.

We walked around the front of the van. I made a mental note of the licence plate and the make and model—a GMC Safari, boxy-looking, old enough to pre-date the redesign that made newer models more rounded.

"Got another transponder?" Ryan asked.

"No. They didn't have a two-for-one special."

I went to have a look through the back windows. There were two panes, one on each of the rear doors.

"Keep walking," Ryan said. "Company's coming."

The back door of the QAQ office had just opened and Luc
Lortie was coming out, followed by another man his age, also
dressed in a T-shirt and jeans. The one who'd been helping him
unload the cartons the day before.

I kept walking.

Ryan caught up with me and as soon as we were around
the corner, we sprinted to the car. I was barely in my seat when
he started his U-turn, ready to pick up the van when it exited
the lane onto St-Hubert.

When you have a hemi-powered Charger, who needs a
second transponder?

"We okay for gas?" I asked.

"Yeah, why?"

We were going north on Christophe-Colombe, a few car
lengths behind the van, the elevated Metropolitan in sight up
ahead. "In case he gets on the highway."

"Let him," Ryan said.

The van did get onto the highway and took it westbound
as far as the 15 North, onto which it turned. This was the highway that led to the Laurentian Mountains, some forty miles
away. It was easy to hang back and keep the van in sight; it didn't
seem able to muster any great speed. We knew we could catch
up in a hurry if it exited anytime soon. We drove over a bridge
that took us from the island of Montreal into Laval, past low-
rise industrial parks that had pushed all semblance of flora away
from the road. Traffic was light at first but filled in as we continued north, many of the cars pulling boats on trailers or carrying canoes on their rooftops. I guess not everyone was
planning to attend the Fête Nationale celebrations in the city.

Whatever saints we hadn't passed in the city were grouped
along the highway as we continued north: Ste-Thérèse,
St-Jérome, St-Janvier, Ste-Anne-des-Lacs. Ahead of us were ski
hills, bare runs carved through abundant pines on which low grey

clouds seemed trapped. We were approaching St-Sauveur when the van moved into the exit lane without signalling. We followed it up the ramp and onto an eastbound road that curved sharply down toward a secondary highway, the 117, which had once been the only road between Montreal and the Laurentians. There weren't enough cars to provide much cover so Ryan had to stay well back. We went past the kind of businesses that cater to cottage country: fireplace installers, swimming pool sales, rentals of skis and snowmobiles for winter and Jet Skis for summer.

"He's turning off," I said.

"I see."

The van took an eastbound road that started out paved. After about half a mile, it changed to gravel. In drier weather, the van would have kicked up dust that would have made it easier to follow at a distance. But there had been too much rain for that this week. There was thick forest on either side—maples, poplars, birch and conifers vying for light and space—with narrow lanes leading to cabins and cottages hidden by foliage. Some lanes were open, some fenced off with signs saying, "*Privé*." Private. "*Défense de passer*." No trespassing.

At least said they didn't say trespassers would be shot.

The road was hardly straight, so there were long moments when the van was out of sight. After one series of winding curves through thick forest we came to a long straightaway where we could see hundreds of yards ahead. No white van. No vehicles of any kind or colour.

"We lost him," I said. "Shit."

"Not so fast," Ryan said. "There were only a few places he could have turned off."

"And if we follow him down any of them, we'll be easy to spot."

"Not if we go in on foot."

"Find a place to turn around. Maybe one of these lanes will have fresh tracks."

We had to drive another hundred yards before we found a wide spot where Ryan could pull a three-point turn. Then we crept slowly back west. The first place Luc could have turned off, now on our left, was gated and padlocked. No way they could have stopped, unlocked it, driven in and closed up again in the brief time they were out of sight.

The next place, on the right, had no gate. Ryan stopped and I hopped out to take a look. There was a patch of mud that stretched from the edge of road at least a dozen strides in. No tire tracks. I got back in the car.

"You were right," I said. "There's only a few more places they could have gone in."

"If we follow," he said, "you're not going in empty-handed."

"I know, I know."

"You can have the Baby Eagle again, or my spare Beretta."

"Which matches my outfit?"

"If I had something pink—fuck!"

I looked ahead and saw the white van roaring up the road toward us, straddling the yellow line. Ryan wrenched the wheel to the right and the car kicked up a spray of gravel as it went off the road and into a shallow ditch between the roadbed and the trees. The side of my head smacked the window and Ryan almost fell out of his seat, held in place only by his belt. The van ground into the side of the car, metal scraping on metal, pushing us further off the road. I saw Luc Lortie at the wheel, his thick arms straight and stiff as he held the steering wheel at an angle, yelling something as they went past us, his words lost in the grinding roar.

I heard the squeal of brakes as the van came to a stop, and I twisted around to look out the rear window. Luc and the passenger were getting out. Luc had a tire iron in his hand. The passenger was dangling a crowbar.

The way we were tipped, I was trapped in my seat between the window and Ryan's weight on my left arm. "They're coming," I said.

"Can you open your door?"

I tried the handle. It wouldn't budge.

He reached over and undid his belt and slid even closer to me. He said, "Hang on," and unlatched his door, turned his back to me and pushed with his feet. The door swung open and closed so quickly under its own weight that he had to pull his legs back before they got slammed. He tried it again with the same result. Then Luc's face and shoulders filled the frame as he swung the tire iron, shattering the glass into fragments that fell in on us like a sudden burst of hail. His partner couldn't get around to my side; he swung his crowbar and the back window broke. Luc shifted his iron in his hands and tried to gouge Ryan with the narrow end. He blocked it with his leg and howled as it dug into the flesh along his shin.

He leaned back against me and clawed his Glock out of the holster and fired out the open window. The gunfire roared through the interior of the car but Luc saw it coming and leaned away. And laughed. I felt a burn on my arm where the hot shell casing landed. I shook it off and turned to see the passenger running full speed back toward the van. Luc just backed away, almost taunting Ryan, like a fighter calling out an opponent, wanting him to come to the centre of the ring and fight.

Ryan grabbed the steering wheel to get some purchase, trying to lift his head and shoulders out. I saw blood seeping out of his torn pant leg.

The van engine revved; the passenger was now the driver. I heard him call something out in French; Luc just smirked.

"Hold this," Ryan said, handing me the warm pistol. He got both hands on the wheel and pulled again. When he was clear of the broken window, he held out his hand and I returned the gun. I saw Luc hop in the passenger side of the van as its engine whined. Ryan's finger slipped into the trigger guard and was about to fire when the driver slammed the van into reverse and tore along the side of the Charger again. Ryan had to fall back in to avoid getting his head and arm crushed. There was another screech of metal as the van lurched forward. By the time Ryan got back into shooting position, it was heading east, kicking up gravel as it sped away.

Ryan fired anyway. His first shot hit nothing. Same for the second one. He didn't fire a third. The van was out of range and Ryan wasn't one to waste bullets.

I've heard creative strings of profanity out of Ryan's mouth before but nothing to compare to what he spewed when he finally got out of the car and examined its ruined side. No body part, male or female, was spared. No sexual act left out. Luc's mother—birth and/or adopted—was targeted, as was his sister—all sisters—and several orders of nuns. It was like watching *The Aristocrats* on fast forward.

Then he lifted his pant leg to examine the bloody cut. "We catch up to him," he said, "he's gonna pray to every saint we passed on this road, and every one we saw in Montreal, that he has a fucking heart attack before I'm through killing him."

We couldn't get the car out of the ditch without a tow truck. And we couldn't get cellphone reception on that stretch of country road. We were going to have to go on foot, maybe all the way back to the 117.

"Can you walk?" I asked him.

"Yes, I can fucking walk. It's just a scratch."

"Looks deeper than a scratch."

"Anger is a terrific healer. A hell of a lot better than faith."

So we walked west, keeping an eye out for any vehicles that might give us a ride. When we got to the next laneway, I checked it for tire tracks, and saw fresh ones deep in the mud, with bits of gravel on top of the impressions.

In we walked, past strawberry plants heavy with red berries, our shoes sinking into muddy ruts. Bugs swarmed around us in the humid air. Ryan pulled his Glock and kept it by his side.

"You think there's more men here?" I whispered.

"I'm a city boy," he said. "I don't know what the fuck there is. Could be guard dogs. Could be bears, for all I know."

Maybe Ryan was the smart one. If a bear came crashing out of the growth, he'd have a gun. I'd have karate and Krav Maga and a trove of Jewish lore.

The narrow lane curved down a hill and to the left and then widened into a clearing. There was a small A-frame cabin ahead, built of thick, dark timber with stripes of white mortar in between. It looked at least a century old, with sagging shutters beside the windows and a porch bowed in the centre. Behind it the clearing widened to reveal a sloping lawn that swept down to a weathered dock and boathouse. The roadside foliage had been so thick there'd been no hint of a lake down below, no glitter of blue between the pine and spruce. Amazing what you find when you walk down the right road.

The cabin had no alarm system we could see. Ryan used the butt end of his gun to break one of the old sash windows and we climbed inside. It was all one big room, with a kitchen on the right, a living room on the left and straight ahead a ladder leading up to a sleeping loft. Columns of dust swarmed in the light as we moved through. There was a tang of body odour in the air and a musty smell from a stained sofa that faced a stone fireplace across a scratched wood coffee table. Two ashtrays on the table were filled with cigarette butts—two different brands—and a few roaches burned down to their handmade cardboard filters.

A bookshelf against the wall behind the loft ladder was filled with books on politics and philosophy, all of them worn and well-read. There were French translations of *Das Kapital* and other Marxist writings. A rare copy of *The Anarchist's Cookbook*. Novels by Albert Camus, the plays of Jean Genet, essays by Sartre and Arthur Koestler. Biographies of the former Quebec premier René Lévesque and Paul Rose, one of the leaders of the Front de Libération du Québec cell that kidnapped and murdered a cabinet minister during the 1970 October Crisis. A copy of *Nègres blancs d'Amérique*— White Niggers of America—in which Pierre Vallières famously compared the lot of the Québécois working class to that of African-Americans during segregation and called for armed revolution. I pulled it out of the shelf and fanned through its pages, many of which had passages underlined and notes scrawled in the margins. So did many of the other texts, including the Rose biography, *The Anarchist's Cookbook* and a biography of Anders Breivik, the Norwegian mass murderer who claimed to have acted to protect his country against Muslim influence.

Up in the sleeping loft, there was a thin futon with twisted sheets, and a milk crate that served as a bedside table. On it was another ashtray, an English copy of Geert Wilders's book *Marked for Death*, and a sheet of paper in which a rectangle had been drawn in pencil. In the lower left corner, a semicircle had been traced from the bottom line up to the middle of the left side. There were a few other markings—arrows and Xs along the top and left sides of the rectangle and what looked like sunbeams extending from a circle in the top of the middle of the frame.

I climbed down and showed it to Ryan: "What do you make of that?"

He studied it a moment and said, "A baseball field? The half circle is the infield and the rest . . ."

"The rest is the wrong shape," I said. "A rectangle instead of a diamond."

"We're dealing with a dickhead. Maybe he's too dumb to know the right shape. He was dumb enough to fuck with my car."

"That's what worries me."

"Why?"

"We keep hearing he's dumb. But if this is his place, and these books are all his, then Luc Lortie isn't a dumb guy trying to act smart. He's a smart guy trying to act dumb. Which goes against human nature."

We looked through the kitchen, found nothing. There was no desk or any other place where he might have left some sort of writing behind, something to give us a clearer idea of who he was, what he thought, what he might be doing.

"This can't be his only place," I said. "It's too far to go back and forth every day."

"The guy looks poor as a leper. You think he has this and a place in the city?"

"I don't know what to think. But his father or sister would know."

"Except we can't call," Ryan said. "Not in these fucking woods. You want to start walking back? See if the reception improves?"

"Let's check the boathouse first," I said.

I haven't spent enough time lakeside to know what should or shouldn't be in a boathouse. The only boat of any kind was an old canoe overturned on two sawhorses off to one side. There were some paddles, their flat ends darkened by water and scored from pushing against rocks. A few life vests on hooks. Some tools and a shelf of screws, anchors and other fasteners. A caulking gun. Some gardening tools and bags of topsoil, also pushed to the right. Otherwise, it was empty, except for a pile of white plastic bags. I turned one over and read the label and felt my arms go stiff with tension.

Each empty bag had held five kilos of ammonium nitrate and there were at least twenty of them left behind.

"Look here," Ryan said. He was pointing to a series of circular marks on the floor of the boathouse, each with a radius of a foot and a half or so. I'd seen circles like that before, at the home of a friend who'd invited me for a barbecue; more specifically, in the garden shed where he kept his spare tank of propane.

CHAPTER 17

I t took us about thirty minutes to walk up the leaf-shrouded lane and back along the side road to a point where we had cell-phone reception. Of course that didn't help much because we didn't know who to call for a tow in the middle of nowhere. So we kept walking, Ryan favouring his left leg but giving nothing away in his expression or speed. I'd have been complaining but that's my nature, not his. So I just brooded about Luc Lortie, what we had and had not seen, wondering what he was involved in. He could simply have been a screwed-up young man who didn't know how to please his father, who wasn't presentable in the way politicians like their kids to be, the way his sister so obviously was. He could have issues only a bevy of shrinks would be able to resolve, or he might be up to something seriously deranged. He could be someone who loved baseball but couldn't draw a proper field.

But he had also bought a hundred kilos of a compound that could be used to make a fertilizer bomb. Timothy McVeigh had used ammonium nitrate to blow up the Alfred P. Murrah building in Oklahoma City. Sales were supposed to be restricted, the key word being "supposed."

It was close to noon by the time we came to the 117, where the owner of a Jet Ski dealership gave us the number of a local tow truck driver and let us use his phone. I could barely under-stand the driver's French, but the dealer took the phone from me and explained exactly where we were.

"Gonna be at least half an hour before he gets here," the dealer said. "What kind of car you have?"

"A Charger," Ryan said. "Less than a week old."

"Sorry to hear that. But there's no Dodge dealership around here," the man said. "You gonna have to go to St-Jérôme, probably. How bad is the damage?"

"No idea. It might just be cosmetic, but the way we went into the ditch, we might have busted a wheel. Or worse."

"Too bad. It's a nice car, the Charger. Me, I'd like to have one from the old days, eh? Lots of muscle on that one."

"This one too."

The dealer let Ryan use his washroom. He spent a good ten minutes in there, washing the wound on his leg.

"You going to need stitches?" I asked when he got out.

"I don't think so."

"The bleeding stopped?"

"Until we find Luc."

Forty minutes passed before a tow truck pulled into the dealership lot and honked twice. We thanked the man for his help and squeezed into the front seat of the truck. The driver was around fifty, with a huge gut that strained against his seat belt, his left arm tanned a dozen shades darker than his right. We directed him to the spot where the Charger sat on a thirty-degree angle and stood out of his way while he got it hooked up and slowly eased it back onto the road. I asked in my best French if he knew where there was a Dodge-Chrysler dealership in St-Jérôme. He said yes—*Ouai*—and we got back in and drove south on the 117 with French rock blaring through tinny speak-ers in the truck. The dealership we were looking for was right on the 117. The driver took us around back to the service entrance and lowered the battered car. Ryan paid him in cash, then unlocked the trunk, in which we had secured our matching Halliburton cases and my laptop. When he went inside to speak to the service manager, I checked my cell for messages.

An hour earlier, while we'd been trudging along the fly-infested country road, Jenn Raudsepp had called.

"Where the hell are you?" she said when I got her on her cell. "I tried your hotel, your cell, Ryan's cell."

"We were on the road and had car trouble," I said. "Wound up in a reception-free zone." I didn't go into details about what happened. Didn't want her to know there had been any kind of trouble. Or that there was likely to be a whole lot more.

"So where are you now?"

"Outside Montreal. A place called St-Jérôme. Did you speak to Arthur Moscoe?"

"Oh, yeah."

"What does that mean?"

"Two things," she said. "One, it wasn't easy. The reason he wasn't returning your calls, he had a minor heart attack."

"When?"

"Couple nights ago."

"He okay?"

"For his age and condition, yeah, he's doing all right. They've moved him out of the coronary care ICU and into a regular room."

"What's the other thing?"

"He had quite the story to tell," she said.

"You going to dish or leave me hanging?"

"When will you be at your hotel?"

"Why?"

"I'd rather tell you when you're back there."

"I have time now."

"I don't."

"Come on, Jenn."

"Sorry. There's something I have to do right now. When will you be back?"

"About an hour. Actually two. I think we're going to have to leave Ryan's car here and get a rental. Then we have a stop to make on the way."

"You boys okay?"

"We're fine."

"Then I'll talk to you soon."

"Jenn?"

"What?"

"When you say quite a story . . ."

"You'll stay awake until the end."

The mechanic who examined the Charger told Ryan he had a broken tie rod. "You drive with that," he'd said, "your front wheel gonna come off."

So we left it there for repair and headed back to the city in a loaner they provided, a three-year-old black Jeep 4x4. "Perfect for running someone over," Ryan said.

I knew who he had in mind.

It took us less than an hour to get back to Montreal. I spent most of it on my tablet, looking up ammonium nitrate. It was first and foremost a fertilizer, used to combat the loss of nitrogen in soil, especially in the fall. In somewhat larger amounts, it could be used to blast away tree stumps or create ponds. The amount Luc had stashed in his boathouse could create a pond the size of Lake Superior. All he needed was the right mix of fuel, like propane, and a detonator. The pressure waves emanating from the explosion would travel at the speed of sound, with enough force to decimate nearby structures and blow human beings to pieces the size of stewing beef.

I called Reynald Paquette and got his voice mail. "This is Jonah Geller," I said. "I've just been to a property in the Laurentians which I think is owned or rented by Luc Lortie.

I found evidence that he might be building a bomb—a big one. You need to get up there with a search warrant and check it out. It's on Chemin Gosselin, about two miles east of the 117, off Autoroute 15, exit 60. I can tell you precisely where when we talk. Which needs to be soon."

When we got to the QAQ office on Mont-Royal, Ryan left the Jeep in a bus zone and we marched in like we owned the place. I saw Gabriel Archambault leaning over the shoulder of an elderly volunteer—and a quick glance showed they were mostly older and conservatively dressed—and interrupted his conversation.

"I need to speak to Monsieur Lortie," I said. "Now."

"Excuse me," he said, "but we are in the middle of something."

"Nothing compared to what I'm in. Get him out here."

His lips pursed and went missing. "He is not here now, and even if he were—"

"What about Lucienne?"

"She is not here either. They're both out doing media interviews and cannot be interrupted."

"You'd better find them," I said. "And interrupt them."

"I will not."

Ryan stepped forward but I put out a hand to stop him. "Tell them Luc's had an accident."

"What! Is he okay?"

"Just get one of them on the phone and tell them to call me. You already have my number."

"I can't promise anything," Gabriel said. "Their phones might be turned off."

"They'll check in at some point."

I turned to leave. Gabriel said, "Wait! What kind of accident?"

Ryan pushed past me and got up in Gabriel's face, close enough to give him beard burn. "My kind," he said.

———

At the hotel, we parked underground and took all our gear upstairs. I had to find one of the Lorties and get a line on where Luc might be and what he was planning. There was no professional baseball team anymore, so if the drawing we'd found was indeed a ballpark, it wasn't Olympic Stadium. If he was building a bomb, what other target might he have in mind?

We took the elevator up to our floor. Ryan's limp seemed to be worse, his gashed leg stiffening up on him. I didn't mention it and neither did he.

Outside our room, I got out my key card and slid it into the lock. It disengaged and I opened the door, held it open for Ryan.

"Why don't you get out of those pants," I said. "Let me have a look."

"Jesus Christ," a woman said. "I knew it. I knew you two were lovers."

I almost dropped my metal case when I looked up and saw Jenn sitting at the edge of my bed.

I said, "What the hell?"

"No, no," she said. "Don't let me interrupt. Why exactly is Ryan dropping his pants and what were you hoping to see?"

I turned to Ryan, who looked every bit as stunned as I felt.

"And you," she said to him, with that evil grin I'd missed so much. "Always trying to get me to switch teams. Look who switched first."

I said, "How did you—"

"What?"

"Get here so fast?"

"There was a seat sale and I jumped on it first thing this morning. I was already here when we spoke."

"I thought you were with Arthur Moscoe this morning."

"No, you assumed. I actually saw him last night. Well, yesterday afternoon and last night. His story took a while to tell and he didn't have the strength to tell it in one sitting."

I walked over to the bed and held out my arms and she stood and hugged me for the first time in ages. It felt so good to hold her, to feel strength in her arms. I'd been so worried about her for so many weeks, had been picturing her wasted, worn down by what had happened to her. And here she was in blue jeans and an oversized man's blue Oxford shirt, hiding her figure a little—something she needed to do these days—but still looking fit and tanned like she'd just hitched a ride from the family farm.

She let go of me and held her arms out to Ryan and gave him a briefer hug. Patted his shoulder. "Hey, you," she said.

"Hey."

"You both look like slack-jawed idiots," she said.

"I just can't believe you're here," I said.

"The truth is, I needed to get out. Finally. And I didn't know it until you called. I've been so trapped inside myself since Boston—treating myself like a Fabergé egg, Sierra treating me like one. Feeling like if I left the house, left our little neighbourhood, something horrible would descend and carry me off. Like I was on pterodactyl watch. Then I spoke to you and realized how much I've missed you, missed working. You know me, I've never been one to sit around feeling sorry for myself. And that's all I've done for so fucking long."

"But why come here? I mean, I'm thrilled to see you but we could have done this over the phone."

"I know. But I figured, once I was stepping out, I might as well go all the way. And once I heard Arthur's story, and saw how much he loved his grandson and how heartbroken he was over his murder, I just decided I'd get on the plane. See if you needed me."

"I always need you," I said.

"Cue the sappy music," Ryan said.

"You're as big a sap as Jonah," she said.

"Like fuck. Now if you'll excuse me, I'm going to go drop my pants in the bathroom and look at my own fucking leg."

When the door slammed shut behind him, she grinned and said, "Someone hasn't changed a bit."

"His marriage is over," I said.

"I know."

"He says he's okay with it but he's not."

"He shot anyone yet?"

"Not for lack of interest."

"And his leg?"

"Nothing serious."

"He hurt it in the car?"

"You could say that."

"Jonah . . . was there mayhem?"

"A little."

"Because there is one thing I promised Sierra when I left. And promised myself too, if I'm honest. I'm here to help out. Support you however I can. But I'm not ready for anything crazy, okay?"

"I know."

"I'm not sure you do. I talk a good game, but when I said I was ready for action, I meant helping out on the computer. Making phone calls. Research. Maybe batting an eyelash or two. That's about it."

"I get it."

"Things get crazy, I'm staying on the sidelines."

"Of course."

"So what happened in the car? The truth, please."

I told her. I told her everything that had happened from the time we'd arrived.

"So you think one of these two stories led to his murder," she said. "This family of politicians or maybe some kind of arms deal."

"Yes."

"Obviously, I don't know anything about the Afghans and Syrians," she said. "But I can shed a little light on the Lortie side of it."

"Go ahead."

"As soon as Ryan's done. It's too long to tell it twice."

When he got out of the bathroom, he lay on his bed, Jenn sat on mine, and I took one of the chairs by the window. We were all hungry by then, so we called room service and ordered hamburgers and fries all around, then settled in to hear her story. I was so eager to hear it, I didn't ask Jenn how she knew Ryan's marriage was over.

CHAPTER 18

Artie Moscoe was nineteen years old in the summer of 1950. Still living in his parents' cold-water flat on De Bullion Street, the rent forty-two dollars a month, and still there were months when the family couldn't pay. Cold months, winter months, when bailiffs piled their furniture in the snow at the curb and Artie had to check all the different clubs above shops on St. Lawrence where his father might be playing pinochle, to pry out that extra ten or twenty dollars his mother needed to pay the landlord. He was still sharing a room with his two brothers, Abie and Bernie. And despite being engaged to be married, still a virgin.

He was working two jobs then. Five days a week he was a shipper at the Dominion Dress Company, owned by his mother's first cousin, Irving Schiff. Dominion was a going concern then, selling its wares to the big department stores: Eaton's, Simpson's, Morgan's and Ogilvy's. Like most of the garment companies on St. Urbain, the Main and surrounding streets—in their case, in the new Peck Building—it had a number of different divisions: Miss Montreal for higher-end fashions; Stay-in-Style for everyday wear; Working Woman for business suits; and Parapluie for raincoats and other outerwear.

Mr. Schiff had promised to move Artie into sales once he had learned the back-room ropes, knew every model number in every line, how they were made, from what fabric, with what pattern. That summer, he was still in shipping, laying dresses in cartons, sealing them with tape, making sure the orders matched their packing slips. He worked eight to six five days a week and on Saturdays from eight to noon, when the factory opened its back doors and sold seconds for cash to customers who couldn't afford to buy the items in the stores. His mother gave him grief for working on Shabbos, but always relented when he put eight extra dollars in the kitty. On Sundays, he worked noon to nine at Hammerman's soda fountain on Park Avenue, corner Villeneuve, scooping ice cream into cones and mixing various flavours of syrup with seltzer water, mostly for rich kids who drifted over from Outremont, along with the neighbourhood kids who'd saved their pennies all week.

His older brother, Abie, had been accepted to McGill University in medicine, despite the quotas that had been established to keep Jewish students to a minimum. Bernie was still in high school at Baron Byng. What was going to be with him? He was a *vilder*, a wild one, smoking and drinking and skipping school to play pool on Rachel with an older crowd. It was up to Artie to help keep the family afloat, and his resentment sometimes burned in his gut like a cloud of gas on fire.

His fiancée was Esther Felberbaum, one year his junior, a girl from a slightly better neighbourhood—Rue Jeanne-Mance, just two streets in from Park. Her father worked in his father's fur business and was making a good living, so good the Felberbaums were planning to move to Outremont themselves. Esther was a pretty girl, with auburn hair and dark eyes and a cute figure under the sweaters and plaid skirts she wore. But eyeballing was about as far as Artie was getting. Esther was very firm—emphatic—that there'd be nothing hot and heavy until they were married. Oh, they kissed, they petted, they rubbed against each other. And he'd practically limp home after, his groin aching with frustrated desire. Sharing a bedroom with two brothers, afraid he'd be caught in the act and endure endless teasing and shame, he'd sequester himself in the bathroom to relieve his burning need. In his mind, everyone was having sex but him. Abie for sure, being two years older. Probably Bernie even, given the crowd he ran with. Artie thought he loved Esther. He was going to marry her, for God's sake, once they had a little more money saved. She was working as a secretary in her grandfather's company and didn't have to help her parents with rent and groceries. Her salary was going toward her future—their future—which meant their own flat in the area or maybe, if her parents kicked in something, a semi-detached bungalow in Ville St-Laurent.

Later on he wondered what would have happened if Esther had been more forthcoming. He wasn't expecting her to go all the way, but if she'd at least given him maybe a hand job once in a while, in the darkness of Fletcher's Field at night, away from the lights of the street, the touch of a hand that wasn't his own to take the edge off. Wasn't he responsible, working the way he did to help support his family? Day in, day out, seven days a week—didn't that entitle him to more than necking and a feel outside the bra? But always she refused. "When we're married," she'd say, "you get the whole package. Until then, only the wrapping."

In the factory there were girls who flirted with him. French-Canadians who packed dresses under his direction, who wore light cotton dresses in summer and called him Ar-*tie*, laughing at the French he tried to speak, correcting his pronunciation so he sounded more like them. One girl named Francine—he was sure she'd go to bed with him if he asked her out. Sometimes when they worked side by side he'd smell a musky odour coming off her body and he'd get an erection and have to lean against the shipping table to hide it. She had jet-black hair, shiny and straight, and a round, pleasant face. Lousy teeth but that was par for the course with the Frenchies back then. A little bit plumper than he liked but if she were naked underneath him, God, he'd take that extra flesh, take it in his mouth and—and—Jesus, he had to stop thinking about it. Sometimes had to disappear into the dingy little bathroom at the back and masturbate as fast as he could.

If he and Esther didn't set a wedding date soon, he thought his head or his body would explode, maybe both in quick succession. So on a Friday night in July, at her parents' dinner table, all the windows open to get a cross-breeze going in the heat, the white lace curtains hanging limp, not moving an inch, he spoke to her father, laid out his financial situation, and it was agreed they would get married the following April. Not the 20th because that was Hitler's birthday and who wanted that as an anniversary, but the 27th, at the Chevra Kadisha synagogue. Nine months to go. He had waited this long, what was nine months more?

Nothing. A blink of an eye in the long run. But a week later, Francine called him aside to say one of the other girls was quitting, moving back to Lac-St.-Jean to care for her father, an asbestos miner who had some kind of lung cancer. Was it possible, Francine asked, that her own sister Micheline could take her place? She was eighteen and a hard worker, Francine said. A high school graduate who was good with numbers and writing, who'd even make a good secretary once she improved her English. Artie said it wasn't up to him, he'd have to speak to Mr. Schiff. Couldn't he just say hello to her, Francine asked. She was right outside. Just a quick word and he would see what a good prospect she was, someone he could recommend to the boss. So Artie said okay, just for a minute because they had a big order to get out to Eaton's, and the truck was already at the loading dock and you *never* wanted to be late for Eaton's because they might refuse the order, and then their buyers wouldn't take your calls anymore.

One minute, he told her. No more. Francine thanked him and went out to the loading dock and came back in, leading her sister by the hand.

Micheline had the same dark hair as her sister, shiny like the mane of a coal-black horse. But her eyes were blue, her cheek-bones high, and when she smiled her cheeks dimpled, and her teeth were white and straight. The dress she wore was a vivid flower print, sleeveless with a V-neck. Nothing plunging or untoward, just low enough to reveal a fine gold chain with a small cross that hung above her breasts. Her legs were bare and her feet visible through white sandals that looked like wicker. She held out her hand and Artie shook it. He smelled something light and floral, what he imagined rosewater would smell like. He felt his heart beat faster. He knew he should say something but couldn't think what that should be or what language it should be in. The floor might just as well have opened like a trap door and sent him plunging to the basement. Or some-where farther down.

"Wait here," he said. He turned and walked out the door that led to the front office and showroom and told Mr. Schiff a girl was quitting but he had found a fitting replacement.

Micheline proved to be as good a worker as Francine sug-gested. She was prompt, polite and precise. A little shy, com-pared to her older sister, never one to make jokes, but when she laughed, Artie laughed too, even if he didn't get the joke. He started shifting his work in ways that brought him closer to her. He'd ask her to help him prepare orders so they could stand side by side at a table, lost in the light scent of roses. To put her hand on the seam of the box as he wet the thick, fibrous tape they used to seal it. To come down to the basement to help load bolts of cloth into the freight elevator to take up to the cutters.

He asked everything but what he really wanted to ask, which was whether she'd go out with him sometime. He couldn't; he was engaged, for God's sake. And she probably had a boyfriend. How could she not, as pretty as she was? He thought of roundabout ways he could find out, like asking her what she was doing on the weekend, seeing if she said, "My boyfriend and me, we're going to the movies . . ." Francine always talked about her boyfriend, Vincent, and the dances they went to, the movies they'd seen.

But he never asked Micheline and she never volunteered.

About three weeks after Micheline was hired, on a sweltering Sunday night in August at Hammerman's soda shop, so hot behind the counter that Artie had to keep putting Johnson's baby powder on his forehead and forearms so sweat wouldn't run into the drinks he was mixing, the bell rang over the door and three girls came giggling in, speaking French. You didn't hear much French on Park Avenue in those days. That's where the Jewish kids hung out, walking along holding hands, driving their father's cars—those few whose fathers had cars—up and down, back and forth, calling out to friends or groups of girls on the sidewalk.

When Artie looked up and saw Micheline with two friends, his heart fluttered, then quickly sank. Seeing her outside the factory was something he had thought about constantly, but not like this; not with powder on his arms and face like a clown, serving cones and squirting coloured syrup into glasses. He'd wanted her to see him dressed in his best poplin jacket, striding up the avenue, ordering in a restaurant.

Damn it. Damn it damn it damn it.

So pretty, so light on her feet. He made himself smile and say "*Bonsoir*" to her and her friends, and she gave him a beautiful smile in return, a real hummer, and said, "Ar-*tie*," the way her sister did, with the accent on the second syllable. "How many jobs you have?"

He took their orders, scooped ice cream into their cones—she ordered strawberry, of course she did, and he bet her lips tasted like strawberries the rest of the night. Maybe always. He was glad they went to sit at one of the rickety white tables outside because the sweat was running freely and he had to powder up again.

The next morning he wasn't sure what he should say to her

about it. Maybe nothing. Maybe avoid her completely. But she spoke first, saying he was lucky to work at an ice cream shop where he could probably have all he wanted. "Me, I love ice cream," she said. "I would have one every night if I could."

"Always strawberry?" he said.

She smiled and said, "*Ben, non.* I would have a different one each time. Strawberry one night, chocolate the next. Then vanilla, pistachio—what else you have at that place?"

He stammered out the complete list of flavours, watching her eyes sparkle with each new one. And couldn't help himself, didn't want to stop himself, and said, "Come next Sunday night and I'll make you something special. A triple scoop with strawberry, chocolate and vanilla."

"*Non!*"

"Yes."

"*Oh, mon Dieu,* that sounds great. I'm gonna do that. I'm gonna see you there next Sunday."

The week dragged by. There were orders to fill, the fall lineup going out to the stores, wool dresses and skirt-jacket combos much heavier than what the girls were wearing now in the summer heat. Micheline almost always wore something light and sleeveless. Micheline. What do you look like naked, he wondered. What do you smell like when a man holds you in his arms and breathes in the tang of your sweat, the musk of your— oh, God, he had to stop himself and march off to the washroom, splash cold water on his face. And quickly touch himself.

On Friday night he had dinner with Esther and her parents and they took a walk after, the two of them, and necked awhile in Fletcher's Field. For the first time in months he didn't try to feel her up. And the kissing grew tiresome after a while. Too much spittle passing between them, pooling in the corners of his mouth. He walked her home to Jeanne-Mance after half an hour, saying he was tired and needed sleep before going into the factory for the eight-to-noon shift.

"My parents don't like that you work Saturdays," Esther said.
"Mine neither."

"Once we're married, I hope you won't have to. It would
be nice to go to synagogue together. Especially once we have
children. That's how you meet other families," she said. "The
kind we want to be friends with."

That Saturday morning, after his half-day selling goods
for cash, Irving Schiff paid him eight dollars, as always, and
Artie gave his mother seven.

"Not eight?" she asked.

"I need one," he said. "To buy something for Esther." But
it wasn't for Esther. It was to buy ice cream for Micheline and
maybe something else.

Sunday wasn't as hot as the week before so he didn't need
the baby powder. He just worked his shift, pocketing the odd
penny tip he got, keeping his eye on the door, looking up every
time the bell chimed.

"Watch it, sport," one customer said. "You almost got
black cherry on my shirt."

By eight-thirty, he started to wonder if she would come.
At quarter to nine, he decided she wouldn't. Why the hell would
she? He was English, Jewish, not bad-looking but no Cary
Grant. Working in a factory and a soda fountain. If she was ever
going to take a second look at a Jew, wouldn't it make sense to
go for a lawyer, a doctor, an accountant? Even the salesmen at
Dominion Dress made good money and drove nice cars. They
wore suits and ties and some of them had pinkie rings that spar-
kled, maybe with real diamonds.

Not a minute later he heard the doorbell chime and she
walked in alone, in a peach coloured dress, her gold cross shining against her flawless skin. She sat at the counter right in front
of him and said, "You have something for me?"

Willy Hammerman, the owner of the shop, let him leave
early that night. While Micheline had her three-scoop cone, he

washed up, put on the fresh white shirt he had brought with him just in case, sucked on a mint and combed his hair, and by nine-fifteen they were walking together east on Villeneuve toward the Main. Away from Park Avenue, where someone might see him and say to Esther, "Who was that Artie was walking with last night? The *shiksa* with the cross around her neck?"

They kept going past the Main to St-Denis, then along Gilford, a quiet street, with small two-storey flats crowding close to the sidewalk. As the sky darkened behind them, they spoke to each other in English, because Micheline wanted hers to improve. "Tell me when I make errors," she said. "I'm not going to stay a shipper, you know. I can type good and I am learning about bookkeeping too."

Should he tell her that "type good" wasn't correct, that she should say "type well" instead? No. Nothing she said tonight could be wrong, not when she was walking at his side.

He walked her all the way home to a cold-water flat not unlike his, on Rue Chabot, not far from Delorimier Stadium where the Dodgers' top farm team, the Montreal Royals, played. She said thank you for the ice cream and he said, "*De rien.*"

"English only, please," she said. "Okay, Ar-*tie*?"

"Okay."

The first kiss came three days later. It came because it had to, because he couldn't stand it anymore. They were in the basement together, hauling out bolts of light blue wool—one of this year's big colours, something a woman could match with a white blouse, or cream or navy—and his blood was pounding through his veins, rushing like the St. Lawrence River in spring. He looked at her hand first, pale against the cloth, and he put his hand over it. She turned and looked at him and he knew it was going to happen and when it did the sweetness of it almost made him fall over. Their lips met, her teeth parted, her tongue slipped out and their bodies pressed together. His erection sprang up almost immediately and he pulled away from her but she moved with him. His back was against the wall then, he had nowhere else to go, and their bodies pressed so close, so completely, that all he could do was whisper her name into her ear and breathe in her scent like he'd dreamed of doing and it was as warm and rich and beguiling as he'd imagined.

That's as far as it went that day. They broke off the kiss and she smiled and put her hand on his cheek and then they brought the cloth up in the freight elevator. He was sure everyone in the shipping room could see right through him. "I kissed Micheline Mercier" might as well have been stamped on his forehead. And his heart.

Esther could have been in China for all he thought of her. Yes, he had dinner there on Friday, he had to, but on Saturday night, instead of taking Esther to see *All About Eve* as he had promised, he begged off sick.

"But it has Bette Davis," she complained.

"Next week, okay? I promise. It's just I don't feel so good."

That night, he took Micheline to a place called Rockhead's Paradise, where they saw a young pianist named Oscar Peterson, along with a bass player, drummer and saxophonist. Abie had told him about Peterson—"A genius, Artie, I swear to God, the Mozart of our time"—and they walked out of there so feverish, so electric, that they were wrapped in each other's arms the minute they hit the sidewalk.

One week later, on Friday night, after dinner at Esther's but no trip to Fletcher's Field, Artie Moscoe lost his virginity to Micheline. They did it in the showroom of Dominion Dress, on the couch where Irving Schiff sat with buyers as his salesmen showed samples of the new lines, the couch covered with a sheet Artie had brought from home. Artie had let them in the back door of the factory with a key Mr. Schiff had given him for early Saturday openings.

He ejaculated almost as soon as he entered her. He barely got to enjoy the sensation, the warmth and wetness of her. Still, it was like the first breath of air a miner takes in when he emerges from the dark underground, the first pearls of water a man feels on his tongue when he crawls out of the desert into the green of an oasis.

"I'm sorry," she said.

"Why?"

"That you are not my first."

So she knew. Knew that this was his first time. But it didn't matter. She stroked his back and his neck and it wasn't long before his desire returned and the second time, it all took longer. Now he felt like a lover, in control of himself. What did he know at that age? What did he understand about women's bodies and orgasms? Nothing. She looked happy enough, naked beneath him, wearing nothing but her cross on its chain.

"Micheline," he said after coming the second time.

"Ar-*tie*," she said.

He told her how beautiful she looked and she smiled.

All the next month, he teetered between ecstasy and agony. Ecstasy when they were together, agony when they were apart— especially when he was with Esther, going through the motions, playing the role of fiancé. He saw Micheline at least two or three times a week. He held back more of the money he was making, telling his mother he needed to save for his wedding.

"But her father's paying," his mother said.

"For the house then, Ma."

He used the money to take Micheline to dinner, to Rockhead's, even once to the Gayety Theatre for a burlesque show. They went for walks, they stole into the showroom. They used the apartment of one of Micheline's neighbours when they went to the Laurentians for a week.

Miss Montreal, he called her sometimes.

"Because it's the company name?" she asked.

"Because you're the prettiest girl in the city."

"*Ben, non.*"

"Oh, yes. If they had a contest you'd win."

"I'm too skinny. The girls who win the Miss America, they have big curves. They have more up here."

"You don't need more. You're perfect the way you are."

The High Holidays came early that year and things were busy at home in September as his mother cooked and cleaned in preparation for Rosh Hashanah. There were errands he had to run, shopping to help with, floors to sweep, services to attend, relatives to visit. An entire week went by without seeing Micheline once. And before he knew it, it was Yom Kippur. More services, more relatives, more things to help out with.

And after the holidays, back at work, Micheline seemed distant. They never showed affection openly in the factory—Mr. Schiff knew Esther's father—but he could tell something was wrong. She came out of the washroom one morning crying. She huddled with her sister more than usual. She didn't want to go down to the basement when cloth needed to be brought up. She didn't come to the ice cream store on Sunday.

He wondered if she had another boyfriend.

Technically, he had no right to be jealous if she did. He had never told her about Esther, that he was engaged to be married. In the first weeks of infatuation, he never thought anything would actually happen between them, and didn't want to burst the bubble around him. Then, when the affair began, he didn't want to say or do anything that would send her running. And it wasn't like he was sleeping with Esther, so he didn't feel like he was betraying Micheline. The fact that he was betraying Esther—well, a lot of guys he knew were doing the same thing. Engaged to Jewish girls who wouldn't have sex, running after French girls who'd go all the way.

None of this mattered. The thought of Micheline with another man filled him with anxiety, sadness, rage. He pictured some smooth French lover seducing her, whispering things in her native tongue that he could never master, taking her to the finest clubs and restaurants, driving her around in a Packard convertible, her hair streaming behind her in the moonlight. Pictured himself lying in wait, surprising them, beating the man senseless and reclaiming Micheline as his own, crowning her Miss Montreal with a diamond tiara.

It wasn't until October that she finally took him aside and told him she was pregnant.

I was thinking about the implications of that, the timing, when Reynald Paquette called.

"That's a pretty wild story you told," he said. "What's this evidence you found?"

"You're familiar with ammonium nitrate? How it can be used to make bombs?"

"We had a seminar on it a couple of years ago."

"Luc has a hundred kilos of it. I found the empty bags in the boathouse of the place I searched."

"That you searched," he said. "Illegally. Broke in, I suppose?"

"You going to pull out the rule book now? Play word games with me?"

"Shut up for once. This isn't a game to me, it's my job. How am I supposed to get a search warrant? Tell a judge you broke into someone's property—what did you do, smash a window or break down a door?"

"Window."

"Great. At a property which may or may not be owned, rented or otherwise occupied by a member of the Lortie family—and found, what? Some empty bags."

"You could do a title search on the property."

"What's the address?"

"I don't know the exact address. It was an A-frame cabin on a country road. Chemin Gosselin. I told you this."

"You told me nothing I can act on. Am I supposed to send officers into the mountains to track down a rural address, based on that? It's Friday of the long weekend. I'd be lucky to get two guys on bikes."

"Isn't there a municipal force there? They're probably familiar with the local owners."

"That's part of the problem right there," he said. "Say I call them and ask if the Lortie family owns property up there. The minute I hang up, rumours will start. Why was the Crimes Majeurs squad calling about them? I start to drag that name through the mud, I'll have problems of my own."

"Bigger than a bomb levelling a city block? Because the amount of stuff he had, that's what he can do."

"All right," he sighed. "Let me see what I can find. If I need you to pinpoint the location if this cabin, you could do it?"

"Yes. I'll email you a satellite image that shows exactly where it is."

Micheline's pregnancy threw her relationship with Artie into turmoil. For all the romance of it, all the grandness, there were harsh realities to deal with. In 1950, in the small village that was Jewish Montreal, ending his engagement to Esther Felberbaum and marrying a French-Canadian—a Catholic—who was already pregnant would have led to virtual excommunication. His family, her family, his employer, all would have turned against him and turfed him. Maybe not his mother, and probably not his brothers—Bernie probably would have clapped him on the back and said something crude about him finally getting some—but the rest of them? He would cease to exist. His father would say Kaddish over him as if he were already dead.

Despite all that, he was willing to go ahead. He told her so. But Micheline said no. Her family would not have been any more understanding or welcoming, she told him. "I never said nothing to you about this," she said, "but my father, he hates the Jews. When he was younger, he was a follower of Adrien Arcand and Lionel Groulx. He believed all what they wrote and said about Jewish people, that we should not shop in their stores or have anything to do with them. When Abbé Groulx supported Vichy France during the war, my father supported it too."

"It doesn't matter," Artie said.

"But it does! If we have a baby together and your family won't have us and mine won't either, what would we do? Two people alone can't raise a child. You need grandparents, uncles, aunts, cousins. You need friends and neighbours. We would have nothing but the two of us."

"That's enough for me," he told her.

"But not me," she said.

Abortion was out of the question. Even though Artie's brother Abie, the med student, knew someone who knew someone who could perform the procedure, almost certainly safely, he knew Micheline wouldn't hear of it. Maybe she wasn't the staunchest Catholic, but she had been raised to believe in certain fundamentals, one of them being the wrath of God, the hell that would await her if she committed such a sin.

The only option was to have the baby and give it up for adoption. Even this was not without its trials. To be pregnant and unmarried in Quebec in those days was to invite derision from all concerned. Most girls would be sent away to live with relatives once they started to show, usually somewhere in the country, away from the prying eyes and flapping lips of the neighbourhood. And once they gave birth, they had to give up the baby whether they wanted to or not. Adoptions were often forced on them. Sometimes they'd be told the babies had been stillborn. They never knew the warmth of the newborn at their breast. And neither did the infants. They'd be placed with Catholic agencies by the sisters who usually helped in the deliveries.

And sometimes, if the doctor knew of a good family that wanted a child, he would arrange a private adoption himself.

"Jesus Christ," I said. "It's Laurent. Not his kids. He's the one who was adopted."

"You mean this right-wing nut with all his anti-immigrant bullshit," Ryan said, "his big Quebec for old-time Quebecers line, he's got a Jewish father?"

"So it would seem."

"Well if that ain't a motive, what the fuck is?"

"Wait a minute," I said. "I doubt very much that Arthur's name ever went on the birth certificate. The social worker told me how strict the laws are around reunifications. Did Arthur tell you anything else?" I asked Jenn.

"Not really. What he told me was, he only really started thinking about it last year, after his wife died. As long as she was alive, he never allowed himself to pursue it. But once she was gone, he couldn't help wondering what happened to this child he fathered. He didn't even know if it was a boy or girl, or what had become of Micheline. He said he thought of hiring a private detective at one point, but couldn't bring himself to do it. Even if Micheline was still alive, he was hesitant to contact her after all these years. He said, 'What if her life turned out badly? What if she's dirt poor or lived a life of abuse, all because I didn't have the courage to see things through?'"

"We have to assume Sammy found out somehow," I said. "He knew the month and year of the birth. Knew the mother's name. There must be archives he could have gone to, records he could consult. If she married, he could have tracked her down. Maybe convinced her to file a reunification request."

"Which means we can find her too," Jenn said. "I'm good at that kind of thing. I don't mind getting dusty."

"You might not have to," I said. I had a sudden vision of the list of names and numbers on Sammy's fridge, all beginning with the letter M. What if it didn't stand for Monsieur?

What if it stood for Micheline?

————

It took nearly half an hour to drive to Sammy's flat. Every street leading there was mobbed with people carrying Quebec flags, white fleurs-de-lys on blue backgrounds. Cars were honking, their passengers leaning out of windows, waving their flags, trying to high-five each other. Canada Day never seemed to create this level of excitement and participation, at least not outside officially sanctioned events. There was genuine electricity in the air.

Even the clouds seemed to have burned away. The late-afternoon sun was shining for the first time in a week, promising a perfect evening for the big concert in Parc Maisonneuve and whatever other events were planned.

When I got back to the hotel with Sammy's list in hand, the three of us started calling the names on it, working three cellphones at a time, crossing off those that had no one named Micheline living there.

It was Ryan who hit the right house: M. Grenier. He handed me the phone while the man who answered walked off calling, "*Maman. Téléphone!*"

I waited about thirty seconds before footsteps sounded at the other end, starting off faint and getting only a little louder before someone picked up the handset and said in a light, breathy voice: "*Oui?*"

"*Madame Grenier?*"

"*Oui, c'est moi.*"

"*Micheline Grenier?*"

"*Oui, monsieur.*"

"*Est-ce que votre nom de fille était Mercier?*"

"*Qui êtes vous?*" she said.

"*Un ami de Sam Adler.*"

"*Oh, mon Dieu,*" she breathed. "*Pauvre Monsieur Adlair.*"

Poor Mr. Adler indeed.

CHAPTER 19

She still lived in the house where she had been born, in a neighbourhood so far east the tendrils of gentrification had yet to curl around it. The streets were crowded and narrow, with two-storey houses that showed no outward signs of renovation. No expensive German casement windows or sanded, refinished doors. Most of the parked cars were older, showing rust and unrepaired damage. People sitting out on stoops to escape the heat of flats that had no air conditioning, eyeing the Jeep as I backed into a parking spot.

Jenn had come with me. She spoke better French than any of us and I thought her presence would serve the situation better than Ryan's. She had also heard Arthur Moscoe's story first-hand and might be able to prompt Micheline if her memory faltered.

A man answered the door. He looked to be in his late forties, with greying whiskers and thin hair and a paunch that hung over stained sweatpants. He held a bottle of Molson Export in one hand.

He turned and called, *"Maman!"* and walked away toward the kitchen at the rear.

What if she's dirt poor, Artie had wondered. Maybe she wasn't quite that, but neither had she lived a life like his. Or that of her hidden son.

I knew that the woman who came to the door was eighty-two. Her face was deeply lined and spotted, her hair white and thin, but she carried herself well, if slowly, and when she smiled I saw the fine bones of her face, how lovely she must have been in her time. When she was Artie's Miss Montreal. And there around her neck, in a crevice of tired, blemished skin, was the gold cross she had worn when Artie first laid eyes on her.

"*Entrez, je vous en prie,*" she said, indicating we should come in.

"*Merci,*" I said.

The ground-floor apartment was small, with a dropped ceiling that made it feel even smaller. In the parlour on the right were two old red leather chairs with brass studs and scuffed legs, as well as a couch that faced a small television on a wood-veneer stand. The coffee table had white lace doilies on it and there was a plate of chocolate-chip cookies laid out, along with a pot of tea and white china cups with gold edging around the rims. Propped up in a frame on the table was a black-and-white photo of a younger Micheline, maybe forty years old, next to a burly man with thick black hair combed into a pompadour. His arm was around her shoulder and he wore a heavy gold watch and a ring with a gold face about an inch square.

She pointed to the red chairs and Jenn and I sat. She lowered herself onto the couch, bracing herself on the bolstered arm, the soft cushion almost swallowing her thin body.

"*Mon mari,*" she said, pointing at the photo. "*Il est mort depuis vingt ans. Cancer du poumon.*" My husband. Dead for twenty years. Cancer of what—the lungs?

I wasn't sure how to say sorry in this context. *Je regrette? J'ai des regrets?*

She saw me faltering and said, "Would it be better to continue in English? I don't speak it like I used to, you know, but most of it is still there."

"If that would be okay."

"Let's try. You want to ask about Mr. Adlair, yes?"

"Please."

"So sad about him. I only met him a few times but he seemed very nice. Very *sympathique*."

"He was. How did he find you, do you know?"

She leaned forward and edged the plate of cookies closer to us. "It would not be so hard. I was not hiding, you know. I am living in the same house my parents owned. I moved back here after my husband died. Only my name changed and Mr. Adlair, he looked up marriage records from the early fifties and I suppose there were not that many Micheline Merciers to search through."

"When was this?"

"A few months ago. It was still cold, I remember. Snowing. I do not drive and neither did he, so when we went to see Madame Boily, he had to pay for a taxi."

"He convinced you to initiate a reunification?"

"It did not take much to convince me," she said. "My husband was gone. My daughter has—I am not sure of the English word—*la schizophrénie*—and will never have children. My son, who lives here with me, he never got married neither. Doesn't want children. It's so different now from when I was a girl and everyone had big families. Five kids, ten. More than that in the country. Even fifteen was not unusual in my mother's time because many did not survive. So when Mr. Adlair called me and asked if I wanted to contact my child, see if he would like to meet me, I took the chance. Took it very quickly."

Jenn said, "He had no idea then who this child was?"

"Of course not. Neither one of us knew. So we made the application and a month or two later I was told, yes, my son would meet me."

"Laurent Lortie," I said.

"Yes. What a surprise that was. It was amazing to me what he had become. What a fine family had taken him in. It was a big relief to me to know that things had gone well for him. A big success in business. Two kids of his own. And now the leader of a party in the election. It gave me a lot of pride."

"You shared this with Mr. Adler?"

She looked down at the plate of cookies. "Maybe I should not have done that. The confidentiality, they say, is very important in these affairs. But without him, it would not have happened. I would not have taken the steps. So I told him. But that cannot be why he was killed."

"Of course not," I said. Nothing to gain by implying there was. "Tell me, what was Monsieur Lortie's reaction when he found out who his father was?"

"I don't know," she said. "I did not tell him that."

"Why not?" Jenn asked.

"I had not spoken to Artie in—what, sixty years? His name never went on the certificate of birth. Without his permission, I did not think it would be right to involve him in that way."

"Is it possible Mr. Adler told him?"

"Told Monsieur Lortie? Maybe. I know they met sometime later, because Mr. Adler wanted to write something about Laurent and his daughter. But I told him he should not write anything about me being Laurent's mother. Not as long as I'm still alive."

Jenn said, "Did you meet your grandchildren? Luc and Lucienne?"

"Only Lucienne," she said. "Maybe one month ago, Laurent took me to lunch with her at the nice hotel on Rue Sherbrooke, the Ritz-Carlton. Luc was not able to attend."

Not able? More likely, Laurent would have been embarrassed to take him to the Ritz.

"How did that go?" Jenn asked.

"So lovely," she smiled. "All my life in Montreal, I never once went into a place like that. I'm going to always remember that day. They treat you so nice and the food is so good. I had the most wonderful salad with—*les artichauts*?"

"Artichokes," Jenn said.

"Yes, and then poached cod with little baby squids. I would have had the steak but at my age, it does not agree with me so well. Or my teeth. I even had some wine, which my doctor doesn't like me to take. A white Burgundy. I was embarrassed at how much it cost. More than the whole meal, I think. And I had two glasses."

That was a week before Sammy died, I thought. What if the wine had loosened her tongue and something had slipped out about Artie? And if she hadn't told Laurent who his father was, I was almost certain Sammy had. The irony of it, the inherent hypocrisy of the *pure laine* Québécois, supposedly from a faultless line of early settlers, fathered instead by a hustling Jewish kid from the poorest part of the ghetto. I thought about the article he'd written about the veterinarian opposed to eating halal meat. If that situation had raised his ire, this would have sent him into the state of high dudgeon Holly Napier had recalled with such fondness.

Laurent would not have wanted that published. Even if Sammy had told Micheline he wouldn't write about it until she was dead, he could have written something without mentioning her name. He was who he was. Was it possible Laurent had had Sammy killed for it? He could have hired it out. Or he could have sent Luc. Strong, muscular Luc, who'd rushed Ryan's car with a wild look in his eyes, smashed its window, gone after Ryan with a crowbar. Who practically laughed when a gun came out. I could picture him and his friend bundling Sammy out of his apartment with a sack over his head, barefoot, taking him somewhere—maybe to the cabin—and then beating him and dumping him in an Arab neighbourhood, a Magen David carved in his chest to throw blame on the Muslims he detested.

Then I didn't want to picture it anymore.

Back at the hotel, we told Ryan about our visit to Micheline.

"And your client, Moscoe, he doesn't know any of this?

Doesn't know his long-lost son turned out to be a right-wing redneck?"

"He would have told me if he'd known," I said.

"Well, I wouldn't tell him now," Ryan said. "Probably give him another heart attack."

"Maybe that's why Sammy didn't tell him. Arthur lived through a lot of anti-Semitism in Montreal in the thirties and forties. He saw first-hand what ultra-nationalists were capable of."

"But Sammy promised Micheline he wouldn't write about it," Jenn said. "Not while she was alive."

"It doesn't mean he never broached the subject with the Lorties," I said.

"He's moving," Ryan said.

I said, "Who?"

"The Syrian. His car is heading south." He was sitting at the desk where my laptop was open, pointing at the pulsing image being sent by my transponder.

Shit. I had forgotten about the planned meeting between Mehrdad and Mohammed. "We're going to have to finish this later," I said to Jenn.

"Where are you going?"

"A prior engagement."

"To which I'm not invited?"

"To which you can't come."

"It's dangerous?"

"I don't think it's going to be civil."

"Okay," she said. "Fine. I'm going to go downstairs and book a room."

I said, "Oh."

"What?"

"They're full up. This holiday weekend—we only got in because there was a cancellation."

"The Sheraton isn't far."

"They're full too."

"Do we call up for a cot?"

Somehow I couldn't picture the three of us sharing a room. Just Ryan and I made it crowded. And Jenn was not a small girl: six feet of solid Estonian farm stock.

"I have an idea," I said, and called Holly Napier.

"You changing plans on me?" Holly asked.

"I was actually calling to see if you had room for a house guest."

"Uh, Jonah . . . I like you well enough so far, but I'm not sure I'm ready to jump into bed with you."

"It's actually for my partner."

"Ryan?" she said. "Are you nuts?"

"My real partner. Her name is Jenn Raudsepp and she turned up in Montreal unexpectedly and hotel rooms are impossible to find."

"Oh. Well. Okay, I guess. But I'm heading out to catch the end of the parade and the concert."

"Hang on a sec." I covered the mouthpiece and said to Jenn, "Want to go to a concert? It's big and it's free."

She shrugged and said, "Why not? I'm in Montreal, I might as well do what they do."

I asked Holly if Jenn could meet her at the press pit.

"It's going to be crazy near the stage," Holly said. "What does she look like?"

"Tall and blonde. Wearing a blue shirt and blue jeans."

"The right colours, at least. So is she your business partner or partner partner?"

"Business," I said.

"That's it?"

"That's all."

"You and I still going to meet later?"

"One way or the other."

CHAPTER 20

Whoever said you should cross that bridge when you come to it wasn't thinking of the Champlain Bridge. After forty years of salt and weather damage, and the beating it took from handling fifty million vehicles a year, it was undergoing major repairs, narrowed to one lane going south. The north-bound lanes had reopened, cars speeding along new asphalt with burring sounds, but we were bumper to bumper. A soldier crab-crawling on his belly would have left us in his painstaking dust. The only saving grace was that Mohammed al-Haddad's car couldn't go any faster. The transponder showed he was ahead of us by a few hundred yards, creeping just like us.

Halfway across the bridge, another two miles to go, the black water of the St. Lawrence River swirled against the pilings of the huge concrete supports. An endless line of cars inched along next to an equally endless line of orange pylons, on the other side of which sat empty construction vehicles, the workers long gone for the night.

"I don't even know why we're following this guy," Ryan said. "You seem pretty sure one Lortie or another killed Sammy."

"Pretty sure isn't the same as certain. It's still possible the Syrians did it. Sammy could have known about their business."

"It was Luc's van in the alley that night."

"We think."

"You think. I know. The way that little fucker ran us off the road, then tried to pry my leg apart."

"And Mohammed and his brother came after us with guns. So let's stay with him for the moment. We have no idea where Luc is right now, but we know where to find Laurent later."

"Yeah, at a concert with a hundred thousand people."

"He'll be getting up on the stage at some point," I said. "We'll just listen for the sound of booing."

Ten minutes later we were off the bridge and into the South Shore town of Brossard, following the silver Lexus as it exited onto Boulevard Milan and then curled east to Boulevard Grande Allée. A few blocks later, the car turned right onto Chevrier. We hung back on Grande Allée, not wanting to get too close. The transponder showed the car turning right on the next major street, Boulevard Lapinière, and coming to a stop. We moved ahead slowly past a hydro transmission station, transformers grouped like soldiers awaiting orders, and made the same turn onto Lapinière. In the shadow of an elevated stretch of the Eastern Townships Autoroute was a small group of warehouses and industrial buildings.

"Right there," I said. The Lexus had parked outside one of the warehouses and Mohammed himself was getting out of the driver's side. Three other men, including Faisal, got out the other doors. A sign on the warehouse wall said Entrepôt de Tapis. This, then, was the warehouse Mehrdad Aziz had spoken of. We saw Mohammed ring a bell outside the entrance. When it opened, he and two of the other three entered. One took up position at the door.

We crept north on Lapinière until we got to a service road and stopped. No one from the warehouse would see us there. Its north-facing wall was all brick, no windows. And the only car Mohammed had seen us in was the Charger, not the Jeep.

Ryan didn't offer me the Baby Eagle this time. He kept it in its ankle holster and got me his Beretta from the gun case. I wasn't going to argue about carrying it, not if we were entering a place bristling with armed men.

"This one has a safety where'd you expect it," he said.

"I see it."

"On or off?"

"On."

"Take it off."

"Okay."

Off we went, walking slowly and quietly under the scarred belly of the highway overhead.

We approached the warehouse from the south, creeping in the shadows cast by neighbouring buildings, our footsteps drowned out by the rush of cars along the highway to our left. There was a loading dock at the rear, its doors rolled down to the concrete lip. An unmarked half-ton truck was backed up to it, the cab empty, the engine silent. Next to the dock was a metal door, lit by an overhead light, where the fourth brother stood with one hand at his side, the other inside his jacket. I didn't think it was there so he could scratch himself.

Ryan whispered, "You think you can come up on him from his left?"

"If he's distracted."

He took out his Glock and threaded a suppressor onto the barrel. "I'm nothing if not distracting. Watch the light over his head. When it goes out, make your move."

The building that faced the south side of the warehouse was a manufacturer of storm doors and windows. It clearly had a night shift operating; its parking lot was half full and the windows I could see were all lit. On this long summer night, the sky was just beginning to darken and the moon was not yet up.

I moved along its wall until I came to the next street, then turned north, staying in whatever shadows I could find.

When I could see the truck, and not the guard, I turned left. If I couldn't see him, he couldn't see me. I hoped. I kept the Beretta where it was, in the small of my back, and crouched forward slowly. I avoided pebbles, bits of broken glass, food wrappers, anything that might make a noise underfoot. When a string of tractor-trailers roared down the highway, I moved a little faster and made it to the side of the truck. I peered under it and saw the legs of the guard at the door. He was shifting his weight from foot to foot. Restless. Bored. I moved to the very back of the truck and waited. Getting myself ready for a fast break.

When Ryan shot out the light over the guard's head, all I heard was *pfft*, no louder than a cough. Then the sound of glass falling and the guard's grunt of surprise. I came running around the back of the truck while he was still brushing bits of glass out of his hair. He saw me way too late. Before he could raise his weapon, I threw a hard left into his solar plexus, taking every bit of breath out of him, then stepped into the back of one knee, forcing him to the ground. As he fell, I caught the machine pistol he'd been hiding under his jacket. It had two grips, one at the rear and one at the front. A long ammunition clip stuck out of the rear.

Ryan jogged up to my side, put the barrel of his gun against the man's head and said, "You going to stay quiet or take a bullet?"

He gasped for air, still winded.

"I'll take that as a yes." Then he holstered his gun and said to me, "Let me see that a sec."

I gave him the machine pistol. He turned it over in his hands. "This is nice. I really fucking like this."

"What is it?"

"The Steyr TMP. I've seen the civilian model but this is genuine military. We get out of here alive, I'm taking this home."

"You are truly a man of the world."

"Just not the right world all the time."

"Ready?" I said.

"Get your gun out. Then we'll be ready."

I hauled the guard to his feet and held his jacket collar. Ryan eased the door open and went in first, pointing the Steyr ahead of him. He didn't fire so I assumed there was no one there to shoot and followed him in, moving the guard ahead of me. His legs were still wobbly from a lack of air so I kept enough pressure on his neck to propel him forward.

The hallway ahead was plain drywall. For a moment, I thought back to the corridor we'd walked down in Boston, so richly panelled in wood, lined with portraits of the men who'd built that business. There was nothing like that here, no investment of time or taste. The only thing on the walls was one calendar held by a push-pin.

Ahead we heard voices, loud ones, hiding nothing.

"If this is an arms deal," I whispered, "we could be walking straight into a shitstorm."

"When guns come in crates," Ryan whispered back, "they're never loaded. They could have a hundred AK-47s, it don't fucking matter if we can get the drop on them."

A hundred AKs. Why didn't I find that comforting?

We moved as silently as possible along the tiled floor, no carpet here to absorb the sound, past an office on one side, a washroom on the other. The voices grew louder. At least two men talking. But I knew there'd be more. At least three Haddad brothers, and probably three on Mehrdad's side. Getting the drop on them sounded good in principle. How the fuck was it going to work in practice?

Whatever space lay ahead of us, either the main storage area or a showroom, was behind double doors that could open either way. Perfect for pushing hand trucks or dollies through in either direction.

"I'll go first," Ryan whispered. "You come in right behind. If we need to get their attention, settle them down, I'm gonna fire a burst at the ceiling. Or rip a pricey carpet. Ready?"

My heart said no but my lips whispered, "Yes."

Ryan pushed his hip against the door and went through it, the Steyr gripped in both hands. I charged in behind him, ready to blast a carpet or ceiling tile.

"All of you fucking freeze!" Ryan yelled.

I took in the scene in front of us. A large open space lit by fluorescent lights in fixtures that hung on short chains from a concrete ceiling. The walls I could see all had built-in bins stacked with rugs wrapped in brown paper. Halfway across the room were six men huddled around stacked wooden crates, examining the contents.

Mohammed al-Haddad held an AR-15 assault rifle that gleamed with a light sheen of oil. So did his brother Faisal and a third man who must have been one of their brothers.

Mehrdad Aziz was there too, his jaw agape as he saw Ryan and me. The two men from his store were behind him.

I hoped Ryan was right about the weapons being empty.

"Put the guns back in the crate," Ryan said. "Now."

Mohammed said, "What you did to my brother, asshole? You hurt him, you motherfucker?" There were deep blue bruises under both his eyes, and the left was shot through with blood.

I shoved the guard ahead and he stumbled and stayed down on one knee. Mohammed said something to him in their language and pulled him up by the elbow.

"He's fine," I said. "Just winded."

"So what is this, a hijack? You here to steal our guns?"

"No," I said. "Just to ask you something. Since I have you and Mehrdad in the same room."

"Just to ask!" Mohammed laughed. "You assholes try to kill me yesterday, you break in here like this just to ask? Fuck your ask and fuck you."

"If we'd tried to kill you, you would have been dead," Ryan said. "So put the guns down. The trigger on the Steyr doesn't need much pressure. You should know."

Mohammed tossed his rifle carelessly into the crate. Faisal set his down more carefully and wiped his hands on the seat of his pants. The third man hesitated and Ryan pointed the gun at the ceiling and fired a burst. Plaster fell where they stood, dusting their hair and the shoulders of their jackets.

"Okay, okay," the third man said and he stowed his rifle on top of the others.

Ryan said to me, "Pat them down."

While he held the Steyr at waist level, I stowed the Beretta in the small of my back and patted Mohammed first. He had a pistol in his waistband, a Beretta clone called a Taurus. Faisal had one too. Maybe the same guns they'd had at the Jean-Talon Market, if they'd had time to recover them. Maybe others from some private stock. The third man wasn't carrying anything, just a wallet that showed he was Sayeed al-Haddad. That meant the outside guard was Omar.

Neither Mehrdad nor his boys had guns. Careless? Or faith in this particular Mohammed?

I put all the guns on a table behind me and looked into the open crate, in which at least a dozen AR-15s were stowed. One other crate, also open, was filled with more of the Steyr machine pistols. The other crates were still nailed shut.

"Now we can talk," I said.

"Let me guess," Mehrdad said. "You have more wild accusations to make. More murders to accuse me of."

"No. I want to ask about Sammy Adler."

"Ask the crack of my ass," Mohammed said. "You are not real police. I don't have to answer you nothing."

My phone vibrated and I debated letting it go but knew I had to at least check.

Lucienne.

"Keep them covered a minute," I told Ryan.

"What the hell is this about my brother having an accident?" she said.

"Where are you?" I asked.

"Where—at the offices of Radio-Canada," she said. "I'm going to be on air when my father delivers his speech. Now what about Luc?"

"Have you talked to him?"

"No, I haven't been able to reach him. His cellphone is off and he never came back to the office. Was he really in an accident?"

"Yes. A car accident."

"Oh, God—"

"Relax," I said. "He wasn't hurt. He caused the accident."

"What!"

"He ran a car off the road. One I was in at the time."

"Were you hurt?"

"Not for lack of trying."

"Where?"

"Up in the Laurentians, around nine this morning."

"But that's impossible. He was picking up brochures and posters from our printer and taking them to Parc Maisonneuve for our volunteers."

"Maybe that's supposed to be where he was, but trust me, he was on a country road east of St-Sauveur, driving an old white van."

There was a brief pause and she sounded less strident, less sure of herself, when she said, "St-Sauveur?"

"A small cabin with a dock and a boathouse. You know it?"

"Hey! You!" Mohammed called. "You going to be all day? If that's your mother on the phone, tell her I'm going to fuck her, right after I fuck you in the ass."

Lucienne said, "What was that?"

I covered the receiver and said to Ryan, "If he opens that

toilet again, shoot him." Then to Lucienne, "Nothing. You know what I'm talking about."

"Yes," she said. "I know the place. My grandfather left it to Luc when he passed away four years ago."

"Just to Luc? You don't share it?"

"No. Grandpère knew Luc had fewer opportunities than I. That he would need something to provide stability, or an income if ever he needed it."

"I was there today, inside," I said. "I searched it."

"And?"

"I think he's making a bomb. A big one."

"Luc? That's crazy. What would he know about bombs?"

Not would he make one, but could he?

"I don't have time to go into it right now, but I found both ingredients and directions."

"He's not that kind of—"

"He's exactly that kind. You didn't see him when he smashed our car window with a crowbar and tried to gut my partner with it. You've heard of Anders Breivik?"

"The Norwegian killer?"

"He and your brother would make great cellmates."

"Luc is the complete opposite of—"

"Yeah, yeah. He's shy and quiet, keeps to himself. Wouldn't hurt a fly. I'm telling you, he's going to set off a bomb somewhere and blame it on Muslim extremists. To prove your father's point about them, rally public opinion against them, and help him get elected. And there's a good chance he killed Sammy Adler."

I heard Mohammed laugh and say, "Everybody killed this Adler. A fucking popular guy."

"What possible reason would he have?" said Lucienne.

"Sammy knew about your father being adopted. And who his birth parents were."

There was a long pause, long enough I thought the connection had been lost. "Lucienne?"

"Yes. I'm here."

"You know what I'm talking about, don't you? That your real grandfather was a man named Arthur Moscoe?"

"That's what Mr. Adler claimed. Without proof."

"Forget proof for a second. Did Luc know about it?"

"Possibly."

"Just possibly?"

"We didn't talk about it."

"But he's around you and your father all day. He could have heard something."

"Like I said, it's possible."

"Say he did know. Would he have done something about it? To please your father, eliminate a threat to him?"

"You're asking me if my own brother is a murderer. Or a mad bomber of some kind."

"That drawing," Ryan said. "Ask her about baseball."

"Lucienne, does your brother have any connection to baseball?"

"In what sense?"

"I don't know. Did he play it? Was he ever kicked off a team?"

"Luc? No, he was never one for team sports. He was strong but not well coordinated."

"Did he attend games?

"Not that I know of. Why?"

"There was a drawing in his cabin that resembled a baseball field. A large rectangle with a semicircle down in the left corner."

I heard a sharp intake of breath on the other end. "But— but that's impossible," she said.

"What is?"

"I am looking at an image like that right now."

"Where?"

"On a monitor at Radio-Canada. They're showing a map of Parc Maisonneuve, where the parade is ending and the concert will begin. That's just what it looks like."

"Hold on a minute. Ryan," I said, "give me your phone."

"I don't believe this," Mohammed laughed. "More phone calls."

"He told me to shoot you if you spoke again," Ryan said, handing me his phone. "Don't think I need to be told twice."

I opened his browser and found a satellite map of Parc Maisonneuve. As I zoomed in, I saw images of the park as it normally was, a large green rectangle. Then an image of the way it had been set up for the concert, with a large bandshell in the southwest corner. A half-circle that looked like a base-ball infield.

I said to Lucienne, "Get hold of your father."

"I've been trying ever since I got Gabriel's voice mail but Papa's phone is turned off. He does that when he's in interviews."

"Keep trying. Tell him to stay the hell away from the park."

"You really think that's Luc's target?"

"Why not? It would be the worst atrocity in the history of Montreal. And if blame is placed on Muslim extremists—it would play right into your father's hands."

"But Papa could be killed too."

"Not if the bomb goes off away from the stage."

The drawing. Rays shooting out of a sunbeam. Not near what had been, in my mind, the infield. Off to the top side. Where he would take out even more of the crowd.

"Oh Christ," she said. She'd been so cool, so controlled when I'd met her at her office. Now her voice was soft, almost breaking.

"When is your father due to go on?" I asked.

"During Johnny Rivard's set."

"Who's that?"

"An old-time star in Quebec. A rock-and-roller, you would call him. He shares some of our views and agreed to call Papa up at the end of his set."

"What time?"

"He's one of the last acts. Radio-Canada expects him to go on around ten."

It was just after eight.

"I have to go," she said.

"Not to the concert."

"Yes. I have to."

"Wait!"

"For what?" she said.

"Do you have a picture of Luc? Something you can email me?"

"I—yes, of course."

"Send it," I said. "Right now."

As soon as I ended the call, I called Jenn's cell. Got her voice mail. *Fuck!*

"Get out of the park," I said. "The minute you get this message. You and Holly both. Call me and tell me you got this message, okay? But get out of the park first. Get completely clear of it."

I tried Holly's phone too. More voice mail. I left her the same message.

I was about to dial Reynald Paquette when a crazy thought took hold of me.

I put my phone away and stowed Ryan's too, so as not to distract him.

"Change of plan," I said to Mohammed and Mehrdad. "Forget Sammy Adler for the moment."

"How can I?" Mohammed said. "No one shuts up about him."

"I need your help."

"My help!" Mohammed roared. "To do what? Go fuck yourself? Kill yourself?"

"To stop an attack that will kill hundreds, maybe thousands of people. And made to look like Muslims did it."

Mehrdad said, "What are you talking about?"

"Have you heard of Laurent Lortic? Québec aux Québécois?"

"Of course," he said. "I read newspapers. He and his daughter, they are the party of hatemongers and Islamophobia."

"That was the daughter on the phone just now. And her brother is going to detonate a bomb at tonight's big concert." I unfolded the creased pamphlet I had found in the lane outside Sammy's apartment, the one purportedly from the Quebec Muslim Liberation Front, and handed it to him. "He's going to put the blame on you Muslims to help his father get elected. By this time tomorrow, the city will be out for blood."

"The West has been out for Muslim blood for centuries," Mohammed said.

"Not like this. Nothing like this. Young people are going to die in this blast. Teenagers, children, all civilians."

"What kind of help are you asking for?" Mehrdad asked.

"Looking for him. And getting two friends of mine out of the park."

"Watch," Mohammed said. "He'll ask you to throw yourself on the bomb while he helps the friends."

I ignored him and the urge to tell Ryan to let her rip. "You do that, I won't call the cops here to bust up your deal. The amount of guns you got here, you would do serious time."

"You call the cops here," Mohammed said, "there is nowhere you can hide from me. From any jail in the world, I can order you killed."

"Just help us find him," I said. "There are seven of you."

"Let the police do that instead of coming here. That's where they should be. I pay fucking taxes."

"I will call them. From the road. Now come on."

"Cops if I go, cops if I don't go. I tell you what I think. I think I take my chances right here."

Mehrdad said, "My men and I will come."

That got two fast conversations going, one in Dari and the other in Arabic. Mehrdad shushed them. "It's the best way," he said. "The wire transfer is complete. We three will come with you to help. Mohammed can stay out of it. No police are called here. Deal?"

CHAPTER 21

We drove out of the industrial park and back toward the bridge, the three Afghans stiff and silent in the back. The smaller of Mehrdad's helpers was Rashid, the big one Kamal. When I dialled Paquette's number, I got voice mail. Same with his cell. Why didn't anybody answer their phones? What was the point in having one if no one fucking answered?

I had promised Sierra, promised Jenn, that nothing would happen to her, and in trying to keep her out of danger I had plunged her right in the middle of it.

I used the browser on my phone to find the general number for the Major Crime Squad. Someone there said, "*Un instant*," and a dial tone burred in my ear.

"*Crimes Majeurs*," a man said. "*Chênevert à l'appareil*."

Great. The partner from hell. "*C'est Jonah Geller*."

It took a second for the name to click, and it must have clicked loudly because he practically snarled in my ear: "*Geller? Qu'est-ce que tu veux maintenant?*"

"*Votre aide*."

"*Ah, oui? Avec quoi? Ton Italien?*"

"Detective, please—"

"We have an Italian investigator on our team, you know. He explained to me what your friend said. *Minchia*, he called me, yes? And a few other things? My friend here says they were all big insults."

"Forget that, okay? Someone is planning to bomb the Fête Nationale concert tonight."

"Paquette told me you had a crazy story about a bomb builder. Luc Lortie, you said?"

"It's not a story, it's the truth."

"Based on empty bags in someone's cabin?"

"It's his cabin. His sister just confirmed it. And the bags held enough ammonium nitrate to build a massive bomb."

"What reason would he have for this alleged plan?"

"To blame it on Muslim extremists. Help get his father elected. You need to get people out of the park. Then send in bomb technicians. Dogs that sniff out explosives."

"Or other dog's assholes. Which would take them straight to you."

"Shut up and do something, for Christ's sake. You want this much blood on your hands?"

"I'll see if I can find Paquette," he said. "I'm not authorizing nothing just on your word." And he hung up.

I closed my phone and screamed, "Fuck! How does a moron like this become a cop!"

"You're asking the wrong person," Ryan said.

I tried Jenn. I tried Holly. Why weren't their phones at least on vibrate?

No one called back. Ryan shifted lanes to get around hogs. The arc of the bridge took us closer to the darkening sky. Maybe ninety minutes to detonation. A hundred thousand people in harm's way.

"How did you get mixed up with Mohammed?" I asked Mehrdad. "Running guns to a gangster, that's not the impression I had of you."

"No, you took me for a murderer."

"I told you, I don't believe you killed Sammy."

"Not now, maybe."

"Back to my question."

"Mohammed is sending the weapons home to Syria, to help the people fighting the regime there. The odds are so much against them. They need support, modern weapons, and he is providing whatever he can."

"And you just happened to have a few crates full?" I said.

"No. This is not my business, not usually. But I still have contacts back home, people with access to weapons. And I understand what it is like to fight an enemy who hates you for what you are. Just like you Jews, right? "

"Yes."

"The fight against the Soviets, that was before my time. When they left in 1989, I was still young, not even a teenager. The Taliban, though, them I remember very well. You want to talk about hate, fanaticism—you won't find anywhere people more filled with hate. Families like mine, with education, with culture, we became the enemy in our own home. In Kabul, especially. Having to leave our country, run away first to Pakistan, then here. I know what the Syrians are going through. Just because they are not Alawite or members of the Ba'athist party, they have been oppressed, tortured, murdered."

"You did it all for the cause?"

He smiled and said, "No. I won't pretend that. Mohammed is paying me very well. And the irony—that is the right word?—the irony is that he first came to me to take money from us. Protection, he called it. There was no way I could pay him. No way I would. That is not how Afghans are. But times have been very hard for us. Since the economy became so bad, people are not buying rugs like they did before. We were in danger of losing our business. So we came to a different arrangement."

I was going to ask him how exactly that had happened when my cell rang. Unknown number. I was hoping it was

Holly Napier, telling me she and Jenn were well away from the stage.

It was Paquette. "What were you telling Chênevert about the Fête concert?"

"That's Luc's target. I'm sure of it."

"Based on what?"

"A drawing I found at his cabin. It's a sketch of the concert site."

"That's it?"

"It's enough. He wants an atrocity he can blame on Muslim extremists. What better target than this?"

"Where are you now?"

"On the Champlain Bridge. Trying to get to the site. Is there a way you can clear the area?"

"Of a hundred thousand people? Not without a stampede. Or a riot. And Montreal has had enough of those this year. There's nothing else I can go on?"

"His sister believed me," I said. "And she knows him better than anyone."

"*Merde*. Okay. I'm going to go there myself. When you're going to get there?"

"Less than half an hour, I hope. Which gives us less than half an hour to find the bomb."

"How so?"

"I think Luc will set it off while Lortie speaks, which is around ten-fifteen. A singer named Johnny Rivard is supposed to bring him up on stage."

"Christ."

"Tell your people to look for a white van, might be parked along the north side of the park."

"Why there?"

"Luc can blow up the crowd but not the stage where his father will be. Listen, his sister just emailed me his picture. I'm sending it to you right now. Get some plainclothes men to look for him. The van is an older Safari with recent damage on its left side."

"Which matches the paint on my fucking car," Ryan said.

"I'm putting the plate number in the email," I said.

"Good. There's already a big police presence there. They can start to search the crowd."

"He'll be somewhere on the fringes. Close enough to see the blast, far enough he doesn't get caught in it. Or the stampede it causes."

"All right," he said. "I'm on my way. See you at the party."

Once we were finally off the bridge and heading east on Notre-Dame, I called Jenn's cell again and was surprised to feel tears in my eyes as I dialled the familiar number. When it went to voice mail, I hesitated. I wanted to tell her I loved her. That I wanted her to be safe and happy, content with Sierra, thriving in her work and her life. All that came out was, "Call me. Please. Tell me you're safe."

At ten o'clock, we were at the corner of Sherbrooke and Pie-IX, as close to the park as we were going to get by car. Ryan pulled onto a side street and blocked a hydrant, and we spilled out into the warm night, all five of us, the Afghans looking cramped and hobbled as they pulled themselves of the back seat and took their first steps. We walked north in the shadow of Olympic Stadium, its concrete shell and unfinished tower looming cold and grey against the starless sky. Up ahead to our left was Le Jardin Botanique, Montreal's botanical gardens, silent, mostly deserted, except for people walking toward the park. Still a few acts to catch.

Still a climax to come.

Straight ahead I could hear electrified fiddle music and see blue strobe lights flashing from the bandshell. Crowds of people walked along with us; even more were streaming out of the park, having already partied long enough. Some looked sunburned, some looked drunk, their arms around each other. Faces painted blue and white, hair dyed bright blue, many wearing identical white T-shirts with blue hearts in which was written, "*Québec à nous.*"

Quebec for us.

How different was that from Laurent Lortie's idea that Quebec belonged more to some people than to others?

Across Sherbrooke, the crowd was massed like an army awaiting orders. I've been at Canada Day parades, Israeli Independence Day festivals, but never in my life had I seen so many waving flags. Every other person seemed to have one, forming a sea of blue and white, moving back and forth as if a conductor somewhere was directing them with a baton. I saw huge puppets made of papier mâché towering over the crowd. Some were familiar figures from Quebec's past, like René Lévesque and Maurice Richard. Others went much farther back in time, wearing the rough clothes of voyageurs and explorers.

I tried to make out where the press pen was, but the area close to the stage was completely jammed with people shoulder to shoulder, bouncing up and down to the music, waving their arms, transported by the sound, the closeness of others, the community around them.

They could all be dead in minutes if we didn't find Luc's van. If that was the vehicle he was using to deliver the blast. It could also turn out to be something entirely different: something stolen, rented, borrowed or bought.

"Mr. Geller!" a woman cried.

Lucienne Lortie was moving along the sidewalk toward me, pushing people aside, ignoring their angry glances. Her face still bore pancake makeup from the television interview she had been preparing for. Tears had streaked down her cheeks at some point, turning the powder to something like clay. "Have you seen my father? Or Luc?"

"We just got here."

"I have to find them," she said, her chin trembling. "My father, I think, is waiting behind the stage until Johnny Rivard goes on. My brother—he could be anywhere."

"We'll find him," I said. "Now stand a little to your right."

"For what?"

"Just hold still." I took out my cell and took her picture with the stage and its blue lights clear in the background.

"What's that for?"

"Just something I might need. Go find your father. And keep him off the stage. If Luc is waiting for him to go on before he sets off the explosion, maybe it will buy us some time."

I watched her walk to a gate behind the stage, manned by burly men in bright yellow jackets with "*Sécurité*" lettered on the back. I kept watching. Hoping to see Paquette materialize. He didn't.

"All right," I said to Ryan and Mehrdad. "The press pen is at the front of the stage."

"We're going to have to get through ten thousand people," Ryan said.

"I don't care if it's twenty thousand. Jenn is in there somewhere."

"Then let's get moving. You," he said to Kamal. "You're the biggest. Get in front and start pushing."

Kamal hesitated until Mehrdad urged him forward with a nod. Ryan and I got behind him. Mehrdad and Rashid backed us up until we were a tight wedge and then we started pushing our way through the mass of people facing the stage. We were trying to create a perpendicular path, coming at them from the side. Stepping on feet. Making them step back. Elbowing their sides. Someone kicked me in the side of the leg. Someone else swore and clapped the back of my head. I kept pushing against Kamal's broad back, making him go forward even when the wall of people didn't want to give way. I wished I were taller, tall as one of the giant puppets I'd seen, able to see out over the crowd, spot Jenn's shining blonde hair or Holly's pile of curls. I wished my arms were long enough, strong enough, to sweep aside the people blocking our path. That I were Moses, able to part this sea and find a clear path forward.

I put my arms on Kamal's shoulders and drove with my legs.

"Easy," he shouted. The first indication that he spoke English.

"I'll take it easy if you keep moving. Use your legs. Come on, push."

I could smell my own sweat running down my sides. It was too hot, too close, too many people getting angry, pushing back. Someone threw a plastic cup at me and I felt ice and liquid run down my back. Ryan was grunting beside me, swearing under his breath. I wondered how far we had come. What if it were only a few feet? It felt like we'd been moving an hour. Sisyphus had it easy compared to us; he only had to push rocks up a hill. We were pushing people who didn't want to be pushed. I felt another blow to my neck as someone cursed and struck out at me. I ignored it and kept my arms up, my head down. The music was getting louder as we got closer to the towers of speakers facing the crowd. I could feel drums and bass pounding up from the earth, resonating in my chest. I wished they'd turn the sound down, gag the singer, so I could shout out Jenn's name. Hear her call mine if she saw me. I should have asked Holly exactly where the press pen was. With so many people around us, so many flags, we could be going right past it.

Kamal stopped. He was panting and his shirt was soaked through with sweat.

"Keep going," I said.

"You get in the front."

"We're halfway," I said. A look to my left showed we were at centre stage. I could see the band now, a singer with an electric guitar at a microphone, waving his hands over his head, getting the crowd to wave along. Which didn't help us, since it made it harder to see where we were going. More hands slapped against me inadvertently. Someone's long fingernail poked my right eye and it teared up. I blinked a dozen times, trying to clear it, then walked into a cloud of exhaled smoke. I put my hand on Kamal's shoulder and trusted him to be my eyes.

"Up ahead," Ryan said. "I think I see a fence."

I wiped my eye and looked ahead. Had to close the blurred right and peer through the left. Inside a fenced-off area were cameras mounted on tripods. A mike boom held high above a techie's head. We shifted direction slightly and kept pushing, Kamal grunting like he was dragging a plow through rock-hard earth. Sweat dripping off his chin.

Seconds later, our forward movement stopped. We had hit the metal gate enclosing the press. Ryan shouldered his way in front of Kamal and we both bellied up to the gate and scanned the people inside the enclosure.

"You see her?" I yelled.

"No."

"Hang on." I crouched down and stuck my head between his legs, took a deep breath and rose with him up on my shoulders. People behind us booed and yelled at us as we blocked their view. "*Descends!*" a hoarse voice yelled. "Get down." Someone shoved me and I almost fell over but Kamal caught me and kept us upright. And smiled at me, flashes of gold in a few lower molars.

"There," Ryan said. "Jenn! Hey, Jenn!"

"Can she hear you?" I panted.

"No," he said and then yelled, "Jenn! Jenn Raudsepp!"

"Now?"

"Fuck it," he said. "We're going over."

The fence was only chest high. I boosted him onto the other side and followed him over.

"Thank you," I said to Kamal, and to Rashid and Mehrdad behind him. They were sweating and breathing hard too.

"We'll go look for the van along Rosemont," Mehrdad said. "If we see nothing by Viau, we'll turn south. Check the back of the crowd."

"We'll be right behind you," I said. "As soon as I get my friends to a safe place."

"I see the crazy brother or his van, I call your cell."

I gave him the number and he and his boys started making their way through the crowd, this time away from the stage. People moved aside instinctively, less resistant to people who weren't trying to usurp the space they'd fought so hard to get.

"There she is," Ryan said.

I turned and saw Jenn and Holly: Jenn rapt as she watched the band on stage, no idea what was going on or what it had taken to come find her; Holly taking notes in a narrow reporter's pad, flipping the page and scrawling away on a fresh one.

We hadn't taken a step before a man in a yellow Sécurité jacket blocked our path. He was over six feet and broad as a Douglas fir. He said something I couldn't hear.

I said, "What?"

He leaned in closer and said, "I saw you climb the fence. This is for journalists only."

"We'll be out in a minute."

"You have accreditation?"

"My name is on a list."

"Then why did you come over the fence?"

"We're just picking up a friend."

"Out. Now." He put a big hand on my chest and pushed.

I had spent the last twenty minutes pushing and being pushed. I'd had more than enough. I kneed him in the balls and he doubled over and clutched his groin in the expected way and we moved quickly around him. A cameraman swore at me as I moved through his field of vision, ruining whatever shot he was taking. I left his balls unkicked.

"Jenn!" I yelled, and this time we were close enough for

her to hear me. She turned with a look of surprise, a what-are-you-doing-here look. I rushed up to her and said, "Your phone turned off?"

She said into my ear, "Huh? No. Except—no, maybe it is, I forgot to charge it when I got in. Why?"

Why. "We're leaving," I said.

"What's happening?"

"The bomb, honey. It's here. Holly!"

She turned and gave me the same surprised look that Jenn had, a spotlight illuminating her tangle of red hair.

"You're early," she said with a smile.

"We have to go."

"I can't. I'm covering this for—"

"Holly, remember Luc Lortie? The brother who's supposedly slow?"

"Of course."

"He's planted a bomb here. And it's going to go off once Laurent gets up on that stage."

She pulled back and looked me in the eyes. "You're serious," she said. A statement, not a question. And could tell from my look back that I was.

I turned around and saw the guard I had kneed getting to his feet. "Is there a faster way out of here than the way we just came?"

"Yes," she said, pointing to the far side of the press pen. "There's the stage door to the left and an exit to the street."

"Then let's exit. Now."

She shoved her notebook into her shoulder bag and led us out a break in the gate that opened onto the backstage area. I wished we'd seen it from the street—getting into the press pen by that route would have saved us a lot of time and energy. We passed through it and out another gate onto a paved path bordering the grounds of the Botanical Garden.

"Don't you have a cell?" I asked Holly.

"I had my hands full taking notes and photos," she said. "It was in the outside pocket of my purse."

I filled them both in and we strode quickly along the path. When we were at least a few hundred yards away, beyond what I judged to be the ring of any explosion, I pointed Jenn toward the street and said, "Take a taxi or the Metro, either one. Wait for us at the hotel."

"You're not coming?" Jenn asked.

"I need to find Luc."

"Let the police find him."

"I can't just walk away."

"But you expect me to?"

"I promised you nothing would happen."

"But it's okay if it happens to you?"

"Just go."

"Not unless you come."

"Does anyone give a shit if I come?" Ryan said.

"I meant you too," Jenn said.

I pulled her close and kissed her hair. "Go. I'll see you soon."

"No you won't, you dumb shit." She tried to blink back tears but they fell anyway.

I turned to Ryan and said, "Take them out of here."

"I'm with you," he said.

"You don't have to."

"This is what you brought me here for, right? To have your back? Let's find this punk and get his shit over with."

Behind us I heard a wave of applause as the singer on stage finished his number. Then a man with a voice made for radio took the mike and called out to the crowd and they roared as one.

"*Et maintenant*," I heard him say, followed by something that echoed through the park. I couldn't catch the meaning. I strained to hear it but all I heard was disembodied words.

And then the name Johnny Rivard.

CHAPTER 22

A bass drum started thumping a four-four beat. A guitar joined in charged with treble, a full-on country twang, followed by honky-tonk piano and bass. A rockabilly quartet, old-time, led by a singer old enough to believe in Laurent Lortie's message and want to bring him up to speak to the great mass of people still packing the grounds.

I was hoping like hell Lucienne had found her father and convinced him to stay off the stage.

Ryan and I were on Boulevard Rosemont on the north side of the park, panting a little from a fast run up the long paved path bordering the gardens. We stayed at a jog, checking both sides of the street for Luc's van. And what if we found it? I knew nothing about bombs. Certainly not how to disarm one. I didn't think Ryan knew any more than I did. Guns were his thing.

"There!" Ryan said, pointing at a white van parked on the north side. We jogged toward it but halfway could see it was a well-kept recent Sienna. We kept going, staying at a trot. I noticed the Sienna and most of the other cars had blue permit parking stickers in their windshields.

"*Bonsoir,*" a man yelled onstage. "*Bonne Fête tout le monde.*"

The crowd roared back at him as one.

And then he launched into a song. Okay. He was doing at

least one number before he called Laurent up to join him. Make it a long one, I thought. Make it "In-a-Gadda-da-Vida" or "Whipping Post"—give us seventeen or eighteen minutes more to find the misfit boy and his bomb.

I didn't hear my phone ring but I felt it vibrate in my pocket.

It was Reynald Paquette.

"Where are you?" he shouted. I could hear the same music that was playing around us over the phone, so he was somewhere on the scene.

"On Rosemont, going east. You?"

"Approaching backstage. Waiting for the bomb technicians. If you see anything, don't touch it. Don't even approach it. Call me direct."

"Fine. Have you circulated Luc's picture?"

"As widely as I can. But the patrol officers, they have to stay at their posts, keep the crowd under control."

"There won't be a crowd if a bomb goes off."

"Just remember what I said. You find something, don't touch it. I'd rather see a robot camera blow up than a person."

"Even me?"

"Don't ask Chênevert that."

The first song ended and the crowd erupted in applause. I heard a chant go up: "Joh-nee! Joh-nee!" I looked right and saw people waving their flags, pumping their fists, lighting lighters. One man was bouncing a child on his shoulders, a boy no more than three or four, blond curls spilling out of a blue ball cap with a fleur-de-lys on the front. The father was holding the boy's legs so he wouldn't fall. The boy gripped his father's shirt tightly with one hand and with the other held his hat firmly on his head.

I waited to hear what was coming next. Play it again, Johnny. Fast or slow, sad or not, it doesn't fucking matter. Play something so the crowd keeps on cheering, the boy keeps bouncing, his hat stays on his head.

We were getting close to the back of the crowd. Still no white vans. The only van of any colour was a panel truck, the kind a baker or florist would use, and it was blue. It also had two parking tickets under the front right wiper. No resident permit. And a lot more interior space than a van: more than enough for a load of sacks and cylinders.

"Hang on," I said.

We walked over to the truck and peered through the windows, Ryan on the street side, me on the sidewalk. The space to the rear had been covered over with a tarp. There was nothing personal of note in the front, other than a coffee cup. A pink rental agreement.

I jumped a foot back when the truck's parking lights flashed and its horn chirped and Luc Lortie laughed behind me.

"Imagine if I had pressed the wrong button," he said.

He came out into view from beyond a tangled hedge about four car lengths east, a cellphone in one hand, his car fob in the other. Ryan took out his Glock but wisely didn't extend it at Luc, not with so many people who might see it and run. Or try to.

Luc smiled and said, "Point it, go ahead. I showed you already, your gun doesn't scare me."

"I didn't have this clear a shot last time," Ryan said. "And you were trying to take my leg off."

"I can take more than that off now," he said. "I can take it all, debone you both like chickens."

He held up the cellphone, his thumb obscuring one of the top buttons. "This activates the detonator. I've already dialled the number, all I have to do is press send. This truck will be gone, along with everyone within two hundred metres."

"Including you," I said.

He shrugged. "Do I look like I love my life so much? You presumably searched my cabin. Is it the home of a contented man?"

"You don't want to live to see your father succeed? And your sister?"

"I'll still know, even if I die."

"And what if Lucienne dies?" I said.

"Why would she?"

"Because she's here. In the crowd, looking for you."

For the first time, he lost his cocky grin. "You're lying. She is at Radio-Canada. It's miles away."

"She's here," I said, holding up my phone. "And I can prove it." Jesus, a war fought with cellphones, mine and his. One a detonator, one a reminder.

"You call anyone and we die."

"I'm not calling, okay?" I brought up the photo I'd taken of Lucienne moments ago, and held it out in front of me.

"I can't see that," he said. "It could be anything."

"Here." I started walking toward him.

"Stop!"

"No tricks," I said. I took one step at a time, as if the pavement beneath my feet were mined. When I got close enough to slide the phone in a straight line along the sidewalk, I knelt and did it. It skittered to within a few feet.

"Pick it up. Look at it."

He stared at the phone without moving.

"Look at it. I won't move."

He pocketed his keys, crouched down and picked up the phone and stared at the image of his beloved sister, lit from behind by blue strobes. Could he see the tears streaking her makeup, the agony straining her face?

"You detonate the bomb, you'll kill her too," I said.

"Why? Why did she come?"

"To stop you. I told her about it and she wants you to stop."

"I can't stop. I am what this family needs. Can't she see that? For my father to lead this province, and for her to take over when he retires, it is up to me to act."

"She doesn't want it to happen this way," I said.

"It won't happen any other way! The sheep will keep on

voting for the same stupid people. They need me to provide the spark."

"That's not what Lucienne believes. She knows your father can succeed without this kind of violence."

"He can't, I'm telling you. Without me, at best he'll place third and be the swing player in a minority government. I'm the only one who can take him to the top."

"Not without killing your sister."

"Call her," he said. "Tell her to get away. Do it now, or I swear I'll—"

"She won't go. I already asked her and she stayed. And even if she left, everyone would know it was you who set off the bomb. The people would shun your family forever. The party would be destroyed. Think of Anders Breivik. You think his father could get elected in Norway? Ever?"

"No one will know," he said. "Not if you die with me."

"The police know," I said. "They're here looking for you."

"I don't see them."

"You never do. But they're here. I told them about the bomb. And about Sammy Adler. They know you killed him."

"For all the good it did," he said. "There was supposed to be outrage. A beloved Jew writer killed by vicious Muslims. But the police never came out and said that's how it happened. There wasn't the outcry there should have been."

"There will be now," I said. "But not the one you hoped for. Now do the right thing. For Lucienne."

"There is no right thing anymore."

He was standing completely still. Maybe here in body but his mind miles away. Maybe in a cold home where love was conditional, the bar always set too high for him.

"Give me your phone," I said.

"To spend twenty-five years in prison?" he whispered. "See my sister once a year? My father, I bet he wouldn't come at all."

"She'd come more often," I said.

"Suppose she did." His body shivered as though a dust devil had blown up around him, swirled into him and moved on. "Nobody ever cared for me like Lucienne. No one protected me like her. When my father would make me feel so small, so dark, like a little stranger in my own house, it was always Lucienne who made him stop. Who said, 'Be nice to Luc. He needs love,' she'd say. 'Encouragement and love, that's all . . .'"

He reached into the pocket of his pants. I felt Ryan tense in his shooting stance. But Luc was just getting his keys. "This way, she'll never forget me."

"What way is that?"

"What do I do?" Ryan hissed.

"Hold on."

Luc started walking toward the driver's-side door, holding the detonator cellphone up by his head. The keys jangled as he wiped his cheek with the back of his other hand.

"Luc?" I said. "I can't let you drive away in this."

"Then come for the ride," he said. "It's going to be a short one." He looked behind him, across the end of the park and Rue Viau. On its far side was a small municipal golf course, dark, empty.

He shook the dark hair out of his eyes. "Why go out with a whimper? Come on, get in, Geller," he said. "Get in or go home."

I stepped back and let him get in.

He opened the door, got in and turned the key. The door locks engaged. The engine roared and the tires screeched as he pulled away from the curb and barrelled along Rosemont toward Viau. He ran the red light there and almost hit a small white Fiat going north, regained control and jumped the curb into the golf course. I hopped up onto the hood of a parked Subaru wagon, then onto its roof, and watched as the van kept going for another ten or fifteen seconds, then stopped.

The explosion came a few seconds later.

CHAPTER 23

The blast blew out every window in every house bordering the golf course. We found out later that many suffered structural damage as well but mercifully no one was killed—except Luc Lortie, who was incinerated. Somehow only one person was seriously injured in the stampede that followed, a woman whose head was stomped after she was knocked to the ground by people rushing toward the stage, perhaps fearing another explosion would follow. They also ran toward Boulevard Rosemont, pushing each other, dropping their signs, blankets, water bottles and other belongings, leaving the field littered with fallen flags, as if an army had retreated in sullen defeat. Ryan and I kept to the north side of the street, braced against the tide of people moving toward us, running past us, some holding their children. I wanted to tell them it was okay, the danger was past, but why would they believe me?

Only now did I feel exhaustion in my limbs from our earlier push through the crowd. The adrenalin that had kept me going all day was draining fast. I wanted to call Jenn, tell her we were okay, then remembered Luc had dropped my phone on the sidewalk. A thousand running feet had probably reduced it to chips and shards of plastic. I borrowed Ryan's phone and called her.

"Ryan!" she shouted. "Are you okay? Where's Jonah? Why isn't he calling?"

"He is," I said. "It's me."

"What about Ryan? Did—"

"He's fine. We both are."

"Thank God," she said. "When I saw the explosion, I—"

"What do you mean, saw? You're not still here, are you? You were supposed to get the hell out of here!"

"What are you, mad at me? I couldn't just leave."

"Where are you now?"

"Behind the stage. In the Botanical Garden. Now get over here. If you're going to yell at me, please do it in person. I need to see you're okay."

It took fifteen minutes to make our way past the stage and into the gardens where Jenn and Holly Napier were waiting. Dozens of other people stood in knots, their faces wrung with disbelief at what had just happened. Some of them were nursing scrapes or brushing off grass stains, anxiously scanning the crowd for missing friends or family. Others just wept or trembled as if seized by chills.

Jenn hugged me fiercely, then gave Ryan the same treatment.

"The man of the hour," Holly said and hugged me too. There was a charge there I couldn't ever feel with Jenn. It surprised me with its strength and then her mouth was on mine. Not for long but long enough.

"Definitely not your average bear," she whispered.

"I'd say get a room but I know there's none to be had," Jenn said.

"Quiet, you. Listen," I said. "Can you guys hang here a minute? I need to find Lucienne and Laurent."

"We'll wait," Jenn said.

I turned and made my way against the crowd toward the back of the stage.

———

Laurent Lortie was sitting on the ground, his back against the rear wall of the stage, his knees up, his head buried in his hands. Lucienne was standing nearby, but looking away, holding herself as she cried.

Why the hell wasn't her father holding her now? This, I thought, was the man who had driven Luc to commit his crime. Sorry for himself, unavailable to everyone else.

I walked up to Lucienne and said, "Hey," as softly as I could.

She looked at me, eyes red as a demon's, fists clenched so tightly the bones looked like porcelain. "Is he dead?"

"Yes." I moved toward her but she put up a hand to stop me.

"Wasn't there another way?" she said.

"No. He was very determined to do what he did."

"For us," she said. "For me. How am I going to live with that?"

"You will. You're strong."

"Oh, everyone thinks so. Lucienne Lortie, so strong, so full of resolve, a will of steel. Nothing can hurt her, nothing pierces her shield. That's what they think, but I am just like everyone else. I feel pain, and not just my own. I always felt Luc's too. He had so much, he couldn't handle it all. And now everyone will think of him as a criminal, a maniac. A terrorist."

"Because that's what he was!" Laurent cut in.

I looked at him, stunned that he would talk about his son that way, in that moment.

"Papa, please," Lucienne said.

"We were getting so close," he said. "If people had just had the chance to hear me speak. I worked so hard on that speech, it had everything in it. All the hope I have for this province, all the will I would bring to the position. They will never hear it now because of that wretched misfit."

Lucienne began to sob and I said to Laurent, "Take it easy, for God's sake."

"I will not." He struggled to his feet and brushed his clothes, smoothed his hair. But no smoothing could erase the tired lines in his face. "I don't want to be associated with him anymore, not for a minute. I should have disowned him in life. I will certainly do it in death."

"I was certain for a while that he was the adopted one," I said. "He seemed so unlike you. Now I see he was your son, to the marrow. You helped make him exactly what he was."

"He was nothing like me. Nothing like Lucienne."

"That's not true," she said. "He was a lot like me. He just couldn't find room in our family to grow."

"And I suppose that's my fault?" Laurent said.

"It's not a matter of fault," she said. "Just don't blame Luc for everything. Mourn him a moment. Grieve, Papa."

"I can't," he said. "Perhaps I should but I can't. I don't have it in me. I can't find it there."

"Try grieving for your nephew," I said. "Maybe that'll work."

"My nephew?"

"Sammy Adler. Arthur Moscoe's grandson. Luc killed him. Luc wanted to keep your birth father secret and throw the blame onto Muslims."

"Nothing can surprise me about him," Laurent said. "Nothing can lower him further in my estimation."

"Please," Lucienne said to me. "That is enough for tonight." She put her arm around her father's unyielding shoulder and said, "Don't worry, Papa. I have enough grief for us both."

Sitting on the back bumper of one of the rented trucks was Reynald Paquette. His jacket was off, his tie was at half-mast and his sleeves were rolled up to the elbows. I looked around for Chênevert but didn't see him.

Paquette held out his hand and we shook. "You did well for an amateur," he said.

"Thank you. Thank you for coming out here. For believing me."

He grinned and said, "It was too fucked-up a story to be lies." Wasn't it just?

"It was Luc driving that van?"

I said, "Yes. Forensics will confirm it, if there's enough left of him. But I saw him get in."

"Christ," he said. "That's going to end his father's campaign for sure. And stir up a lot of other pots."

"He also killed Sammy Adler. He confessed to it before he ran. And he had help from a friend I can identify."

"We'll need a full statement."

"As long as you don't need it tonight."

"Tomorrow will be fine. Have you seen the Lorties?"

"They're backstage."

"How are they taking it?"

"She is upset," I said. "He looks like he couldn't give a shit, the heartless prick."

"He wanted to go up on the stage and give his speech," Paquette said. "Show he was not afraid. She's the one who wouldn't let him go. Hung on to him like she was drowning."

He was pushing his tie back into place when René Chênevert strode into view. He stopped and crossed his arms when he saw me. He wasn't going to shake my hand unless someone put a gun to his head. Too bad Ryan had stayed behind.

"This must be bad news for you," I said.

"*Quoi, lui?*"

"The end of Québec aux Québécois."

He shrugged and said, "What do I care?"

"You cared enough to follow us when Laurent told you to."

"What I do is my business," Chênevert said.

"And mine," Paquette said. "Is it true?"

"Has to be," I said. "How else did he know where I was staying? He is the one who told you, right?"

Paquette nodded.

"The minute I told Lortie what I was looking for, Chênevert was on our tail."

Chênevert's face turned red and he uncrossed his arms. Oh dear. His jacket fell open and I could see the butt of his pistol turned forward on his belt. "I don't have to listen to this shit from you. Any shit," he said.

"Then stop listening and start talking," Paquette said. "Is it true Lortie called you? Come on, René, if it is true, I'll find it out, you know that."

"*Puis?*" Chênevert said. "What if he did call me? So what? Maybe I support some of his ideas. Maybe I wanted to see his party succeed."

"And then what?" I said. "A job as his chief of security? Perfect. You could quit pretending to be a detective and run around covering ass. His and hers."

"*Maudite crotte de chien,*" he said. "Get out of here before I break your neck."

"With your gun and badge on?"

He pulled his holster off his belt and handed it to Paquette. It looked like a Glock 17.

"What about your badge?"

He took a black leather folder out of his jacket pocket and handed that over too. Then he shrugged out of the jacket, tossed it well away to one side and put up his hands in a boxer's stance.

I laughed and started walking away.

"Where you going, piece of shit? You scared?"

"I have no intention of fighting you," I said. "I just think you look better without the badge."

I heard his feet pound the ground and turned to see him rushing in a crouch, going for a takedown. Maybe I had no intention of fighting him; I also wasn't going to get tackled. I grabbed his head with both arms and bent it downward, cutting off his air, then rolled onto my back and flipped him hard onto his. His breath went out of him as he hit the ground. I got up onto my feet, ready for more.

"Don't tell me that's it," I said.

He rolled onto his side, then onto his hands and knees. He spat into the dirt and stood slowly.

I said, "That's the way," moved in and hit him hard twice in the chest with open palms. He staggered back but stayed on his feet. His eyes looked glassy and he was breathing hard.

I faked a shot to the head and when he raised his hands, slammed him in the solar plexus. Whatever air he had left in him rushed out and he bent over and vomited. I jumped back to avoid getting sprayed.

I brushed the dirt off my clothes, shook Paquette's hand again and started walking toward the Botanical Garden.

"My office," he called. "Tomorrow morning."

"Afternoon," I said. "I seriously need some sleep."

The four of us went back to the hotel and proceeded to empty the mini-bar of all things alcoholic, along with most of the snacks. Arthur Moscoe was paying for it and we had earned every pricey ounce. At one o'clock, we turned on the TV. The bombing was on every channel, French and English. One French station showed a graphic of the Front de Libération des Musulmans du Québec's poster and reported the group had claimed responsibility for the atrocity. By tomorrow, I figured, there'd be a different story. For tonight, people could sleep tight— or not—with their prejudices confirmed. At one point, Jenn remembered that she had called Sierra earlier and told her she was going to the Fête concert and went into the bathroom to call home, reassure her lover she was safe.

"I wish I had someone to call," Ryan muttered. "Someone who gave a shit."

"I do," I said.

"I'm thinking of somebody else," he said, and cracked

open another bottle of vodka. "Shit," he said. "We need more ice." And he went down the hall to find some.

I turned off the TV and sat next to Holly on one of the queen beds. "Did you know," I said, feeling every one of the drinks I'd had, "Ryan and I have known each other exactly a year? This time last year was when we met."

"I'm sure it's quite the story."

"It is."

"Want to come home with me and tell it?"

"I do."

"Jenn won't mind?"

"She might. But I was not your average bear tonight."

"No."

"I saved a lot of people."

"You did."

She leaned over and kissed me, a longer, sweeter kiss than the one we'd had in the park. She smelled good. Her hair, her skin. Something like coconut. Maybe traces of sunscreen. For a moment, I thought of Arthur Moscoe, the young Artie, lost in the rosewater scent of Micheline Mercier in the basement of Dominion Dress.

CHAPTER 24

We left Ryan and Jenn a note saying, "Figure it out," and took a cab to her place. I'd like to say we spent the rest of the night making mad, passionate love. We didn't. We did get naked together and got into her bed and kissed and pressed against each other and that is as much as I remember because I fell asleep in about three minutes. It was delicious anyway. I woke up around four-thirty, totally disoriented—then realized where I was and curled into the small of Holly's back. She stirred and took my hand and pressed it to her breast. It felt good to be in a woman's bed, to feel the curves of her body, smell her soap. In the grey light of the false dawn I saw a long hair on her pillow and thought of the darker one we had found in Sammy's bed and how it had led us to Mehri Aziz. Then I fell back asleep for another two hours.

I woke to the smell of coffee. I sat up and was rubbing sleep from my eyes when Holly came in wearing a white terry-cloth robe tied loosely at the waist.

"Good morning," she said. "Sleep okay?"

"I did."

"I guess stopping a mad bomber tired you out."

"Sorry."

"Don't be," she said. "It was nice having you here. How do you take your coffee?"

"A little milk would be good."

"Be right back."

She padded out in bare feet and I looked around the room. It was a good-sized room with a south-facing window, the walls covered with black-and-white photos of famous writers: the creased, worn face of Ezra Pound; Karsh's portrait of Hemingway in his fisherman's sweater; a sleepy-eyed Salman Rushdie; Émile Zola, whom I wouldn't have recognized except for his signature; Gertrude Stein and Alice B. Toklas with a standard poodle between them, the poodle the best-looking of the three.

When Holly came back, she had a steaming mug in each hand. And no robe.

The coffee was cold when we finally got to it.

On the way back to the hotel, Holly drove us to St-Viateur Bagel, where they had been baking bagels in wood-fired ovens for decades. We picked up a mixed dozen—half with poppy seeds, half with sesame—along with cream cheese and lox, and took it all up to the room.

Ryan was in the bathroom, humming above the sound of the shower. Jenn didn't look thrilled to see us.

"He snores," she said. "And he sleeps with a gun under his pillow, so what am I gonna do—give him an elbow in the ribs?"

"I know. I've been sharing a room with him."

"What's in the bag?"

"Bagels, cream cheese and lox."

"Poppy or sesame?"

"Both."

"You're halfway forgiven." Then she grinned at Holly and said, "You, on the other hand, have nothing to atone for."

Holly said, "Thank you."

"Want to tell me about his prowess now or wait until we're alone?"

"Alone," I said.

"Did I ask you?"

Sister, my sister. It was great to have her back.

While Jenn spread out the food on the small round table by the window, I went down to the lobby café and got four large coffees to go. And a copy of the Montreal *Gazette*. The front-page headline read "CONCERT CHAOS" and showed a woman running with a child in her arms just ahead of a throng of people. Flames and a huge plume of black smoke boiled up against the sky behind them. I scanned the lead story in the elevator. It quoted a shaken Johnny Rivard, who'd been on stage at the time of the blast; festival organizers, who vowed next year's party would go on without a hitch; and plenty of bystanders who'd fled the scene. A grim police commander in charge of media relations was quoted as saying all angles of investigation were being pursued but it was too soon to point fingers at any individual or group. Asked about rumours Muslim extremists were behind it, he said detectives were considering all leads at this time.

No one mentioned any member of the Lortie family, living or dead. Maybe identifying the bits and pieces left of Luc was going to take a while.

Back in the room, we went through most of the bagels, swept up the crumbs and considered what to do next. Holly said she needed to go to her office and plan how *Moment* was going to cover the story of the bombing.

"There are a few things you need to leave out," I said.

"What things?"

"Me. Some of what I know. Most of what I did."

"You don't want publicity?"

"Not this kind."

"But I need to finish Sammy's stories. Both of them. I owe him that much. You understand that, right?"

"Yes. But first we need to know how the story ends."

———

After Holly left, the three of us sat in the room deciding what to do next. "I'm going to have to see Paquette soon," I said. "Which means staying one more night."

"And I share with Ryan again?"

"No reason you can't fly home today," I said. "You bought a return ticket, right?"

"Of course."

"So use it. Go home. It's better than six hours in the car with us."

"You don't need me for anything?"

"We did what we came to do. All that's left is to tell Arthur what happened, and that can wait one more day."

"All right," she said. "Let me see what flight I can get on."

She was searching her options on my laptop when Mehrdad Aziz called and asked me to come by the store. "It would be my honour to have tea with you," he said. "To thank you for what you did. If that bomb had gone off as intended, Muslims would be waking up to a very different day."

"I'm the one who needs to thank you. You and your big goofy pal."

"Kamal? He is a cousin, actually."

"Okay, cousin. Without you, I wouldn't have reached my friends."

"Yes, you would. But maybe we helped make it easier. Please say you will come."

"All right."

"Your friend Mr. Ryan will come too?"

"I'll ask him."

"The earlier the better," he said. "Saturdays are often busy after lunch."

"Give us an hour," I said.

"Fine. We will see you then."

He hung up and I told Ryan about the invitation. He shrugged. "You sure you want to go? I don't know about you, but I'm still stuffed from those bagels."

"It's just for tea. And I want to get my sphere cam back. It cost too much to leave behind."

"Okay."

"What about me?" Jenn asked.

"We could take you to the airport first," I said. "Go to the store from there."

"I can't get on a flight until at least three. I'll hang here until you get back, if that's okay. Then either you can drive me or I'll take a cab."

"Sure."

"What about your transponder?" Ryan asked. "Want to get that too?"

"I'm in no rush to see Mohammed again."

"I didn't think so. Maybe Moscoe will reimburse you for the cost."

"Maybe."

"You think he'll contact Micheline?" Jenn asked.

"Wouldn't that be interesting? Artie Moscoe and Miss Montreal, together again for the first time since 1950."

"Stranger things have happened," she said. "I mean I walked in on Ryan dropping his pants and it just got nuttier from there."

CHAPTER 25

Mehrdad unlocked the front door of Les Tapis Kabul when Ryan and I arrived. Mehri was nowhere in sight. He stood back and waved us in without making eye contact and relocked the door.

"I thought you were open this morning," I said.

"It is quiet," he said. "And I don't want us to be disturbed while we have our tea."

"Where's Mehri?"

"In the back room. Waiting for us."

"And Kamal and Rashid?"

"No, they don't work today."

"Just the four of us."

"Yes."

We walked to the back of the store. So much beauty around us, all the hanging carpets in lush shades of crimson, scarlet, vermilion: the colour of wine, roses, rubies. The work of men, women and children in dusty rooms half a world away. Soft carpets made for bare feet, for making love on in front of a fire.

"Please," Mehrdad said. "This way."

He led us behind the counter and opened the door to the storeroom. Once again he held the door for us, waiting until we were all the way in before closing it behind us. Once it was shut, he said, "I am sorry."

I could see why. Mohammed and his brother Faisal were standing behind a shipping table. His left hand was on Mehri's shoulder. A gun filled his right. He shoved Mehri toward her brother and levelled the pistol at us.

"He said he would kill Mehri if I didn't call you," Mehrdad said.

"It's all right," I said.

"All right?" Mohammed said. "It is excellent. Now you are here, come all the way in. Faisal, take their guns."

Faisal wasn't wearing his neck brace anymore. He walked up to me and ran his hands down my sides, found nothing. Then he opened Ryan's jacket and reached in for his Glock. Ryan leaned his head forward and yelled, "Boo!" and Faisal flinched. Ryan bared his teeth in a chilling laugh.

"Faisal!" Mohammed barked. "Be a man and take the gun." Faisal did. He handed the Glock to Mohammed, who hefted it, decided he liked it, then stepped forward and slammed the butt into my nose. I felt a shock of pain through my face as the cartilage broke. Blood rushed down my face and the back of my throat. I didn't care. Because in his rush to repay me for breaking his nose, he had overlooked the Baby Eagle in Ryan's ankle holster.

I spat blood on the floor. More took its place in my throat. "You happy now?" I said to Mohammed. It hurt to talk. Every move I made sent more pain through my sinuses and cheekbone.

"Only partly," he said. "Only a nose's worth. You have more yet to pay for what you did."

"What I did? You mean saving your community from a mob?"

"My community is my family. My brothers. You hurt Faisal's neck. You hurt Omar last night. You abused me. These things cannot go unanswered. People see us injured and no one pays for it, what are they going to think?"

"That you're a gutless asshole?" Ryan said.

"Shut up, you. You want your nose broken too?"

"Wouldn't be the first time."

"There is a first time for everything," Mohammed said. "When I'm done with you, you won't have such a smart mouth."

Mehrdad said, "Please, Mohammed. That is enough. You took your revenge. It's over."

Mohammed laughed and said, "Over? I thought you knew revenge, you Afghans. Or maybe you're worried we'll mess up your store. Don't worry about that, okay? We will take them to your warehouse and finish them there. Show them how Syrians do things. Let's go." He pointed the gun at me.

"There's something you should know," I said.

"No stalling. Come on. Out the back."

"Mehrdad," I said. "That bin of carpets on your right. Reach inside the one with the blue edging."

Mohammed swivelled and pointed his gun at Mehrdad. "If there is a gun in there," he said, "you'd better leave it where it is. Or else I shoot you and your sister."

Mehrdad said, "It is not a gun. It's a ball."

"It's a camera," I said.

"What use is a camera inside a carpet?" Mohammed said.

"It records picture *and* voice," I said. "Every word you've said since you walked in has been recorded."

Mohammed strode over to Mehrdad and slapped the camera out of his hand, then stomped it with his heel. "There's your fucking camera now. No pictures. No voice. Now shut your mouth and walk toward the door. Hands over your head."

"You're not exactly up on current technology, are you?"

"Fuck you and your technology. Move."

"The camera doesn't just record. It transmits."

"Transmits what?"

"This conversation to a computer. Which my friend is listening to in our hotel room right now. Hearing every word you said. Sending the police."

It would have been nice if it were true. I had no idea what Jenn was doing, Maybe taking a shower or watching TV or chatting with Sierra. Or shopping for something frilly on Rue Ste-Catherine.

"You are a lying shithead Jew motherfucker."

"How else did I know about your meeting last night? We heard Mehrdad call you. Heard every word he said."

He paused for a moment, then said, "Even if it is true, we will be gone when they arrive. All of us, including you two." Pointing the gun at Mehrdad and Mehri.

Mehrdad stepped in front of Mehri and spread his hands. "Why?"

"If the police come, I don't want you here when they arrive. Also, I want you to see what happens to these guys. So you will know what happens to you if you talk."

"We won't say a word. I have never talked to police in my life, not in Kabul and not here."

"I'm not asking."

"Then I will go," Mehrdad said. "Let Mehri go home."

"She comes too. Faisal, you will drive with these Afghans. In the back seat with your gun at the woman's head. If her brother does anything stupid, shoot her. You," he said to me, "you and your friend go with us, in the back of the truck. Now start walking. Hands on your heads. Whoever makes a stupid move gets a bullet in the face."

We started walking.

Mohammed walked backwards, keeping his gun on us. I tried to think of something I could do to distract him long enough for Ryan to claw the gun out of his ankle holster and fire. But there was nothing at hand, nothing I could throw. Just empty space between us. Feeling like I was choking on bloody spittle and snot.

"Faisal," he said, followed by something in Arabic. It must have meant open the back door because that's what Faisal did.

He was no more than a step outside when he started backing into the room, slowly putting his hands in the air. Then I saw a glinting tube come through the door.

Shiny steel.

Inches and inches of it.

Ryan's Smith & Wesson Classic revolver, the biggest gun he owned. An eight-and-three-eighths barrel.

Jenn Raudsepp was holding it, fully cocked. She kicked the door shut behind her and pointed the Smith at Mohammed and said, "Drop it."

Mohammed laughed. "Or what? You going to shoot? You fire that gun, it's going to knock you over. Break your shoulder."

"I'm six feet tall, asshole," she said. "And I've trained with it. You want to see? Jonah," she said, "don't stand in back of him. I put a round in him, it's going to keep going to the street."

She was in a proper shooting stance, right arm extended, right hand cupped in her left. I moved a couple of feet to one side.

Mohammed said, "How much you want to bet I can shoot you twice before you squeeze the trigger?"

She said nothing. Stayed in her stance, the fearsome barrel holding steady.

"Or your boyfriend. Or this Afghan whore. Any of this I could do. You don't believe me? Watch." He looked over and started to raise his gun.

It was a feint. I could tell by how deliberately he was moving. He was betting Jenn would look down at Mehri too and then he'd change speed and direction and gun her down.

I started to shout a warning to Jenn. "Don't—" was as far as I got before she fired. She held her stance and the roar filled my ears as a round tore past Mohammed's head and smashed into the plaster wall behind me and into the front of the store. Maybe into the next municipality.

Mohammed yelled something in Arabic, what had to be a curse with all its harsh consonants, and let his gun fall. Jenn kept the Smith trained on him as I kicked Mohammed's gun to the side. I retrieved Ryan's Glock and handed it to him. He seemed less surprised than I was by Jenn's sudden appearance.

I said to Mohammed and Faisal, "On the ground, both of you."

Jenn said, "Wait a minute. Ryan, you have him covered?"

"Yeah."

She walked up to Mohammed and slammed his broken nose with the long barrel of the Smith. Mohammed howled as a fresh mix of blood and tears ran freely down his chin. "That's for hurting my friend."

"Now get down," Ryan said, pointing his Glock at both brothers.

Faisal got down quickly and laced his hands behind his head without having to be told to do so. Mohammed got down on one knee, one hand cupped over his nose like he could catch the blood streaming out and put it back inside. Ryan kicked him in the side to hurry him along.

"You understand now," he said, when Mohammed was prone. "We're all squared up. Whatever you think you were owed, you just got it."

Mohammed's voice, strained and hoarse, told him to go fuck himself.

Ryan laid the Glock against the cheek that was turned up to the ceiling. "Here's the deal. We're going back to Toronto. We're leaving you dirtbags to your city. You want to come down our way, on my turf, take whatever revenge you think you got coming, try. I'll kill you before you get your bearings. Understand? Before you know which way Yonge Street runs, you'll be in a body bag."

"I cannot let this stand," Mohammed grunted. "Everyone will know I was disrespected."

"Broken noses heal," I said. "Yours and mine, a month from now, we'll both be back to gorgeous."

"But that hole in your head won't heal so fast," Ryan said.

"What hole—"

"The one I'll make if you don't shut up and get lost."

Mohammed was about to launch a reply that would be either profane, stupid or fatal when Mehrdad stepped in.

"Take his deal, Mohammed. End it here peacefully. Because even if you retaliate, even if you kill them all, your shame will not end."

"Why not?"

"I told you I would never talk to the police. And I won't. But the community, that is a different story. Unless you make peace, I promise you: Word will get out that a woman broke your nose."

Ryan retrieved the transponder for me. I didn't think bending down, letting blood rush into my head and out my nose, was in my best interest. Once we were sure the Haddads were gone, we said a quick and final goodbye to Mehrdad and Mehri, and walked to the Jeep.

"Shit," Ryan said. The back window was broken; inside was the chunk of cinderblock Jenn had used to get to Ryan's gun case.

"Another day," he said, "another damaged car."

We plotted a route that would take us to the closest hospital, the Jewish General, so I could get X-rays. I had no doubt my nose was broken but I thought the gun butt might also have fractured my orbital bone. We stopped at a convenience store and bought a bag of ice, which I held to my face as we drove.

"So what made you come to the store?" I asked Jenn.

"Your transponder. I was booking my flight and the trace program was still open. I saw Mohammed's car parked behind the store and didn't think he was there for the tea."

"You were very convincing with that gun. I thought Mohammed was right, that firing it would knock you on your ass."

"I've had some lessons," she said, looking at Ryan. "From a very good teacher."

"Yeah? Since when?"

"About six weeks," she said.

"Let me guess," I said to Ryan. "That gun range you took me to, the one in that strip mall on Highway 7?"

"Twice a week," he said. "And she's a very quick study. Lights the place up."

"I'm sorry, I'm having a hard time processing this."

"What is there to process?" Jenn said. "All it comes down to is, no one is ever going to hurt me again. Not the way they did in Boston. Not any way. I don't care what I have to do, I'm going to protect myself."

"You should take a page out of her book," Ryan said. "Carry that Beretta I bought you."

"He bought me one too," Jenn said. "I don't carry it, but if I'm home alone, it's where I can get to it fast."

"Jesus," I said. "I feel like I'm at an NRA meeting."

"There are worse places you could be," Ryan said.

"I know," I said. "I've been to enough."

EPILOGUE

I wasn't sure how Arthur Moscoe would take the news. There would surely be some relief or resolution in knowing his grandson's killer had been found and had faced a final, shattering justice. Maybe he would find some solace in the fact that Sammy had not been set upon by a mob, that the Star of David had been carved into his chest not in a virulent, anti-Semitic rage but as a calculated move to shift the blame onto a beleaguered community. And he'd probably be glad to know Sammy had been falling in love again in the days before he died.

But what would he think about Laurent Lortie being his son? Would he feel any kind of warmth toward a man whose politics leaned toward the scary fascism of his youth? And if he did, how would those feelings be tempered knowing one of his grandsons had murdered another?

I wondered if he would call Micheline, revisit the love affair now sixty-three years in the past, or leave it lie as he had done for so many years.

The only way to know was to ask him, but I didn't want to do it over the phone. As I lay on the bed in our hotel, a baggie full of ice leaking slowly down my neck, even the idea of driving back to Toronto was painful. The X-rays had shown two fractures in my nose—one at the bridge and one an inch below—and a third in the right orbital bone. The attending physician had walked his fingers gingerly along my eye socket and said he didn't think I'd need surgery. "Come back when the swelling is down and we'll check it again. In the meantime, stay off your feet and keep icing it."

The hospital had provided a handful of Tylenol 3s, two of which I took, and I dozed for an hour or so while Ryan and Jenn went down to the hotel fitness centre to work out—that or carry out more clandestine target practice. When I woke up, I made the mistake of looking in the mirror. An ugly face looked back: darkening bruises under my eyes, the right side swollen from my eye to my chin, the right eye completely red. I looked like Mohammed's homelier twin.

I called Holly and told her I had to postpone dinner, and why. She said I could come to her place when she was done working and she'd take care of me. With a steady pain throbbing from my right eyebrow down to my jaw, I wanted her nestled next to me, her head against my chest. Her bare feet nudging mine. Her scent filling the air, even if my busted nose wouldn't detect it. But Montreal's potholed streets were too daunting a risk for my busted face. I pictured bones grinding in a jarring ride and said I was staying put.

"Then I'll come there as soon as I'm done," she said.

Ryan took Jenn to dinner in Little Italy, a place he knew up near Jarry Park where half the men in the place looked like wise guys, and the other half actually were. From there, they'd go to Holly's apartment, where she could sleep in the bedroom and Ryan could use a pull-out couch.

I watched Manny Pacquiao knock out opponents in all weight classes on my laptop until Holly got there around nine. Then I found an Atlanta Braves game. In between trips to the ice machine, she sat at the desk, tapping at her laptop, polishing her story on the bombing.

The tapping of her fingers against the keyboard stopped. "How you doing?" she asked.

"Okay."

"I thought I heard you grunt."

"I think it was more of a sigh."

"You need more Tylenol?"

"Do they come in extra-large?"

She got up and went to the bathroom to fill a glass of water and handed it to me along with two capsules.

"Thanks."

"You hungry?"

"It hurts to chew."

"I could order you some soup. Or make a run to Chinatown."

"I'm okay for now. How about you?"

"I'm good." She sat on the bed beside me and gently touched the left side of my face. "You know, you were a lot better looking this morning."

"That's because I was naked. Come to think of it, you were naked too."

"I could be again."

"Wait till the Tylenol kicks in."

"You look sad, Jonah."

I forced a brief smile, which felt okay on one side of my face, not so good on the other. I told her how I was feeling torn about going home: wanting to spend more time with her here, letting my fractures heal; needing to tell Arthur how and why Sammy's life had ended.

"You don't want to call him?" she said.

"It's the kind of thing I need to do in person."

"So go home tomorrow and talk to him and fly back here on Monday."

"Really?"

"Why not? The jazz festival starts Thursday. There are Canada Day events Friday. A fireworks show. We could go down to the port, take a calèche ride through Old Montreal—all the corny touristy stuff Montrealers never do."

"You think they heal faces at St. Joseph's Oratory?"

"You're not crippled, just temporarily gross."

"What about your story?"

"I'll finish it while you're gone."

"You're on," I said. "As long as nothing comes up at the office." I reached over to the nightstand and got my cellphone and checked the World Repairs voice mail box. The first three messages were all minor things Colin could handle: finalizing a contract, sending out a report on a closed file, preparing a proposal for an industrial espionage gig.

The fourth was from Arthur's lawyer, Henry Geniele. He left three numbers I could try, including his home, which is where I reached him.

In a sombre voice he told me Arthur Moscoe had died of heart failure the previous night.

I had never felt so deflated after a case. Everything we had done that week, we had done so Arthur would know what had happened to Sammy. So he could die knowing he had done everything possible for his grandson's memory. Maybe he had died peacefully anyway. But peace eluded me, as it so often does.

Jenn and Ryan flew home Sunday. He said he'd figure out his car situation later.

She said she'd be in the office when I got back.

I stayed with Holly. When she went to work, I typed my report for Henry Geniele, summarizing the investigation, detailing our expenses, suggesting avenues for follow-up with Reynald Paquette. I emailed it to him and got a reply thanking me for my efforts. "I only wish Arthur had lived one more day, so he could have known what happened," he wrote.

Him and me both.

I debated flying back for Arthur's funeral but I didn't want to complicate the family's grief by immersing them in the details of Sammy's murder, or by sitting there with a face that invited questions or morbid curiosity. I logged on instead to a website set up for the family by the funeral home and left a brief message of regret: "May he rest in eternal peace," it said. "May his memory be a blessing." Both standard formulas of condolence in Judaism. Then I added: "May all his family everywhere be comforted knowing he passed away without pain."

Even Laurent Lortie.

On Monday, I spent two hours in the office of Reynald Paquette, working on my official statement. It wasn't exactly reciprocal. I told him everything I knew about Luc; he told me almost nothing about how the police would proceed from there. Neither the police nor the media had yet identified Luc as the person who had detonated the bomb, but it was going to come out soon enough. In *Montreal Moment* if nowhere else. I kept Ryan's name out of it; when asked about Alessandro Spezza, I said only that I had hired a driver by that name and that the police were welcome to contact him at the address on his driver's licence. And good luck with that.

The trickiest part, it seemed, was connecting Luc in any official way to Sammy's murder. Paquette wanted to close the book on it, but the only evidence supporting the theory was his purported confession to me on Boulevard Rosemont.

"Of course," he said, "if anyone else heard it, that would be more favourable."

Which brought us back to Ryan, which meant it wasn't going to happen.

I went back to the hospital on Tuesday morning. By then the swelling had gone down enough that a consulting surgeon confirmed my orbital fracture was not displaced and no surgery would be needed. He inserted a metal rod into my right nostril, rebroke my nose, packed it with gauze and taped it down. Now I really looked like shit. Scary shit, the right side of my face dark purple. Half man, half eggplant. I doubted Holly would want to look at me, let alone kiss me.

But she did. We made love every day when she came back from work and every night before we fell asleep and every morning before she left. Gently. Me on my back, mostly, to keep my face from throbbing.

On Thursday we went to the jazz festival and listened to free outdoor concerts near Place des Arts. Being jammed into the streets with thousands of other people made me feel uneasy; it was too much like the Fête concert that had almost ended in disaster.

On Friday, we hammed it up and took the promised calèche ride through the old city. I felt the bones in my face jar as the horse-drawn buggy bounced over the cobbled streets, but it was worth it to have Holly close to me, her breast swelling against my ribs with every breath. We walked through the port area and watched fireworks light up the sky over the St. Lawrence River on Canada Day. It was more subdued than the Fête Nationale; no one had their faces painted red and white and no fervour surged through the crowd. Which was just fine.

We went back to the jazz festival on Saturday but opted for one of the ticketed events: Richard Galliano, who made an accordion do things I had never thought possible.

When we got back to her apartment, I booked a flight back to Toronto for the next morning. Later that night, she thumbed through her CD collection until she found Blue Rodeo's *Casino*, and skipped ahead to "Montreal."

> *We met in Montreal*
> *Far from the crime*
> *Moving in circles*
> *Running with so little time*
> *Sat and we talked*
> *About rumours and lies*
> *Stayed til the sun hit the floor . . .*

Late in your bed
You said don't you be sad
Think of how lucky we are
For the things that we've had
Life that's around me I'm letting it go
But you stay up here in my head

Those were the times
That was our life
I probably wouldn't change
One little thing if I tried
Moments together mapped out
Like the stars in the sky
Now you're in the things that I do
Still I miss talking to you.

And we danced.

AUTHOR'S NOTE

Alert readers might note that the passage of time in the Jonah Geller series is somewhat compressed. The first four novels have been published over a six-year span (2008-13), yet Jonah has aged just one year, and makes reference to the fact that he only met Dante Ryan the previous June. This is a deliberate distortion on my part, as I do not want Jonah to age too quickly—he is no more ready to turn forty than I was—and want his cases close enough to each other chronologically that the effects of one spill over to the next. I have also taken the occasional liberty with geography, such as the exact location of the bandshell at the Fête Nationale concert in Parc Maisonneuve and the existence of a certain lake east of St-Sauveur.

ACKNOWLEDGMENTS

Writing crime fiction is a dream come true for me. Without the love and support of my wife Harriet, and my sons Aaron and Jesse, the dream would have remained just that. Thank you so much. It hasn't always been easy but I like to think it's been fun.

Thanks as always to my agent, Helen Heller, for her ongoing support and advocacy on my behalf; publishers Anne Collins (Knopf Random House Canada) and Marion Garner (Vintage Canada) for believing in Jonah Geller; editor Paul Taunton, for making the book leaner and stronger; copy editor Barbara Czarnecki, who helped me deal with an alarming case of geographic dyslexia; and publicists Sheila Kay and Dan Sharpe, for helping to spread the word.

Very special thanks to my sister Barbara and my lovely niece Isadora for proofing the French parts of the book. It's been nearly thirty years since I've lived in Montreal and my French is rustier than a tin man left in the rain. They probably had a good laugh at some of my mistakes but corrected them patiently and thoroughly. My dear friend Jeffrey Harper also provided his usual insight and support, not to mention the occasional bed in New York. Attorney Doreen Brown clarified certain aspects of adoption law in Quebec. Thanks always to my mother and father for supporting my mid-career shift into crime writing; and to my uncles, Harold and Gerald Seidman, for employing me as a shipper in their clothing factory in my youth, which gave me the backdrop of young Artie Moscoe's world.

Most of the draft of *Miss Montreal* was written at the Toronto Writers Centre, a great haven for authors who need a little human contact while they work. Thanks to Mitch Kowalski and all the writers who have made me feel at home there.

I suppose I should thank Pauline Marois, leader of the Parti Québecois; François Legault, leader of the Coalition Avenir Québec; and Jean Charest, leader of the Liberal Party of Québec, for staging an election that would have been achingly funny had it not been so blindingly sad. Guys, you were the collective gift that kept on giving.

And finally my thanks to René Balcer, Linwood Barclay, Sean Chercover, Rob Cohen, Lee Gowan, Kirsten Gunter, Harold Heft, Sarah Heller, Avrum Jacobson, Jon Mendelsohn, Deon Meyer, Jim Napier, Suri Rosen, Will Straw, Beth Sulman, Bill Zaget and Dave Zeltserman: in different ways, over the past year, you helped me keep the fire burning.

ABOUT THE AUTHOR

Howard Shrier is the author of four acclaimed novels featuring Toronto investigator Jonah Geller: *Buffalo Jump*, *High Chicago*, *Boston Cream* and *Miss Montreal*. The only writer to date to ever to win consecutive Arthur Ellis Awards for Best First Novel and Best Novel, his novels have been optioned for a proposed television series by Toronto's Media Headquarters. Howard was born and raised in Montreal, where he earned an Honours Degree in Journalism and Creative Writing at Concordia University. He has since worked in a wide variety of media, including print, magazine and radio journalism, theatre and television, sketch comedy and improv, and corporate and government communications. Howard now lives in Toronto with his wife and two sons and teaches writing at University of Toronto's School of Continuing Studies.

www.howardshrier.com

Miss Montreal has been set in Janson, a misnamed typeface designed in or about 1690 by Nicholas Kis, a Hungarian in Amsterdam. In 1919 the original matrices became the property of the Stempel Foundry in Frankfurt, Germany. Janson is an old-style book face of excellent clarity and sharpness, featuring concave and splayed serifs, and a marked contrast between thick and thin strokes.